"YOU KILLED THOSE MEN."

Her voice quivered between accusation and awe.

He didn't admit it. Not exactly. "I'm sorry. Did you want to get to know them better?"

"You rushed in to take on armed men with your bare hands? You expect me to believe that? Are you insane?"

"Should I have just kept walking?"

His gaze locked into hers, his eyes darkening with something she'd never seen in them before.

"Step back, Savoie."

Her gruff command must have lacked conviction, because his head lowered until his breath feathered against her lips. Soft. Warm.

"Don't." Not quite so tough.

He tasted her slowly, riding the jerk of her chest, gentling his hold on her hands, finally releasing them. Her palms came up to rest against his shoulders, motionless at first, then beginning to push. He lifted off her by a scant inch, his stare delving into hers, his breathing hurried.

"Max, stop."

"I will if you mean it."

And for one startling moment, she didn't.

He stood back from the impossible temptation she'd become. "The next time you come chasing after me, *sha,* you'd best be sure you really want to catch me."

Masked by Moonlight is also available as an eBook

NANCY GIDEON

Masked by Moonlight

POCKET BOOKS

New York   London   Toronto   Sydney

Pocket Books
A Division of Simon & Schuster, Inc.
1230 Avenue of the Americas
New York, NY 10020

First Pocket Books paperback edition June 2010

POCKET and colophon are registered trademarks of Simon & Schuster, Inc.

For information about special discounts for bulk purchases, please contact Simon & Schuster Special Sales at 1-866-506-1949 or business@simonandschuster.com.

The Simon & Schuster Speakers Bureau can bring authors to your live event. For more information or to book an event, contact the Simon & Schuster Speakers Bureau at 1-866-248-3049 or visit our website at www.simonspeakers.com.

Designed by Jacquelynne Hudson
Cover design by Min Choi
Cover art by Craig White

Manufactured in the United States of America

10   9   8   7   6   5   4   3   2   1

ISBN 978-1-4391-4963-8
ISBN 978-1-4391-5540-0 (ebook)

For Patrish. Thanks for seeing me through the rough spots on the way to a dream.

Masked by Moonlight

Prologue

IT WAS A steamy night, the kind New Orleans is known for. The heat of the day rose off the pavement, becoming a dense mist as it met the evening drizzle. Brilliant flashes of lightning strobed across the still Mississippi, warning of a storm that would settle in tight and wail through the early morning hours. Low clouds scudded past the pale moon that hung heavy and full. It was a miserable night for T-Bob Gautreaux, who had empty pockets as he drove his ancient Caddy home along the slick cobbles.

Fifty bucks. That's all he'd needed. A sweet fifty to throw down on a wager that couldn't miss. He'd told Dolores that, but being a woman and an ignorant Cajun to boot, she hadn't understood. She'd cursed him soundly and swore she'd leave him if he sold off any more of her dishes. They were all she had left of her mama—as if her mama was the one paying the bills.

Fifty lousy bucks. She'd started crying, saying he'd promised her he wouldn't gamble no more. Funny how she believed that promise every time;

you'd think she'd catch on that he never meant it for more than a day or two. Well, maybe a week that time he'd knocked her down the stairs when she'd tried to stop him from going to the dog track. She'd said their baby needed to go to the doctor. Their baby. He wasn't even sure the brat was his.

He'd stepped over her sprawled body at the bottom of the stairs. How was he to know she'd busted three ribs? It wasn't like he'd meant for it to happen. Things like that just did, when he was drinking . . . the way he'd been drinking earlier this evening when she'd tried to claw his face as he fished their last twenty out of her purse. He'd hit her once, just hard enough to shut her up. She should have known better than to go at him like that.

But he'd needed more than twenty, and could come up with only one way to get it if he was to make post time. What was he supposed to do? Pass up the chance to get rich? She'd get over it in time—like always.

He frowned slightly, thinking back to the way he'd left her with her face all swollen up with tears, her voice hoarse from pleading with him not to leave her with his friend Telest. But thirty bucks was thirty bucks, and Telest, who'd always fancied her, was quick to pull it out of his pocket. She should have been flattered the man thought she was worth it.

Now that the liquor had mostly worn off, he felt a twinge of guilt. But it was just this one time, because he'd been so close to hitting on a sure thing.

It wouldn't happen again. After all, it wasn't like he was selling her off to a stranger—Telest was almost family. And it was the least she could do, after all he'd done to take care of her and the kid. It was probably no more than a couple of minutes, anyway, considering how drunk Telest was when he'd shown up at their door.

The house was dark when T-Bob cut the engine, leaving the car half in the drive, half on the yard. She'd probably give him the *chew rouge* about tearing up her ratty flower bed, and his mood blackened.

He slammed the Caddy's heavy door and swaggered up to the house. If Telest was still in his bed, he was going to beat the stuff out of him, money or no. For principle's sake. Mad and feeling that gnaw of guilt, he needed something to make him feel better about what he'd done. Especially since his "sure thing" had left him dead broke.

The front door was standing open. He couldn't hear the baby crying, which was unusual enough to make him pause. He stepped in and switched on the light. The first thing he saw was a big empty spot on the wall where Dolores had hung pictures of her folks and the baby. Nothing but faded squares remained on the flowered wallpaper.

The ungrateful little . . . she'd left him!

Swearing fiercely, he stormed into the bedroom to see if her clothes were gone, but his gaze never made it to the closet. It was riveted to the river of blood on their tattered carpet—and to what was left of Telest on their bed. T-Bob's first stunned thought was that Dolores had gone crazy and killed him. One step closer told the truth of it. Telest's mouth was open in a silent scream; silent because his throat was gone.

A glimpse at the great, gaping hole in his friend's chest made T-Bob drop to his knees and spew up all his night's celebrations. Dolores couldn't have done such a thing. Nothing human could have.

Then the truth hit him—a truth so horrifying, he could scarcely force his legs to get him up off the floor. But he did, scrambling, sliding in the blood, choking on his moans of terror. His gaze flashed about the room in panic, but all he saw were quiet shadows.

He never believed she'd do it, even after her veiled threats. He thought he'd knocked that nonsense from her head.

But it wasn't nonsense.

She'd gone back to her own people for help.

The smell of fear rolled off him as he grabbed frantically for air. Surely Dolores hadn't asked for his death, too.

For God's sake, he was the father of their child! Her husband! She wouldn't do that for a few little slaps, or a measly twenty bucks. And it couldn't have been Telest. She'd laid down with plenty of men before him, and he'd never believed that there'd been none after. What had he done, for her to seek out her clan's retribution?

Just wait until he got his hands on her . . . she'd be so damned sorry.

But first he had to get out of this place where death hung thick and sweet in the air.

He made it to the car, the breath tearing from him in ragged gasps. In his haste he nearly flooded the big block engine, but it finally growled to life. Rubber burned as he backed out of the drive, and he was going close to fifty by the time he reached the end of the rain-dampened street. Something huge and dark suddenly appeared in the beam of his lights.

What the . . . ?

He slammed down his foot and the brakes locked, sending the tank of a car into a sideways shimmy. He fought the wheel for control, but there was no regaining it on the wet pavement. The big sedan smashed into a parked delivery truck. The impact crushed the passenger side, sending a shower of glass across the seat. T-Bob's head hit the side window, making the world go temporarily black. As soon as he was able, he wobbled out of the crippled car and began to stagger toward the closest light.

Something struck him between the shoulder blades and he went flat out on the wet stones, the wind knocked out of him. He lay gasping for a long minute, then was aware of another sound close by. Too close. A low, raspy breathing, seething between clenched teeth, then a quiet, rattling growl that made him think of one of those guard dogs that could tear a man to pieces on command. With a wild sort of relief, he wondered if that was what had gotten a hold of Telest. Believing that was better than the alternative.

Then he noticed a sharp, pungent scent, like the musty fur collar on his mama's best coat when it got wet in the rain. Only this was stronger, hotter. Alive.

Panting to get control of his fear, T-Bob flopped onto his back to face his attacker, hoping he could be talked out of setting the dog on him.

But there was no man—no dog, either. Just a huge, hulking shape crouched down on all fours and a horrible gleam of yellow eyes. T-Bob cried out and started to scramble backward on the cobbles as the thing began to rise up and up and up, until it towered over him on hind legs to at least seven feet of massive fur and fury.

"You won't ever misuse her again," came the beast's harsh rumble. "Prepare to pay for your sins."

T-Bob's last sight was of jowls rolling back from a row of mammoth teeth. Then he was screaming as the wide, gaping jaws reached down for him.

One

"Glad I don't have to clean up this mess."

Detective Charlotte Caissie examined an unidentifiable piece of the victim on the bottom of her stiletto-heeled boot before scraping it off on the wet cobblestones. A grimace of distaste shaped her boldly exotic features.

"I've never known you to clean up anything, Cee Cee, darlin'," Alain Babineau said from the other side of the vehicle. "If you'd wear practical shoes to work, you wouldn't be picking up our evidence like a litter sticker and carrying it all over the place."

She studied her stylish footgear, then scowled at her partner. "At least my wardrobe doesn't come straight outta my high school yearbook."

"No, you get yours from the Frederick's of Hollywood catalog. And you wonder why my wife thought you were a hooker the first time you met."

"You're just jealous 'cause your wife prefers to dress like Doris Day." She smoothed the short leather skirt that was several inches from a working girl's advertisement. It wasn't her fault she had legs as long as an NBA star's. Nor would she apologize for her in-your-face looks. The exaggerated bristle of short dark hair, dramatically rimmed kohl-black eyes, the slash of crimson lips, and model-sharp angles under café au lait skin complemented her aggressive no-nonsense attitude. A wardrobe that was more Xena the Warrior Princess than Suzie Homemaker flaunted her strong, curvy build and emphasized what she was inside: tough, confident, and capable. All cop. All the time.

"There's more of him over here. Not exactly sure what, though." Her partner straightened, observing the remains of T-Bob Gautreaux with a sigh. A weary grimness about his eyes toughened the all-American looks that were more suited to a country club than a grisly murder scene. "The ole boy sure did get around. Can't decide whether to call in the coroner or the city sanitation crew."

"What do you make of it, Babs?" Cee Cee's gaze tracked the last frantic moments of the Caddy's ride by the devastation left in its wake. Skid marks, dents, glass, and blood. Lots of blood. "He was in a helluva hurry to get away from something."

"Don't look like the poor bastard had much luck."

"He had luck, all right. All bad." Cee Cee activated her radio. "Boucher, whatchu come up with over there at the house?"

"More of the same, detective." The youthful voice thinned with strain. "I'm almost through taking pictures here."

"I don't think I'll be needing any wallet-size prints." She took a bracing breath before asking, "Any sign of the wife and kid?"

"No, ma'am." Quieter. "Thank God." Then a puzzled tone. "You making the wife for this?"

"I don't think so, Joey. A woman on her worst PMS day couldn't come up with this kind of pissed off."

"I've never seen anything like it." The rookie officer's whisper was laced with horror.

Cee Cee glanced about the gore-strewn street. "I have."

In all her years on the force, the last four of them carrying a shield, Charlotte Caissie had seen all sorts of inhumanity dealt out by her fellow man. Shootings, stabbings, punitive maimings—nothing surprised her any more. But this, this carnage they'd come across now and again, was different in a way that made her scalp prickle viscerally. This wasn't an act of anger or revenge or even ritual. The savagery of it was unthinkable on this side of sanity. The way the victims were torn apart went beyond mutilation, requiring a power and single-minded purpose that was more beast than man. But no animal she knew possessed the kind of foresight and cunning to kill, then lie in wait to kill again. To stalk and pursue with intelligent discrimination. It was a thinking beast who hunted the dark city streets. One with specific targets. One who left a merciless message underlined in entrails. A message meant to be taken seriously.

She took it *very* seriously.

"Finish up, Joey, and get on over here before the rain washes away what's left of Mr. Gautreaux." She switched off the radio and returned to the unmarked car where her partner sat inside to protect his suede varsity jacket as he ran names through their database. She leaned against the door frame, her relaxed posture belying the sharp-edged expectation winding through her. "Find what we both knew we'd find?"

Babineau looked up, a feral smile on his aftershave-ad-smooth face. "Gautreaux and Surette, both low-level gamblers in over their heads to guess who?"

Anticipation had her teeth grinding. "Jimmy Legere. How come his name pops up every time we find ourselves looking down into an empty chest cavity?"

"Nothing says 'I own you' like mortal fear. Shall we go pay him a visit and see what he's been up to?"

Cee Cee checked the crime scene. The tape was up, holding back the swarm of press who managed to scent out the dead like flies. Their people were in control, if any control could be had at the site of such depravity. The forensic team was busy unloading their high-tech gizmos in a focused rapture, making her and Babineau's presence obsolete.

"Let's go." She dropped behind the wheel with a fierce smile. "Let's just stop by uninvited."

THERE WAS NO way to drop in unexpectedly on Jimmy Legere. The eight-foot walls surrounding his sprawling estate were studded with surveillance cameras that could summon a crew of armed men in an instant. But as they approached, the wrought-iron gates stood open, almost as if to welcome guests at four in the morning. As if they'd been expected.

She followed the long drive beneath a heavy lace of live oaks, through the formal gardens where statuary stood like cold, nude ghosts under the waning moonlight. In the daytime, the place had a faded elegance to it. At night, it gave her the creeps. She parked so their vehicle blocked the front steps and hesitated within its safety for a minute. There was enough of the old ways steeped in her heritage to get her nape bristling in uncomfortable wariness—a kind of walking-over-graves nervousness, making her wonder if there were more ghosts roaming behind the pale stucco walls. The ghosts of those Legere had killed.

Shaking off the superstitious shivers, she got out of the car. The sound of the door slamming echoed back off the mist. She didn't bother giving the grand home an admiring glance; she'd been there before. With Babineau following, she marched up the marble steps, surprised that no one had arrived to intercept them. No one ever caught Jimmy napping, which was why he was still alive. The wide porch was darkly shadowed, smelling of verbena and musty wood. She strode across it toward the massive front door.

"Kinda early to be making house calls, isn't it, detective?"

The low voice came out of the blackness, so close that she felt warm breath against her cheek. It took Cee Cee a moment to swallow the heart that had catapulted into her throat. She'd nearly leapt out of her fancy new T-Bob Gautreaux-stained boots.

"But not too early for you to be up and around," she countered in a gruff tone to cover her start of alarm. She could sense rather than see him, standing right at her elbow, a forceful presence cloaked in stillness. No wonder no alert had been spread at their arrival. Jimmy had his big dog out on the porch.

"That's a new perfume you're wearing. I like it. Your hair's different, too."

"All just for you, Max. Now step back or I'm going to have to pat you down."

"Would you?" A flash of white teeth. "I'd like that." But he did glide to a less invasive distance, to where his eyes gleamed from the shadows.

She took a breath, letting the jitters settle, then nodded back toward the road. "Expecting company?"

"I could tell it was you the minute you turned onto River Road."

Max Savoie had a way of saying strange, impossible things like that as if they were true.

"Gonna ask us in, or keep us out here in the rain

like we were trying to sell you something you didn't need?"

His voice was deep and smooth with just a subtle ripple, like rich cognac in a warm glass. "Where are my manners? You know it's always a pleasure to see you, no matter what you're selling."

Because she was still simmering over Babineau's earlier comment, she asked, "You ever mistake me for a hooker, Max?"

Another glint of strong white teeth. "If I had, I'da been counting out twenties."

When he crossed between her and the front door, she got a clear look at Savoie. Dark, tall, and bold. Jimmy Legere's right hand. His silent enforcer. An always-frustrating enigma. No one knew anything about him other than the name he used, a name that led to nothing but dead ends in any of their databases. No birth certificate, no Social Security number, no driver's license, health insurance, tax records—nothing. His past was as inaccessible as the expression on his face when he turned toward her with the door held wide.

"*Après vous.*"

She and Babineau entered the dark, cavernous foyer, Savoie bringing up the rear. She heard him say soft and low to someone unseen, "Wake up, Jimmy. The police are here." Then he preceded them into one of the high-ceilinged parlors and turned up the lights, unmasking himself from the shadows with a dramatic flare.

Cee Cee didn't spend a lot of time admiring men for their looks, but something about Max Savoie's face arrested her each time she saw him.

He wasn't handsome, not even attractive in the traditional sense. He was rugged strength cut into sharp planes and rough angles. Confident without being cocky, powerful without aggression, he exuded complete control over what he allowed the world to see, which was usually damned little.

The fact that he could seem so forceful behind such a calm, immobile front impressed her. Not much did. Max was a man who wasted no unnecessary words or movements, his unblinking stare taking in everything without revealing anything through eyes the color of wet verdigris, beneath lids heavy with guarded disdain.

Or amusement. She often got the feeling that he was laughing at her on some private level, which irritated her. But the odd way he sensed things not apparent to others made her nervous. Sounds, smells, movements. He was alert to them like a mastiff on a short chain. And he missed nothing when it came to her—not the slightest nuance, every tiny alteration, in a way that she'd find alarmingly obsessive if he ever acted on it with more than slightly flirtatious words. Who the hell noticed a new perfume applied modestly to pulse points almost a full day ago? Wondering made those pulse points flutter.

"Coffee?" he asked as they moved toward the center of the big room.

"That would be nice." Babineau spoke up to assert his presence, aware of the way his partner and Legere's bodyguard were atuned to each other, and not liking it.

A slight smile touched Savoie's lips. "I was wondering if you brought any. We weren't exactly expecting company."

"This isn't exactly a social call," Cee Cee corrected.

That cool stare held hers. "Too bad." Without glancing down, he asked, "Who's that on your shoes? Anyone I know?"

She held on to her surprise, drawling, "You tell me."

"DNA isn't exactly my specialty."

"What is, Max?"

The smile remained. He didn't answer.

He was probably a killer. He was probably one of the most dangerous and deadly men she knew, which was why Jimmy Legere kept him so close at hand.

"Is our unnamed friend the reason for your visit?"

This time she didn't answer. She was noting the way he was dressed: quite nicely for almost four in the morning, in a crisp white shirt and black pants. And his inevitable red Converse gym shoes. All fresh and spotless. "Mind telling me what has you up so early?"

"Still up. Playing games of chance."

"Here in the house?"

"Upstairs."

"Witnesses?"

"I'd rather not give her name, unless you need to know it." A pause; then he leaned in close. "I'd rather it was you."

Her insides tightened up unexpectedly, and she was about to tell him off when the shock of his nearness hit home.

He'd intruded into the personal space she held as strictly off-limits, sometimes even with excessive physical force. She didn't like being crowded or handled and wasn't shy about letting that be known. Most didn't need to be told more than once. But for some reason, Savoie never seemed to get the message. Maybe because she let him get away with it.

He was the only man she allowed to move in on her without snapping to immediate back-the-fuck-off defensiveness. She didn't know why she'd never felt threatened by him, this big man who was most likely a ruthless murderer.

She could feel his heat without actual contact, and though it was unsettling, it didn't set off the expected alarm bells. Because it wasn't alarm that unsettled her. It was something else—something quiet, something deep, like a secret her soul knew but wouldn't share with her mind. What was it about him that tugged a blanket of calm over instinctive agitation?

He never touched her, not even a casual brush of his hand or unintentional bump of his body. Sometimes she perversely found herself wondering what it would be like, that contact he withheld so purposefully.

I'd rather it was you.

Though her heart slammed against her ribs, her reply was defensively cold. "That's not going to happen, Max."

He eased back, moving with startling grace for a man his size. "I can dream, can't I?"

She doubted that she was the stuff of his dreams, but her pulse didn't slow down until the arrival of Jimmy Legere. As the crime lord's wheelchair rolled into the room, Max retreated to become a silent, motionless sentinel at his back.

"Detectives. To what do I owe this early-morning wake-up call?"

A slight stroke hadn't slowed Jimmy Legere down or made his stranglehold on the docks of New Orleans any less powerful. If something even slightly unsavory was going on, Jimmy had his hand in it or his hand out to accept a payoff from it. He was a gregarious old man somewhere between sixty and dead, fragile and white haired. He had tons of money but lived in a house as old and broken down as he was getting to be. He donated generously to a variety of humanitarian causes, including, ironically, the fund for families of police officers slain in the line of duty. Probably because the stroke got him thinking about paving his way into Heaven sooner rather than later. Or as a macabre joke.

As long as his people were loyal, he was generous to them as well. But cross him and that's when the legendary Legere surfaced, the man who once threw a lavish wedding for his cousin, then shot him in the eye during the reception because he'd been skimming from that pot of plenty. It was never proven, of course. Few unpleasantries ever got close to Jimmy. One, because he was smart. Two, because Max Savoie was standing behind him, and everyone with a lick of sense was scared to the marrow of Max.

"T-Bob Gautreaux and Telest Surette. Names mean anything to you, Jimmy?" Babineau jumped right in.

"That's Mr. Legere to you," Max said in an inflectionless tone that somehow implied a world of menace.

"Mr. Legere," the detective corrected.

"Be nice to our guests, Max," the old man chided. "I'm sure they've had a long night and are tired and wanting to go home to their families. Jimmy is fine."

"Since when are we guests, Jimmy?" Cee Cee prodded.

"Since you're not here to arrest me. Or are you?"

She gave the old fellow a once-over, noting the striped pajamas over pencil-thin legs peeping out from his silk robe. He wore powder blue terry-cloth slippers. What kind of mobster wore powder blue terry cloth? But she wasn't fooled by his apparent helplessness.

She smiled. "You know everything about everything, Jimmy. What do you know about these two small-timers? Why would someone want to scramble their insides like an omelet and spill them all over my district?"

There was nothing wrong with Legere's ledger-like mind. "T-Bob was in for twenty large. A crude, rather stupid man who used to slap his wife around. Telest, a nobody who bet only when he could pay the interest. Not model citizens, detective, but they paid on their accounts—from what I understand, that is. Dead men don't pay markers."

"But when they die really ugly, they can be an inspiration to those who might consider letting a payment slide."

A rusty chuckle. "Very true, young lady. But these days, considering my health, I search for inspiration at St. Phillip's."

"How . . . admirable."

She let her cool, professional facade slip just long enough for him to see what was behind it: fury, packed in frustration and to-the-ends-of-the-earth determination. She wouldn't rest until she brought him down, until her hand slammed the prison door behind him. He read that promise without taking offense, but without amusement, either. He took her seriously, which was exactly what she wanted. For him to know who was going to lock him away for whatever forever he had left.

"Was there anything else, detective? I should like to get back to my rest."

"I'm sure you'll have no trouble sleeping, Jimmy."

"Never do."

"Must be all that clean living and prayer. You'll let us know if you hear anything?"

"Of course. I'll send Max."

Her gaze flickered to the rough-hewn features, meeting his steady stare. "A phone call will be fine. Sorry to have disturbed you."

"Always a pleasant disruption for an old man like me. Max, see them out."

WHEN MAX SAVOIE returned from that duty, he was met with a no-nonsense stare.

"Max, what have you been up to?"

"WHAT DO YOU think, Ceece?"

Cee Cee started the car and pulled away from the house. She was always glad to have the spooky old place in her rearview mirror. "I think the old man has enough skeletons to supply a medical school, but I don't think our vics are among them."

Though she didn't think Jimmy Legere had any blood on him this time, she was wondering about Max Savoie. For a man who'd been up all night, his clothes had just-pulled-off-the-tag creases still in them. If he'd been romping with a woman, why was he sporting an unwrinkled shirt and smelling of a really nice soap instead of Eau de Sex? He wasn't the only one who had a discriminating nose. Why would he be so well dressed unless what he'd been wearing earlier was covered in T-Bob and Telest? But a gut feeling wasn't enough for a warrant, and she had no desire to be cornered by Legere's slick lawyer before she had her morning coffee.

She made a call to Devlin Dovion, who by now was probably at the scene and up to his elbows in one of the corpses. The medical examiner had been a friend of her father's and always gave her the inside scoop when he could.

"Charlotte," he grumbled, "I'm trying to work here. Let me do my job."

"I can do my job better if you tell me what you've discovered so far. Any idea who killed them, Dev?"

"Who? No. *What* would be the better question."

"What?" She exchanged a puzzled glance with Babineau. "You mean what was used to kill them?"

"Oh, that's easy. Surette had his throat and heart torn out by bare hands."

"Through the rib cage? Is that possible?"

"I'm not saying how it was done, only that that's the way it *was* done."

Cee Cee swallowed. "And Gautreaux?"

"That's a bit more interesting." To Devlin, everything gruesome was interesting. And he liked talking to Charlotte because she seemed to think so, too. They were two of a kind, walking on the dark side of the night.

"Interesting how so?"

"His body was ripped apart by fangs and claws."

"Fangs and . . . claws? Are we talking animal, here? Like some big dog or something?"

"I've got a pretty good bite impression, but off the top of my head, I couldn't tell you what made it. Something big enough to chase and catch a Cadillac going roughly fifty miles an hour, knock down a man weighing more than two hundred pounds, and have enough strength left to tear off his arms."

Damn.

"So we're not talking your run-of-the-mill house pet here."

"Not in my house." Then, to her disappointment, he shut her down. "I'm not doing any more talking until I finish running tests. Every time we get one of these the results come back contaminated by some damn thing or another. This time I want to be extra careful. And keep this just between the two of us for now. Stuff like this always gets the crazies coming out of the woodwork to bay at the next full moon, and I don't need to be that busy cleaning up after you."

She signed off and drove in silence for several blocks.

"So," Babineau began casually, watching her expression as she processed the disturbing information. "Where do we look for this animal? At the pound?"

"Somehow I doubt it."

"Well, I'm out of ideas for the moment and out of energy. What say we call it a night and get started fresh in the morning?"

Out of ideas, maybe. But energy? She doubted it. Her partner had a new bride at home and always seemed in a hurry to punch out.

"Maybe she's waiting up for you wearing something in basic black rubber."

He didn't comment, but the gleam in his eye said that kind of surprise wouldn't be unwelcome.

But just because he had something to go home to didn't mean she was ready to trade their hot lead for her cold sheets.

Her mind was full of questions that needed to be asked—and she had a pretty good idea of where to start looking for answers.

Two

THERE WAS NOTHING glamorous about St. Bart's. There was no stained glass, no fancy silver, no elaborate carvings. Just religion offered plain and simple to the parish poor. Set in the middle of a brutal neighborhood, it was the closest thing to home Cee Cee had ever known.

She'd dropped off Babineau and had stopped at her apartment to change clothes, not wanting to track T-Bob across that holy threshold. She paused just inside the never-locked front doors and breathed in the peace she found nowhere else. It was the scent of polish and oils, incense and melting candle wax, the sound of murmured prayers, of singsong Latin echoing within the soaring walls. The familiar embrace of welcome, of safety.

She strode up the center aisle, instinctively checking out the woman kneeling in silent sorrow and the wino sleeping off his excess in the second pew. No threat there, but something tickled her intuition. She continued along the front of the sanctuary, her eyes restless, but it was a feeling, not a fact, that had her on edge.

A familiar figure was on hands and knees scrubbing the floor with a zealous enthusiasm. Large, lumpy, of indistinguishable age, he didn't look up until she called his name.

"Hello, Benjamin."

Eyes so pale they were almost colorless rose blankly, then lit with recognition. "Oh, it's you Miss Lottie. Kinda early."

Benjamin Spratt was as much a fixture of the church as the hand-carved crucifix presiding over the ragged congregation. He'd shown up one day, a battered and needy stray, when she was little more than a child. St. Bart's became his home, and there was no job too big or small for him to reverently tackle to work off that self-perceived debt. His loving care bestowed a shine to the otherwise humble building.

She smiled at him fondly. "Looks like both of us are getting a jump on the workday. Is she awake?"

"Isn't she always." He chuckled as if that was their private joke. "Go on back. She'll be glad to see you. Mind your steps; it's still wet there."

Cee Cee's anxious spirit quieted the instant she entered the attached building. Memories swirled about her like the warmth of a blanket and a sheltering bed, a full stomach and a tender voice.

St. Bart's had always had a bigger heart than bank account. That hadn't stopped it from opening its arms to a parish in need, providing its children with a safe haven and hot meal when parents, if there were any, couldn't afford day care. Instead of crouching in an empty apartment or roaming the dangerous streets, the innocent had a place to be nurtured and nourished, and to be loved—absolutely and unconditionally.

Spartan but clean and safe accommodations extended that care to another layer of the helpless and the lost, housing victims of spousal abuse and their children. Though only a temporary solution, it provided immediate shelter to those who had nowhere else to go, and hope to those who no longer believed it existed.

Girlish laughter from one of the many tiny rooms made Cee Cee smile, remembering back. She was still smiling when a nun in full regalia stepped into the hall to regard her without surprise. The police weren't the only ones on call 24/7.

"I just put tea on."

"I'd appreciate that, Sister Catherine. It's been a rough night."

"Do you have any other kind?"

Cee Cee chuckled softly as she followed the graceful figure to her private quarters in back. The room was small, sparsely furnished, with no personal effects except two pictures; one of two teenage girls with their arms about each other, and a Polaroid of a couple, its coating now faded and cracked by years. Cee Cee took a seat at the small table, saying nothing as she watched the other woman move efficiently about the kitchen area. Once the cup was placed before her and the scent of Earl Gray filled her nose, she couldn't resist relaxing. But the ugliness of her visit couldn't be kept at bay.

"I'm looking for someone," she began as the young nun took the other seat. "Dolores Gautreaux."

"Why would you look here?"

"Because she's come to you for help before, for her and her baby."

"Lottie, you know I can't discuss those who come here for refuge." Calm eyes lowered to follow the current her spoon created in the cup.

"Her husband beats her, almost kills her, but she keeps going back for more."

"Lottie . . ."

"The man was a real nasty piece of work, but tonight, pieces of him were scattered all over my streets. And I need to find out what she knows about it."

The sister sighed. "They're safe. They're sleeping."

"How long have they been here?"

"I can't—"

Cee Cee didn't have time for formalities of conscience. "Mary Kate, in my opinion, the man got what he deserved. I just want to make sure they're all right. I have some questions. The sooner I talk to her, the better. I don't want them to suffer any more than they already have."

Sister Catherine regarded her somberly, with a

trust that went back through decades of friendship. "I'll speak to her. I'll arrange a time. I'd rather not wake them, considering what they've been through."

"If you'll give me your word that you'll keep them here until I can talk to them."

"More tea?"

Cee Cee made an aggravated sound, then relented. "Sure. You don't have any of Father Furness's whiskey to put in it, do you?"

A giggle reminiscent of the girl Mary Kate had once been made Cee Cee grin. For a second, she saw the free-spirited companion who'd once shared makeup and make-out tips over teen magazines and Top Forty hits. Love rose unbidden, like the fragrant tendrils from the tea, delicate yet hardy and restorative. Then she studied her friend more closely. "You look tired, Mary Kate."

"So do you. There's always too much work to do."

"Amen."

"Have you seen Dr. Forstrom lately?"

Cee Cee stiffened at the mention of the police psychiatrist. "Haven't had anything to discuss lately."

"Would you go to him if you did?" A soft chiding.

Cee Cee considered lying, then remembered where she was. "No."

"Would you come talk to me?"

"To do what, rehash old times?"

Pain flashed across Mary Kate Malone's still-lovely features. Even the scars across her cheek and throat hadn't marred that beauty. Cee Cee's scars were on the inside and hadn't healed quite so neatly. She wanted to feel bad for her friend's anguish but at the moment her frustration was too keen, her anger too acute.

"We've gone over this before, Mary Kate. You handle it your way, and I'll handle it mine."

"Does tracking them down by their own violent means change anything?"

"Does patching up their victims with false hope, before sending them right back home, accomplish anything other than to delay the inevitable?"

Sister Catherine's gaze grew as hard as her tone was gentle. "We do what we can to help."

"It's not helping unless the problem is eliminated."

Mary Kate didn't flinch at that ruthless statement. She argued wearily, "You can't hunt them all down. You can't kill or imprison every man with a heart of evil."

"I can try." Cee Cee pushed away from the table. "Maybe I shouldn't have come."

A warm hand clasped hers. "Sit. Finish your tea. And don't *ever* say you'll stay away. This is your home, your family."

Charlotte squeezed that tenacious hand. "I *am* tired, right down to my bones. Otherwise I wouldn't hurt you with words I don't mean."

"They don't hurt me. Seeing you like this hurts me. How long has it been since you've slept?"

Cee Cee smiled grimly. "Twelve years."

Mary Kate's gaze softened with understanding. "Talk to Dr. Forstrom."

"Dr. Foreplay wants to give me drugs and look down my shirt. I have the feeling he'd like to get in touch with more than just my emotions." A harsh sigh. "If I lose my edge, I can't do my job."

"Talk to him anyway."

"Oh, all right."

"Your word?"

At that tough prompting, Cee Cee smiled. "I guess if I say so here, I have to mean it, don't I?" She drank down the rest of her tea. It was sugary and sweet, just the way she liked it. Mary Kate never forgot those little details. "I'll come by at one to talk to Mrs. Gautreaux."

"She'll be here. But I don't know if she can tell you anything that will help your situation."

"He's dead. I'm sure that's a big help to hers."

Sister Catherine sat silently for a long moment after Charlotte was gone, then she spoke softly to the shadows. "Does she suspect?"

"She's too smart not to," came the quiet response, a deep voice edged with admiration. "Will she figure it out? Maybe someday, but not today. There's no trail for her to follow back here."

"Yet here she is. We can't involve her in this. I *won't* involve her in this. She wouldn't understand that what we're doing is necessary. You know that."

No answer.

Finally she sighed. "Thank you."

Again silence, then a harsh whisper. "You don't need to thank me."

"Yes, I do." She turned toward the darkness that she occasionally called upon. "Keep her safe. She still won't accept that there are so many things out there that can hurt her."

He was one of those things.

"I won't let any harm come to her," he promised fiercely. Not again. Never again.

"Thank you. Go with God."

"Is that who's traveling with me?" She heard a smile in his tone. "I rather doubt that. But you can pray for me anyway if it makes you feel better."

"It does."

It made him feel better, too.

THE RESTLESSNESS RETURNED the second Cee Cee stepped across the threshold. She paused there, leaning against the heavy wood door, holding it open, and pulled a cigarette from her purse. She'd been trying to quit smoking for twelve years. Oh well, what was one more day? She lit the end and took a long drag, then nearly choked as a gasp of surprise sucked the smoke into her lungs.

Inside a man moved quickly across the front of the church. She couldn't see his face, but there was no mistaking the lethal grace of his steps.

The cigarette fell, forgotten, and was quickly crushed beneath her toe as she reentered the sanctuary to race up the wide aisle. Dodging through one of the side doors and down a narrow hall, she burst out into the pale shimmer of dawn. Steam rose off the dirty streets as weak sunlight crept down the sides of nearby buildings, pushing shadows closer to the ground. And out of those shadows, in a swirl of his long black raincoat, Max Savoie disappeared into an alley.

What was Jimmy Legere's henchman doing at St. Bart's, where the wife of a recently murdered man was in hiding?

She sprinted down the sidewalk to ask him, but when she ducked down the alley, there was no sign of him. Just a tight gauntlet of overflowing trash bins and stacks of broken skids. Water dripped down from the air conditioners above, where the buildings leaned in to seal out the new day for a few moments longer. This wasn't the kind of position she liked to get into: no backup, no traffic, and no room to play it safe. But Savoie had gone down this alley, which ended at ten feet of chain-link fence topped with vicious curls of razor wire. The fence wasn't moving, so he still had to be on her side of it. He couldn't have gone up and over it so quickly without leaving a sway in passing.

She unsnapped her holster as she stepped into the dank corridor.

For the first twenty feet, the only sounds were her footsteps on puddled brick. Then she heard a quiet rustling behind one of the Dumpsters. Though she couldn't picture Savoie hiding from her behind a heap of garbage, she continued on, more irritated than cautious.

A man suddenly rose up in front of her, smiling ferociously when his gaze swept over her. His smile never reached the flat soullessness in his eyes.

"Well, hello there, little lady. Don't you know it's not safe to come down here all by yourself, unless you're looking for trouble?"

One hand was on her pistol grip as she reached for her badge with the other. "You don't want my kind of trouble. I'm a—"

His fisted blow caught her in the midsection. The pain was so sudden, so stunning, she doubled up. She hung on tenaciously, swinging an elbow to catch him in the jaw, knocking him back a few steps while she wheezed for breath. *Son of a bitch!* She knew better than to put herself into this kind of situation. She rose above her heaving nausea into a defensive stance.

When he came at her again her fists connected with stunning impact, once, twice, followed by an uppercut that staggered him. As he tried to shake it off, dazed and momentarily malleable, she moved back to put room between them. Angry, still fighting the urge to wretch, she reached for her cuffs.

Large, cruel hands gripped her elbows as another man came in behind her. She was so woozy, she hadn't even heard him. She threw herself back against him, clawing, twisting, kicking, and cursing, inflicting almost enough damage to get free. Then she saw the arc of the first man's hand and the glint of her own weapon in it. The butt smashed into her temple, dropping her to her hands and knees with the other man atop her.

She choked on acidic bile as he tore her shirt, popping all the buttons off, before shoving her face-down. The wet stones were cold and cutting beneath bare skin. And the man straddling her was cold and determined as he yanked on her belt, reached beneath her to fumble with her zipper, and started dragging down her jeans.

A remembered fear, so strong that she couldn't breathe past it, paralyzed her. Her reflexes failed her; her courage curled into a fetal position as she knew with soul-crushing certainty exactly what was going to happen if she couldn't rise above the debilitating horror.

Move now! Do something!

She turned her head to scream, when something wet and hot suddenly splashed her face, blinding her.

The weight lifted off her in an instant. She could hear the man scrambling, trying to run. Then awful screams—first of terror, then of agony that went on and on. She tried to get up, but was trapped by her pants. Dizzy and disoriented, she rolled onto her side and found herself looking into the glassy eyes of her first assailant. His mouth was open in a silent scream; his throat was shredded. And there was nothing beneath that jagged neck wound. Nothing at all.

She must have fainted. A tug on her clothes woke her, but before she could struggle, her pants came sliding up her hips. Firm hands closed on her upper arms, sitting her up. Something damp and revivingly cold swiped across her face and neck. Her senses spun and she clenched her lips tight, afraid she was going to throw up.

Then his voice reached through her fear and pain with a deep, steady familiarity.

"It's all right. No one's going to hurt you."

She made herself open her eyes, and that wonderfully strong face appeared before her in an almost ethereal blur. For a moment, his gaze seemed to glow, hot, bright, iridescent; then she blinked rapidly and it became an intense, steady stare. He wore an expression of grim concern— and a splattering of blood. As she started shuddering involuntarily, he stripped off his raincoat and wrapped it about her shoulders, concealing the rent in the front of her shirt that exposed her muddy bra.

With her breath coming in quick, anxious pulls, she glanced around them—at the headless corpse, at the arm dangling out of the trash bin dripping crimson. Her shaking intensified.

"I came back because I smelled your perfume," he said.

She stared at him for a long minute, then her

laugh sounded thin and a bit crazed. And her arms were around his neck. "Max."

He couldn't move, startled, stunned by the feel of her in his arms.

It had happened so fast, he hadn't paused to think it through. He'd felt her following him, smiling to himself as he easily slipped away. But as that smug amusement warmed him, the hair on his nape prickled and he caught the unpleasant scent and stealthy sounds of two others.

He'd slowed, reluctant to push his way in where she wouldn't want him—Charlotte Caissie was hardly helpless. So he lingered, imagining her knocking the snot out of her would-be attackers. Watching her was always quality entertainment. He'd pay just to stand there, slack-jawed and tongue hanging out, while she pumped gas. The thought of her pumping her fist into some petty criminal was pay-per-view material. The husky growl of her voice was a hand running against the nap of his senses, stirring him up effortlessly into a rough bristle of want.

When her words were abruptly cut off and she moaned in pain, the speed of his rush made the fence shiver as he cleared it. Several powerful bounds brought him onto a scene that burned through him like napalm. She was facedown on the filthy bricks. One of them had rough hands on her, sealing his fate when she cried out in distress. It was the last mistake either of them would ever make, as he tore into them with merciless fury.

He should have disappeared the minute he'd eliminated the danger, before she could gather her wits and identify him. But the sight of her sprawled and vulnerable and cruelly exposed called to him in a way she never would. And he couldn't leave her like that. Never like that.

Then she'd looked up at him and said his name. He was lost in an instant.

Despite her shivering, he noticed that her body was lush and firm and strong, just as he'd imagined when caressing her for years with sidelong glances. He held himself still, calling on rigid self-control as her scent swirled about him, teasing up his nose. Carefully, rapturously, he inhaled. Her heat scalded through his clothing to imprint her shape on his skin. And he would have gladly remained on his knees forever, if it meant indulging his chastely ravenous desires for just a moment longer.

But she was still shaking, in shock. Daylight and discovery were almost upon them.

He stood, lifting her up off the damp stones with him. When she wobbled, he scooped her up into his arms to carry her out of the carnage-strewn alley. She was hardly a small woman, but he carried her as if she were no burden at all.

Cee Cee was too shaken to marvel at his strength or question his intentions. She lay limp and trusting against his chest, her head aching, her heart still racing. His body heat slowly thawed the paralyzing chill, yet she lingered in his powerful embrace, enveloped by a sense of safety. She buried her face against the warm pulse of his throat, her fears vanquished by the rhythm of his breathing, oblivious to her surroundings. He stopped and asked quietly, "Do you think you can drive, or do you want me to sit with you for a while?"

Her fingers tightened in his shirt. She wanted to curl into him, to indulge for just a little bit longer, but her senses began to reassemble and she knew that she couldn't. She shouldn't. Reluctantly she lifted her head from his shoulder, surprised to discover they were beside her car. How had he carried her for such a distance without the slightest strain?

"Put me down."

She must have sounded more capable than she felt, because he eased her down to her feet. She stumbled back to look at him a bit wildly, her gaze touching the blood on his face, on his shirt, on his hands. Feeling traces of it drying on her skin.

"You killed those men." Her voice quivered between accusation and awe.

His eyes were unblinking. He didn't admit it. Not exactly. "I'm sorry. Did you want to get to know them better?"

She tried to speak but had to turn away quickly so she wouldn't vomit on his shoes. She swallowed down the bitter taste, saving her dignity in at least that one thing. His hand touched her shoulder. A surprisingly careful touch, as if she were fragile and he feared she might break. She hadn't expected such gentleness from him, and it made her uncharacteristically compliant—for a moment. She took the handkerchief from him to blot a cold sweat from her face. Then she abruptly straightened, gripping his wrist, wrenching it toward the center of his back as she spun him up against her car. He allowed her to manhandle him with a surprising good grace.

"Where's my gun?"

She patted him down roughly, jerking her revolver from his trouser band before continuing the search.

"I never carry a piece, detective. You know that. I don't like guns."

The image of those dead, staring eyes made her shivering start up again, which agitated her all the more. "You rushed in to take on armed men with your bare hands? You expect me to believe that? Are you insane?"

"Should I have just kept walking?"

She was running her hands up and down his long, muscular legs, over his hips, the movements brusque and impersonal, convinced he had some sort of weapon on him. Something brutal enough to decapitate a man.

As her palms moved up his abdomen, he turned so they were face to face. Her eyes widened in surprise, then objection, as he cuffed her wrists with his hands and reversed their positions to press her back against the car. His gaze locked into hers, his eyes darkening with something she'd never seen in them before but recognized as the rawness of want. Nothing as ugly and degrading as her assailants in the alley, but suddenly just as overwhelming.

He slowly leaned against her, easing his hard contours along her long, lavish ones. Halting when panic flared in her eyes.

"Step back, Savoie."

Her gruff command must have lacked conviction, because his head lowered until his breath feathered against her lips. Soft. Warm.

"Don't."

Not quite so tough.

He tasted her slowly, riding the jerk of her chest, gentling his hold on her hands, finally releasing them. Her palms came up to rest against his shoulders, motionless at first, then beginning to push. He lifted off her by a scant inch, his stare delving into hers, his breathing hurried.

"Max, stop."

That hoarse whisper still didn't convince him. The tip of his tongue lightly traced her full lower lip, the gesture so provokingly intimate, she trembled with helpless response.

His challenge brushed silkily over her damp mouth. "I will if you mean it."

And for one startling moment, she didn't.

Knowing it, he smiled faintly and settled in to kiss her more deeply, druggingly, as if searching for something he was determined to find. And she was willing to let him look, lost to his increasingly urgent explorations. Rough then soft, hungry and hot, then devastatingly sweet.

The aggressive jut of him pressing into her hip shook her. She stiffened into a taut column of denial as he rocked against her, the motion frightening, stirring panic instead of passion. She began struggling, pushing for distance. He left the cushiony softness of her mouth and rubbed his cheek against hers, going completely still when he felt the dampness of her tears.

With a resigned sigh, he stood back from the impossible temptation she'd become. She was so beautiful, so strong yet so alarmingly fragile, her eyes tightly closed, shutting him out with the glistening fan of her lashes. They fluttered open as he stroked his knuckle down her cheek, as soft as sun-warmed satin.

"The next time you come chasing after me, *sha*, you'd best be sure you really want to catch me."

With a small smile, he turned and walked away. In no particular hurry, as if he weren't leaving behind two dead men and a far-from-impartial witness.

Charlotte sank down on suddenly strengthless legs behind the wheel of her car. She instinctively started to reach for her radio, then paused. Max Savoie had come to her rescue and had left the grisly remains of her attackers. He'd killed them without a weapon, with enough brutal strength to separate a man's head from his shoulders. A signature like that would be impossible not to link to the murders she was investigating. He'd saved her life, and she was going to repay him by putting him in jail?

She hadn't actually *seen* him do anything, had she?

Her thoughts took an abrupt detour down a dangerously unfamiliar road as she licked her lips slowly, still feeling the imprint of his kisses. Kisses he'd poured onto the parched earth of her soul, and she'd soaked them up with a greedy desperation.

Just where did he get off, deciding to move their comfortable sparring relationship into treacherous emotional waters? She expelled a shaky breath and leaned back in the seat, closing her eyes to ease the pounding in her head.

Why did he have to complicate everything? First by coming to her aid, when he had no reason to do so and every reason not to. Then he'd slipped through her stony defenses, conquering her not with brute strength, but with calm determination. And she'd let him. She'd *let* him. Then he stopped, even though he hadn't wanted to, because she'd asked.

That hot, compelling light in his eyes had been desire. The kind that accompanied all the cumbersome baggage she'd done her best to avoid.

"Damn you, Max," she whispered.

The last thing on her mind when she'd gotten out of bed that morning was stirring up a mobster's interest in her, be it physical or with all the scary trimmings.

As she started the car, a clear, cold notion clicked in her analytical cop mind.

Max Savoie was her way to Jimmy Legere.

She drove straight to her apartment, stepped into her shower and washed all the DNA evidence down her drain, then threw her torn clothes into the trash. Slipping on a pair of sweats, because she was suddenly chilled to the bone, she wrapped herself up in Max's coat and huddled on the couch with every light blazing. The clock was edging toward seven a.m. when exhaustion pulled her under.

But when she woke from the expected nightmare from the past an hour later, it wasn't to frantic screams. It was to the soothing sound of a low-pitched voice and words that were both so familiar.

Don't be afraid. They won't ever hurt you again. I took care of them for you.

Her eyes sprang open; her fingers clutched the lapels of the coat. Max. Wasn't that what he'd said to her in the alley?

No—not quite the same words.

Had his rescue intruded into her dreams, wishing that he could have saved her then, as he had now?

Or were his words part of a long-hidden memory?

Three

SHE FOLLOWED BABINEAU down the alley, stepping over the tipped trash cans on her way to the plastic-draped form on the bricks. Feeling safe behind dark glasses, with her hair combed artfully over the spectacular bruise on her temple, she sipped her coffee while her partner peered into the Dumpster.

"Yeech."

Joey Boucher caught sight of them and straightened from the small vinyl square that covered the rest of the first victim. "Hey, long time no see."

"Same ole story, Boucher?"

"Same ole song and dance. Got any more of that coffee, detective? I've been here since dawn trying to match part A to victim B, and could really use a jolt of something to tide me over."

Because she was impressed by his steadiness after a rather rocky prior night's performance, Charlotte passed him the half-full cup of espresso. "Help yourself."

Boucher was a homely kid, all ears and nose and Adam's apple, but he had the makings of a fine cop. A little green, a little soft around the edges, but dedicated and smart in all the right ways. He also treated Cee Cee like she could walk on water. She rather liked that about him, too.

"You're a life saver," the young officer sighed after he took his first sip.

Glancing around the alley, Cee Cee could have argued that claim. Struggling to remain dispassionate, she reminded herself why these two men were dead and what they'd planned to do if they hadn't been stopped. "Did they find a weapon?"

"A weapon?"

"A knife, a hatchet, machete? Whatever was used to slice and dice."

"We haven't come up with anything. It looks a little . . . messy to be a blade."

"What are you suggesting, Joey? That these big, hulking guys were pulled apart by brute force?"

"I hate to say it, but yeah. That's what it looks like."

"Just popped that man's head off like a rabbit's?"

Boucher never blinked. "Yeah."

Dovion's words whispered into her mind. *Fangs and claws.*

She gave a snort of disbelief. "Oh, come on. What kind of man has that much strength?" Even as she said the words, she was thinking of powerful arms cradling her close. "How can that happen? How the *hell* can that happen?"

"Don't know, Detective Caissie. But Hammond has someone he likes for it at the station. He supposedly got a tip. Probably while on his knees." That last part was muttered under his breath.

She didn't respond with the usual disgusted agreement, because sudden cold had seeped into her like ice. "Anyone we know?"

"That spooky knee-breaker of Jimmy Legere's. Hey, Cee Cee, don't you want to finish up here?"

She was striding back to the car with a puzzled Babineau in pursuit. "Go ahead, Joey. I'll sign off on it later."

As her partner buckled up, his question was as direct as his stare. "What's going on, Ceece? Something I should know about you and this Savoie character?"

"Don't be stupid, Babs. I have no reason to wish anything but hard time on one of Legere's men. I just think Hammond is making a mistake, is all." She couldn't meet his gaze. She couldn't convince herself that what she was saying was true, so how could she sway him?

Babineau pursed his lips but kept the rest of his comments to himself until they reached the station. She went quickly to Holding Two and stared through the one-way glass. Junior Hammond, a slick third-generation cop looking to make first grade, had his palms braced on the tabletop and was shouting into the calm face of his cuffed prisoner. Max Savoie stared up at his accuser with a flat, unblinking stare.

Suddenly Max's posture stiffened, and his head swiveled sharply. His gaze fixed on the opaque glass.

Cee Cee took a startled step back as his stare seemed to meet hers. Ridiculous, of course. She knew he couldn't see her there, but she recalled his odd claim.

I smelled your perfume . . .

Though his expression didn't change, his attention never left the mirror, even as Hammond was called out by their buzz.

The stocky officer glared at them in irritation. He was built like a Brink's truck, from the squared bulk of his body to the landing strip of his blond buzz cut, a mean aging Hitler youth on steroids. Unfortunately, he could never get his temper locked down tight, which kept him from advancing through the ranks as fast as he'd expected.

His fellow officers didn't like him because there was nothing he wouldn't stoop to for praiseworthy attention, which frequently meant undercutting their solid police work and claiming the results as his own.

Cee Cee didn't like him because he'd had to be told twice about the boundaries of her personal space. The second time had him wearing dark glasses for more than a week. Any fool knew she could drive a railroad spike with her fist; it wasn't her problem that he'd had to learn that hands-on.

"Whatchu mean pulling me off an interrogation?" He started to get up into her face, but caught himself just in time as her eyes narrowed. "You know he'll be lawyered up the minute Legere knows he's here. He was about to break."

Cee Cee laughed. "Into a smile maybe, but certainly not into a sweat. You got nothing, Junior."

"I got a call—"

"From who?"

"A source."

"What source?"

"A reliable source." His jaw hardened like a cement block, daring her to push beyond those boundaries of privilege.

"Uncuff him. Savoie was with me this morning." She heard Babineau choke beside her but continued on. "We were at St. Bartholomew's, discussing theology with Sister Catherine."

"What?" A shriek that quickly dropped in register to a furious growl. "The hell you say." Hammond made a tight circle, chewing on his ire as his "career maker" evaporated right out of his greedy hands. "Theology. Right. Anatomy maybe," he grumbled.

Cee Cee took a step into his path. "Excuse me? Did you say something to me, Officer?"

He drew up short, his eyes blazing. "No, detective. I got nothing to say to you." He stormed back into the interrogation room to grab up Savoie's hands and spring the cuffs. No apology for the inconvenience, just a curt, "Get the fuck outta here."

Rubbing his wrists, Max came out into the hall, stopping when he saw her.

"This is your lucky day," Hammond snarled, shoving past him. "Detective Caissie vouched for your whereabouts. Prayer meeting, my ass." He stalked down the hall.

As she met Max's cool-eyed gaze the corner of his mouth bent up slightly, the only sign that she'd just surprised the hell out of him.

"Alain, I'm going to walk Mr. Savoie out. I'll be right back."

"Sure. You do that." Her partner's look said she wasn't sneaking off without an explanation. "I'm sure he's forgotten the way."

They moved down the crowded hall side by side, not looking at each other.

"Nice coat," he said at last.

"You like it?" She adjusted the lapels of his black trench and stroked her hands over the smooth fabric. The Armani label said it must have cost him a small fortune. "It's hard to find the right fit when you're as tall as I am, and so stain resistant, too. Even the nastiest stains."

"Are you saying I'm the right fit for you, detective?"

"That's not what I'm saying at all, Max."

"When he said he'd gotten an anonymous tip, I thought . . ." He left the rest unspoken.

"You thought I dropped that dime?" Of course he did. Why wouldn't he? She was a cop.

And yet he'd stepped in to save her, knowing who she was, what she was.

He glanced at her, tilting his head to one side as he studied her. She bristled up because his look was asking the same questions she was demanding of herself. And she had no answers. None that made any sense, anyway.

"Max, if I wanted you on the hot seat for it, I'd have snapped the cuffs on you myself. I wouldn't send someone else to do the honors."

He smiled. "Does this mean you were actually impressed by my kisses?" *Enough to lie* for me *to keep me from behind bars?*

The tip of her tongue slipped across her lower lip, as if she could still taste him there. The sensual gesture defused her harsh, "Dream on."

"Was I in them, Charlotte?" There was no tease in that question. He stared at her, his unusual eyes probing.

And she could hear his voice whispering at the edge of her nightmare.

She said tightly, "Sometimes you creep the hell out of me, Max."

"I have that effect on folks. Just a natural talent, I guess."

They stepped out into the hazy heat and Max turned to her. A fresh shirt and jeans replaced the blood-stained garments from the early hours, and he was showered and clean shaven. He'd had time to return to Legere's to wash away any damning evidence and change. When had he gone back to the scene to sanitize it, so no one would find her scattered shirt buttons?

"You're full of surprises yourself, detective," he

said in a light, mocking tone. "Is your career going to survive being linked to me in a purely physical sense?"

She was too startled to be indignant. He *couldn't* have heard them talking. Not through soundproof walls.

I came back because I smelled your perfume.

This was her chance to plant the seeds of favors owed, to curry a gratitude that would be the first weapon in her attack on Legere. But as she looked into those rough-edged features, as she recalled the unconditional security of his embrace, tasted again the conquering heat of his mouth on hers, she couldn't do it, even though the whys and wherefores would have her beating her head against the wall later.

She said coolly, "We're not linked in any sense, Savoie. Not now. This puts us square."

He'd saved her; she'd saved him. The dangerous matter dropped into a confining box with the lid locked down. Case closed.

A slow smile lit his eyes with a smoldering flare of mischief. "Does this mean no more anatomy lessons?"

She almost grinned. "Step back, Max." When he complied, she asked, "You want your coat?"

"You can hang on to it." His gaze swept over her, that small, self-satisfied smile still on his face. "It looks right fine where it is. Think of me when it's wrapped around you."

"Beat it, Savoie. We're going to be having a conversation real soon."

"You know where to find me."

She watched him saunter down to the street, blending into the early tourist bustle without a backward glance.

Charlotte released a weighty sigh. What the hell had possessed her? She'd just lied to let a killer go free. Well, not exactly lied. She and Max *had* been together, and gruesome bits of anatomy *had* been the topic.

But what could she have said if she'd reported the attack, if they asked how she'd been taken down so easily? If they asked why Savoie had to come to her rescue when she'd been armed, trained, and supposedly on her guard? How could she say that a flashback to another weaker time had crushed her courage like an empty cigarette pack? That even after all those hours on Forstrom's couch, she'd folded, and Savoie had picked up the pieces?

That instead of following protocol, she'd destroyed evidence and protected a killer by her grateful silence?

She hadn't asked for his help. And he hadn't asked for hers.

Those men would have killed her; no question about it. But not right away—and Max had stopped that from happening. Fiercely and permanently.

Suddenly the raincoat wasn't enough to keep the chill out.

She went back inside to find Babineau. His suspicious and slighted look was harder to face than her squirming conscience as she announced, "I've got to take off for a while after lunch."

"A little afternoon delight with your new best friend?"

"Don't think you're gonna get away with busting my chops, Babs," she warned, bumping him out of the way as she strode to her desk in the middle of chaos central.

After the strangeness of the last few hours, the familiar noise was a steadying relief. Angry pimp, sulky working girls, sobbing assault victim, anxious parents filing a missing persons report. The usual mix, none of them even remotely suggesting that such a thing as fangs and claws were involved in their problems.

"I can't help it. You don't usually give me much to razz you about," Babineau said.

"Let it go, or I'm gonna have to tell your new Mrs. about your inordinate fondness for the crossdressing decoy detail."

He plopped into his chair at the opposing desk, his good nature restored. "I did look killer in a short skirt and heels. But damn, I hated waxing my legs."

"Oh, how we girls suffer for fashion."

He grinned, and his easy good looks and trusting expression socked her hard beneath the ribs. Why was she risking so much for a troublesome thug like Savoie?

A troublesome thug who could stir up a hornet's nest of confusion beneath the first warm slide of his lips.

One who could open the doors to a revenge she coveted almost beyond her love for her badge.

And suddenly she was walking in those shadowed shades of gray she'd never been tempted into before.

"I've got to go question the wife from the first murder," she told her partner as she checked the messages on her desk as if it were any normal day, and not the day she started deceiving herself that one small lie wouldn't domino into a dozen more compromises. She felt sick and shaky inside.

"And I can't come along?"

She met his expectant look and hated what she was doing. They'd ridden together for years. They had shared cold coffee on long stakeouts, had dodged bullets, had backed each other's plays without question. She'd stood up with him at his wedding, for God's sake.

But this wasn't something she could invite him into. Not because she couldn't trust him, but because she couldn't trust her own instincts when it came to Max Savoie. She was on her own, out on her own limb, and that was a scary place to be.

She smiled grimly. "Ladies only. I know you have a strong feminine side, but what can I say?"

"I say you owe me lunch."

HOURS LATER, A deep, destructive fury built in Charlotte as she listened to the misery that was Dolores Gautreaux's life. Or had been, until someone had done her the monumental favor of killing her husband. Cee Cee wanted to do it herself when she studied the timid creature who sat with her blackened eyes averted, her thin shoulders hunched as if to ward off a blow. Cee Cee spoke quietly, afraid a forceful word would send the anxious wraith scurrying from the room.

"Mrs. Gautreaux . . ."

"Dolores." A cautious strength crept into her voice. "I'm not Mrs. Gautreaux anymore."

"Dolores, did you take a cab?"

"No. I called the Sister. She came and got me."

"And the two of you stripped the house and carried all your belongings and the baby out, while Mr. Surette was doing what?"

"He was passed out in . . . in the bedroom."

"Was he still alive?"

A slight hesitation. "Of course."

Either she wasn't sure, or she knew full well that he was lying on her sheets with his throat and black heart gone. Had she watched as it was done? Charlotte would have wanted to. She could picture Max Savoie jerking that foul organ from the man's chest as a sacrifice to the abused woman, and perversely savored the image the same way she did when she thought of the two men in the alley. But Max wouldn't be so unprofessional as to do murder in front of a woman and child. So maybe Surette was unconscious at the time. A dark part of her thought, *Too bad.*

Maybe it was time to make that appointment with Forstrom.

"Dolores, do know of anyone who would want your husband and his friend dead?"

Her gaze lifted, her eyes glittering. "You mean besides me?"

"Yes."

"No. They'd get into scrapes and mouth off to the wrong sorts, but I don't know of anyone who would kill them. Especially that way." But she didn't wince when she said it. She most likely reveled in it—or would, once she got used to the idea of finally being free.

"Do you know Jimmy Legere?"

"He's the man T-Bob owed money to. I've never met him."

"How about Max Savoie?"

She didn't react. "No." Either she didn't know him or she'd suddenly become a very good liar.

Cee Cee touched the back of her hand. "Do you have somewhere to go when this is all over?"

"I can stay here until . . . until the house is cleaned. Then I'll let it go back to the bank, and the baby and me will go stay with my clan in Lafayette. I should never have left them. In time, maybe I'll forget all this ever happened."

Good luck there. "Of course you will. I don't have any more questions right now. But you understand that you'll have to stay here and be available until the investigation is over."

"Yes. We'll be happy to stay." The look of relief on the poor woman's face twisted around Charlotte's heart like barbed wire. It was a relief she understood all too well.

After thanking Mary Kate for arranging the meeting, Cee Cee strode out into the sun and took a deep breath. Feelings she didn't like to face curled and knotted in her belly. She knew exactly what that woman was feeling. The terror, the dread, the uncertainty, the impotent hatred simmering. If Dolores Gautreaux had hired her husband's murderer, Cee Cee hoped she never found out about it. Sometimes justice had a funny way of taking care of itself and didn't need her at all.

She was about to shake a cigarette from her new pack when she saw Max Savoie standing at the bottom of the church steps. The fact that he'd probably been standing there for some time, just watching her, made the familiar allover crawlies return. She stuffed the pack back in her pocket and stood, fists planted on hips, eyes narrowed, lips thinned as he came up to join her. She did like watching him move. All bold, dark grace. The remembered feel of him, pressed against her, scorched along her skin.

"What do you want, Savoie? Why am I all of a sudden tripping over you every time I turn around?"

"Maybe we're just going in the same direction, detective."

"I doubt that. What are you doing here? And, why were you here early this morning?"

"I'm here on a matter of theology. Don't you think I have a soul, Charlotte?"

"No. Men like you don't have souls, any more than they have consciences." She was tired and grouchy and bothered by Savoie's presence, bothered by her enjoyment watching him come up the steps, but she did have enough decency left to feel bad about her words. Even if they didn't seem to pierce Max's thick skin. Taut, hot flesh that had warmed her so wonderfully when held close in his arms.

She gave herself a harsh mental shake. Those kind of thoughts weren't particularly helpful. Look where wondering about his touch had gotten her. "I wouldn't have pegged you for a religious sort is all I meant." She purposely kept her tone combative, hoping he'd get the hint and back off.

But when had Savoie ever been that obliging? He held his ground just inside the boundaries of her personal space. "Oh, there's a lot about me that you don't know, detective." A small smile. "Now I've got you curious, don't I?"

"You'd be surprised at how rarely thoughts of you cross my mind."

He just laughed. A loud, blow-your-hair-back sound that popped out of him with the startling force of a Jack-in-the-box, alarming because he was so still before and after it leaped out to scare her.

Disconcerted, she said, "So you're here to bribe your way into Heaven? How's that working out for you, Max?"

"I'll get back to you on that, detective."

He just stood there, smiling, driving her absolutely crazy from all the questions swirling around the mysterious way he bobbed in and out of her life, like a weaving, taunting boxer. But was he coaxing her to make a move so he could KO her? Or was it only fancy footwork to distract her from the work she should be doing?

She'd never understood his odd, unreciprocated attraction to her. Why was he still trying to charm her, when he knew she could toss him behind bars and keep him there until he rotted? Didn't he have enough sense to get out while the getting was good?

Apparently not.

"Actually," he said matter-of-factly, "I came to see you. You said we'd have a conversation and I thought maybe we could—"

He paused, going ramrod straight, his palm cupping her elbow. Something in the intensity of his expression made the hairs on her arms stand at attention.

"Max? What is it?" She unsnapped her holster.

He turned in a sudden move, whipping her around in an off-balanced stumble. She never heard anything except his sharp inhalation before he stumbled back into her, falling with her beneath him into the shadows of the worn stone entryway.

Sandwiched between those two solid, immobile objects, it took her a moment to recover her breath. And the first thing she noticed was that Max wasn't stirring.

Wiggling, pushing, she finally managed to clear his unresponsive weight so she could roll up on hands and knees. His eyes were closed. Two things impacted her immediately: He'd taken a bullet to the abdomen, and he'd shoved her out of its path.

She had her gun out, scanning the quiet street even as she pressed shaking fingers to his throat. Finally she found a slow, thready pulse. Her touch brought his eyes open, and he stared up at her with a faint smile.

"Max, don't try to move. You've been shot."

"Okay." Then a slightly dazed, "How bad is it?"

She started to say something to minimize the truth, but the unexpected tears in her eyes betrayed her. "Real bad. I'm sorry."

"Okay," he said again, as his eyes started to slide shut.

"Don't move. I'm going to call the EMTs."

"There's nothing they can do."

She believed him. She'd seen her share of wounds like the one that tore through his midsection, and all of them ended up on Dovion's table. She stroked her hand through his dark rumpled hair, registering on some far plane how soft it was, as she watched his eyes begin to cloud.

"Max, stay with me."

He blinked several times, then fixed on her again. "I never got to ask you."

She dragged up his hand, squeezing it in hers. "Ask me what?"

"To step out with me. To dinner, someplace nice, where you could wear a dress. Something short that would drive me crazy. And we could dance and walk and have that conversation, and maybe even slip in some anatomy lessons." He paused, his breath catching, then hurried on. "What would you have said to that, Charlotte? Would you have said yes?"

Her lips trembled. "Name the date. Anywhere you want to go."

"Tonight. Seven. Sean Paul's."

"I'll be ready." Her tears dotted his cheek. "Hang on. I'm going to get you some help. I've got a great dress. I've been looking for a special occasion to wear it."

"I've never been anyone's special occasion before." He clutched her hand as his bent knees shifted, restlessly at first, then twisted with violent agitation. His head tossed, his gaze dimming. She put her hand to his cheek, stilling his thrashings.

"Don't you die! Don't you die on me, Max. Max?" She shrugged out of his coat, rolling it to slip under his head.

He struggled to say her name. She bent close, tracing the angles of his face with her fingers, thinking he meant to make some last confession.

"Charlotte, listen to me. Do you have a knife?"

"What?"

"A knife. I don't have much time." He squeezed his eyes shut, panting hard.

"I do, Max. Right here." She withdrew a butterfly knife from her bag and flicked the wicked blade open. His hand groped about, finally closing over hers. She gasped. He was still so strong.

"Help me, Charlotte."

"What can I do for you, Max? Anything." She was crying now.

"You have to . . . you have to take the bullet out before it kills me."

"*What?*"

"Listen to me. Don't ask questions."

"Max, I—I can't."

"Do what I tell you. Dammit, just do what—" He broke off, breathing hard. He closed his eyes and when he opened them, they were calm. "Charlotte, I'm sorry. I didn't mean . . . to scare you. I need you to do this for me. Please, do this for me."

She glanced at his wound, thinking of the needless pain and suffering removing the bullet would cause. He had to be out of his mind. He confirmed it with his next statement. "Charlotte, if you care about me . . . if you love me, you'll do this."

Care about him? *Love* him? Her brain slammed on the brakes. She wasn't in love with him!

His body began to jerk in fierce spasms, but his stare remained cool and locked into hers. "Charlotte, do it now. Save my life." His voice roughened. "Do it *now*."

Cursing, wildly upset, yet drawing on a saving detachment, Cee Cee unbuttoned his shirt to lay bare the entry wound. A rifle shot. Professional, clean, silent, and deadly. Shutting down everything but her focus on what she was about to do, she inserted the blade. That was the worst of it, yet he didn't make a sound. Finding the bullet, she dug it out, then clutched it in her fist, weeping over it. Max was so still, she was afraid to look up.

Then, amazingly, his fingertips brushed her shoulder.

Her head jerked up. She hadn't lost him yet. He'd started breathing in shallow snatches, his eyes slitting, glimmering with an odd incandescence. When he spoke his voice was still that raw growl, low and rumbling.

"Go find Sister Catherine."

"Max, I can't leave."

"Go!"

That deep roar backed her onto her heels.

His eyes opened fully. There was something wrong, very wrong with them. They gleamed laser-like, hot, cold, dazzling; frightening her into scrambling to her feet, running into the sanctuary. She opened her mouth to scream for Mary Kate, to come exorcize whatever had inhabited Max Savoie's body.

"Charlotte."

Cee Cee skidded to a stop at the sound of his

voice. She stood frozen, heart pounding, her thoughts flying wildly, irrationally. Then she turned, and her legs buckled.

Max stood just inside the doorway, his long coat closed over the bloodstained shirt, looking as fit and fine as he had that morning. Before someone shot a bullet into him that should have taken his life—but hadn't.

She glanced down at the misshapen lump in her hand that gleamed dully. *Silver.* Why would someone use such an ineffective means, when a high-velocity round would have blasted through his spine and probably have taken her out as well? Why use a bullet made of silver?

Unless . . . the silver was meant to do the damage.

Her gaze rose to meet his with a numbing horror that began to swell like a cold, drowning tide. The horror fed by every story she'd heard as a child made her whisper, "What *are* you?"

He smiled slightly, saying, "Tonight. Seven," before he turned and walked away.

Four

"MAX? THAT YOU, boy?"

Obligingly, Max diverted to the back room Jimmy Legere used as his office. Since his stroke, he'd centralized his hub of power onto the main floor of the house, where he could wheel himself easily from bedroom to workroom to boardroom off the long hall. He'd always preferred to have business come to him, having no great love for city life. And in these huge, nearly empty rooms, Max had grown up tucked safely away from society's notice. Or interference.

Drapes were pulled against the intense afternoon light, making the high-ceilinged room dark and cool. The old man huddled in his favorite chair, his reading glasses down at the end of his nose. A bulky envelope balanced on his spindly knees. Usually his gaze softened fondly when Max entered the room. Today it didn't, and Max approached with puzzled caution.

"Can I get you something, Jimmy?"

"I hear you got an escort downtown. Want to tell me about it?"

Pulling his coat in tighter to conceal the awful stains, Max shrugged. "Nothing to tell, Jimmy. They kicked me loose after a few questions. You know they have a particular lack of imagination that always brings them to me first, anytime there's blood on the ground. I don't take it personally. Nothing to worry about."

He didn't make a conscious decision to keep the attempt on his life to himself. He never kept anything from Jimmy Legere, not ever. Although Max was secretive by nature, his relationship with his mentor had always been one of complete honesty. But some tension underlying this meeting made Max wary without knowing why. Perhaps it was the scent of uncertainty he picked up on the old man. Perhaps it was the horror in Charlotte Caissie's parting words that still had him unsettled. Ruthlessly trained since birth, he let none of his agitation show in stance or attitude. He was a blank, receptive slate, as always, awaiting Jimmy's command.

"This the reason behind the NOPD's surprising courtesy?"

Max took the envelope Jimmy extended and shook out pictures of him and Charlotte Caissie just that morning on the front steps of the police station, looking very friendly with each other. His expression remained unchanged. Something foreign and fiercely protective snapped taut inside him as he spoke with an indifferent calm. "Detective Caissie. We bump shoulders now and again. She did a favor for me, one she owed me. You always told me to keep my enemies close."

"But not close enough to stab you in the heart or cut off anything you're fond of. That all you bumping with her?"

Max blinked once. "Yes."

"Wishing it was more?"

"Absolutely."

Jimmy chuckled at his candor. "She *is* the spicy kinda woman that gets a man's dick in a twist, if he's not careful. She's dangerous, Max. She doesn't dole out favors."

"I know."

"Stay away from her. She's trouble you don't need. You be careful."

"I always am, Jimmy. Anything else?" He waited, an unusual anxiousness kinking his nerves into knots. He'd never had reason to be wary of Jimmy's moods. Since coming to live under his roof as a child, he'd never suffered a harsh word or cruelly dealt punishment, though he'd seen both handed out liberally toward others. He'd never given his protector cause for either. His obedience was unshakable, his loyalty unquestionable. And now he stood before him hiding things, like the blood under his coat and the woman held close to his heart. It didn't sit well with him.

After regarding him for a long moment, Jimmy relaxed. "Get cleaned up. I want you to go along with Paulie. He's got a five-thirty meet down at the docks. Just hang back and let him work, but make sure Vantour sees you."

"Expecting trouble?"

"Vantour might be putting his thumb on the scales."

"You want me to bring back his thumbs for you?" he asked casually.

"Not yet. Just make sure he knows we're watching him. If he's a smart man, he'll play straight with me."

"Whatever you want, Jimmy. Happy to do it for you."

That warm glow kindled in the old man's eyes. "You're a good boy, Max."

He looked down at the top photo, of Charlotte Caissie's sassy smile. With the picture tipped up, Jimmy couldn't see the way he rubbed his thumb along the wide curve of her mouth. "Something else you want to talk about, Jimmy?" His voice was only mildly curious. "Like why you got somebody spying on me?"

"I didn't send anybody to take those."

"Then whatchu doing with them?"

"I've been hearing things, Max. Whispering in my ear like a pesky gnat that you slap away but it keeps coming back. Why you think that is, boy?"

An alarm began to quiver in the region recently perforated by an assassin's bullet. "Depends on who's been whispering and why you've been listening."

"Folks are saying you're not as focused on your work as you should be."

"Who's saying that, Jimmy?"

"They're saying you've been letting your own business interfere with mine. You didn't pick up after yourself, and you made the police look our way. I can't have you getting sloppy and bringing trouble to my door. I've been hearing that I should have doubts about you."

The pictures fell from Max's hands, scattering about his feet. Another man would have shouted and beaten his chest to dramatize his loyalty, or cursed the one who slandered his name or even his boss for paying attention to it. But Jimmy Legere had rescued Max as a desperate child from starvation and madness with one outstretched hand.

He stepped across the photos, crouching down at the old man's feet so they were eye to eye. His glittered with haunted brilliance. Without a word, he reached between the chair cushions for the .38 special Jimmy kept close to him and he pushed the textured grip into one thin hand. Then with both of his wrapped around it, he dragged the pistol up until the stubby barrel rode the jerky motion of his Adam's apple.

"If you have doubts, pull the trigger. *You* do it, Jimmy. Don't send somebody else to put me down in the street like an animal. I won't lie down for them. But if you want my life, it's yours. It always has been. You know that. At least I *thought* you knew. Was I wrong? Has that changed?"

Jimmy's blue-veined hand touched Max's cheek. "You're not wrong, boy. Let go." He tucked the pistol back into its hiding place. "I tell you these things because you've got to be more careful now. I don't have much longer to live."

Max drew a sharp breath, his eyes welling up in surprise and objection as he started to shake his head.

"I need to square things away," Jimmy continued. "To make sure my business is in the right hands. I'm thinking your hands, Max."

"I don't want your business or your money, Jimmy." All the emotions he usually kept tightly compressed knotted up in his expression. Fear, anguish, denial, sorrow, but mostly love for this man who had saved his life and given him a home. "It's not your time yet. It's *not* your time."

"That's not for you or me to decide, boy."

"Who's going to take care of me?"

Such a curious thing to say, but Jimmy smiled. "Max, you've been taking care of all of us for a long time now. And I think it's right that that should continue. You're smart. You're fair. You're respected."

"I'm feared. It's not the same thing. They won't follow me, Jimmy. They don't see me as one of them."

"You'd rather they follow my cousin, T-John? Some say it's right that business stays in the family. *You're* my family, Max. I've always thought of you that way."

He made a soft, choky sound of distress. "Don't do this."

The old man's expression hardened, his tone cracking sharply. "And if I tell you to take it?"

Max rocked back on his heels. In a blink, he was all smooth, impassive control. "Whatever you want, Jimmy. Whatever you want."

And he rose up, a powerful, dangerous man, tightly leashed under Jimmy Legere's control. Without another word he strode to the door, walking over the pictures without a glance.

Jimmy sat staring glumly at the photos as Francis Petitjohn stepped in from the porch. His movements always reminded Jimmy of a crab's sideways scuttle, never straight on. There was no love between him and his cousin but there was blood, and sometimes that counted for more. T-John was clever and quick, but it was a shrewd, selfish intelligence that Jimmy had never trusted. Too much like his brother.

But he was family, and he'd served that family's interests second only to his own at Jimmy's command. Their fathers were brothers, but the only similarities between them were the stringy build and inherent wariness. That Max hadn't picked up on T-John's presence bothered the elder cousin, but his comment was firm.

"See. Nothing to worry about. You were wrong."

"I don't think so, Jimmy. I think you're a fool to trust him as much as you do. You know what he is, what he does."

"For *me*, T-John. For me."

"Maybe once, but maybe not no more. You think he'd be sitting there tame at your feet if he knew the truth? Or would he be going for your throat, like the animal he is?"

Jimmy's expression congealed with fury. And fear. "Who's going to tell him? You? You breathe a word to him and I'll see you planted so far out in the swamps, pieces of you will be showing up in alligator purses for the next ten years." He took a shuddering breath, his calm returning as he addressed his cunningly vicious cousin. And he hated his next necessary words. "Watch him, Johnny. But don't let him catch you doing it."

Jimmy Legere sat for a long while, alone, staring at the photographs on the floor. He hadn't known a peaceful moment since he'd looked at them and had recognized what stirred on Max Savoie's face as he interacted with the policewoman. Something treasured, something hoarded greedily for himself, until this moment.

Love.

ALMOST TOO WEAK to walk upright, Max entered the kitchen. Two of Jimmy's guards lingered over sandwiches at the center table, and their conversation stopped when he appeared. He had known them for more than ten years, but didn't know if he'd ever spoken a single word to them. He had never paid them the slightest bit of attention. Still, they looked at him with badly hidden fear. Wariness. Loathing. Like he was some kind of monster in their midst.

They were right. And Jimmy was wrong. The second he was no longer under Legere's protection, they would rise up and crush him like the village mob in an old horror classic. He'd recognized himself in that black and white truth long ago. He would be Frankenstein's creation, faithfully carrying the deceased doctor in his arms to the safety of the windmill, only to have his good neighbors set fire to it to gleefully watch him burn. Because normal people destroyed what scared them.

As the guards quickly exited the room, he sighed. It was the same way Charlotte Caissie looked at him. Would she show up at his door, waving the first torch?

He had to think who would stage such a blatant attack in a public place. Who wanted to send a harsh message to Jimmy over his corpse? Who would know how to bring him down? He was a target every time he stepped through the gates, but he'd never thought much about it until this minute. He had no fear of guns or knives or greater numbers. But someone had known his one weakness.

Despite the army of men at Jimmy's command, if Max were gone, Jimmy would be vulnerable. And that, Max wouldn't allow. Telling Jimmy about it would just worry him. Max could take care of himself and he would be very, very careful. Because he was not just a dumb beast at Jimmy Legere's back.

He opened the huge stainless-steel refrigerator and was leaning in when he heard a soft step behind him.

"Can I help you find something, Mr. Savoie?"

He glanced back at one of the kitchen people. She was young, pretty, and eager to please, but a residue of fright clouded her stare as if she expected him to gobble her up if she said the wrong thing.

"I'm fine, Jasmine. Just raiding the fridge. Don't tell anyone now, will you?" He smiled and she responded with a tentative one of her own.

"It'll be our secret, Mr. Savoie." She seemed to relax, and he was starting to feel a little better when she happened to look down at his feet and her face paled.

Because the color splashed on his pantlegs was as red as his shoes. He didn't think telling her it was his own blood would take that sudden glaze from her eyes as she took a couple of steps backward then fled the kitchen.

Cursing softly, he turned back to the well-stocked shelves, dragging out a thick slab of beef. For propriety's sake he slapped it into a skillet, and while it was lightly searing he tipped up the foam tray to swallow the red juices. As he was about to lick the last of them up, he heard a gasp. Jasmine had returned to the kitchen and stood transfixed with horror by the sight of blood trickling down his chin.

"What are you looking at?" The low growl tore from him, sending her running.

Why pretend to be what he wasn't?

He snatched the barely warmed beef out of the pan with his bare hands and tore into it with sharp teeth, savoring the raw, restorative taste.

And he knew right then that if he wanted to stay alive, he'd be long gone before that first clod of dirt hit Jimmy Legere's casket.

ALMOST SEVEN-THIRTY.

Max frowned, disappointment swelling. He'd rushed through Jimmy's business to be here on time, apparently for nothing.

What had he expected? Too much. Where she was concerned, it was always too much. She was probably waiting for a warrant right now to bring him in. He was a fool.

He hadn't realized how devastated he was until he glanced up from the bar and saw her standing beneath a light, wreathed in cigarette smoke. The sight of her almost knocked him to his knees.

It took him a long moment to exhale, and the sound shivered noisily.

He'd always thought she was a stunning woman, tall and powerful like an Amazonian queen. With her coffee-with-lots-of-cream Creole coloring, wide slash of lips painted bold crimson, and stare as black and jagged-edged as her short hair, she was impossible to ignore. Bold and black widow devour-your-mate sexy, she probably scared the hell out of most men. On purpose.

But he wasn't most men. And he'd seen her when she wasn't so brave, wasn't so tough and was scared as hell. But he'd never seen her looking the way she did tonight. For him.

The dress was a shiny metallic bronze, textured like chain mail. Thin straps displayed her sleekly muscled shoulders. The gown was gathered down the center in shape-hugging puckers from its low neckline to the minimum of decency, where the skirt split and curved around sweetly to just below the backs of her knees. When she walked, a tease of firm, toned thighs, trim knees, and smooth calves led his gaze down to wicked high-heeled shoes, open in front and laced like an S&M dream about her ankles.

She saw him looking and waited, waited for him to come to her. She held his stare, drawing him across the room with her shielded gaze. There was no fear in those dark eyes. No welcome, either.

When he reached her, she asked, "Is this the kind of dress you had in mind?"

His gaze never left hers. "I want to lick your toes."

"Can we discuss that later? I'm hungry."

He held up two fingers to the maître'd. The man may not have known who he was, but knew from the way he carried himself that he was someone. Plucking up two menus, the man gestured for them to follow. Max let her go first, giving her plenty of space for him to appreciate the way her hips worked the dress, without having her shove his lust down his throat. He could hear her chastising voice: *Step back, Savoie.* As if he were some harmlessly naughty street kid, instead of one of the most feared men in the Crescent City. Thinking she could control him that easily.

And she was right. She could.

They sat on opposite sides of the table, looking fabulous, smelling good, well-groomed and well-mannered strangers. And all Max could think was, when will that other shoe drop? *What are you?*

At that moment, he would have given anything to be some regular guy out on the town with his girl. Not a mob enforcer, a murderer in a fancy suit. And much worse.

Was that what she saw when she looked across the table at him through those heavily fringed, fathomless eyes? Finally, the suspense got the better of him.

"Why are you here, Charlotte?"

"I told you—I'm hungry. And I can't afford to eat here on my salary."

"And you don't care about the company you keep?"

"Why, Max, are you calling me a snob?"

He didn't answer. He suddenly didn't know what to say to her.

She'd had her hair done. He could scent the elaborate, expensive salon products that she usually disdained. Why for him? Why the glamour, the tease? Why share a table with him, when what was foremost in their thoughts kept them from enjoying their usual banter?

The way she was tiptoeing around it made the change in their relationship all the more unbearable. One thing he liked so much about her was her no-holds-barred honesty. The fact that she was withholding that from him, even if the truth was something he didn't want to hear, soured his long-savored anticipation. He sat silent and withdrawn, listening to her talk about the food, about those she recognized in the posh establishment, without really saying anything. Things she might share with a casual acquaintance—not with someone who only hours before had been dying, his blood pumping out beneath her palm.

"Charlotte, look at me."

Her dark eyes lifted, carefully masked.

"What do you see?"

A slight flicker. Then she smiled. "I see a really nice suit. You clean up good, Max."

His expression locked down tight. "You see a thug in a silk tie, a monster in Armani. This was a mistake." He shoved up from the table, and she stilled him with the touch of her hand on his. So warm. So soft.

"You said there'd be dancing."

She rose from her chair, dropping her napkin over the remains of her meal. In the spiky heels, she could almost look him right in the eye. He wanted to put his hands on her in the worst way. Better it be here in public, with all these people around, where he wouldn't be quite so tempted.

Her fingers curled around his. She tugged, he followed, out onto the dance area. No one else was dancing but that didn't matter. Aaron Neville was crooning, "Tell it like it is," as he fit his palm to the curve of her waist. They moved to the seductive song at a cautious distance, close enough to feel each other's heat but far enough apart to retain eye contact. Within a minute, they were joined by other couples who had no such reservations.

Max carefully mimicked the steps of those swaying around them. He'd never danced before. He'd never had reason. He was quick to pick up the natural rhythm of the music, and Cee Cee followed easily. He quit worrying about treading on her sexy shoes and began to eye the other pairs who seemed Velcroed together. What would Cee Cee do if he pulled her up tight against him, tucked her head down on his shoulder, and let his palm prowl over the sweet curve of her rump for a squeeze? Probably crack his nuts with her knee. Dangerous business, sneaking up on any kind of intimacy with her. Kind of like mating with a porcupine. But worth the risk of those painful barbs? Oh, yes.

When he chuckled, she scowled suspiciously. "What?"

He continued to smile. "You're easy to dance with."

"I do have some social graces." Very prickly.

"Do you mind if I look for them?"

"Depends on where you plan to look."

He grinned a bit wolfishly and coaxed her in a bit closer so that their knees brushed and their hips bumped. "You can put your head on my shoulder if you like."

"I'm fine, thanks."

"I seem to remember you kinda liked it before."

Her eyes narrowed at the reference, and he cursed himself for bringing it up. *Stupid, stupid, stupid.*

"Max?" she began after a long silence.

"Charlotte?"

"We need to talk."

"Ah, that conversation." Oddly, he felt himself relax. Even if that other high-heeled shoe was going to drop down hard on the back of his neck, it was better than all this waltzing around with a stranger. "Best it should be in private. Your place is probably closer."

"Will you behave?"

Because there was the slightest catch in that flirty question, he smiled, showing his teeth. "I'll be whatever you want me to be, *sha.*"

She gave him a long look that said the chances of him getting laid out cold were greater than getting laid.

He chuckled. "I'll behave."

She stepped away and returned to the table to retrieve her purse, a bag just big enough to hold her service revolver.

After instructing their server to bill Jimmy's account and to add on something nice for himself, Max waited anxiously for the waiter to clear his request. He hadn't considered how he'd pay the bill until this moment, having no money or plastic himself. He hadn't been thinking about anything except what to say to her, so she wouldn't guess he'd never done this before. Then the server returned with his receipt and a big smile and a "Thank you, Mr. Savoie." He was able to breathe again and follow Charlotte to the door.

She drove a little convertible sports car, fast and aggressively. He didn't know much about cars but thought the tough, curvy lines suited her. Even the temperamental clutch and rough shifting seemed appropriate. He leaned back in his seat, letting the wind cool his face while his gaze grew hot watching her. She concentrated on the traffic and said nothing.

She lived in an old but respectable neighborhood, where houses crowded together, sharing little strips of brownish lawn. She fished out her keys as he climbed the outside stairs behind her. He could scent her nervousness, could hear it in the jingle of her keys, as if this was something she didn't do often. Did that mean she didn't bring men home, or just men like him?

Not that there *were* any others like him.

Her second-floor apartment was a nice place with big, comfortable furniture and lots of bold color. He could smell the river through the open balcony doors. A slight scurrying sound drew his attention to a large cage in the corner and he approached to be regarded by twin pairs of button eyes.

"You have rodents."

"They're guinea pigs. Porky and Baco. They were a gift when I made detective."

The fat little creatures were huddled in the corner, frozen, prey animals sensing they were about to become a meal. He tapped the cage with his fingertip and they let out shrill wheeks of alarm.

Charlotte came up behind him, almost surprising a similar sound from him when she took his jacket by the shoulders and slowly drew it off him. When he turned, she was on his mouth.

She hauled him to her with fingers hooked behind his head, mashing her lips against his before he could suck a startled breath. He'd hoped and dreamed of this, but never expected it in a million years. He let her take what she wanted, his eyes open, breathing light and fast, his hands hanging at his sides while her lips met his with fierce abandon.

Finally, she eased back far enough to free his brain from its vapor lock.

"Well?" Her question caressed his bruised mouth.

"What?" Barely a whisper.

Her fingertips followed the hard line of his jaw. "Aren't you going to kiss me back?"

"Absolutely." And he swooped down on her like a hawk after her little rodents.

As they indulged in deliciously wet, opened-mouth exploration, he was peripherally aware of her hands, busy unknotting his tie, unbuttoning his shirt, pushing it from his shoulders to catch on the cuff links at his wrists. Her palms started charting the furring of his chest and abdomen in a firm, seeking pattern.

He burned beneath her touch, dizzy because she actually had her hands on him, skin to skin. When he started to work free of his shirt, wanting to get a handful of her as quickly as possible, she reached around him to help. As his shirt dropped free, he felt the cold touch of metal and ratcheting circle of her handcuffs. He tried to pull his thoughts from their sensual daze. Kind of kinky, but he'd go along with it. Until something thin and sharp pierced his shoulder.

Charlotte pushed away from him, panting, her lipstick smeared, her eyes wild.

And he realized how deep her clever treachery went as the sliver of silver she'd stuck in his back began to eat through his system like acid. He staggered, stunned and quickly swamped with a weakening sickness.

Over those prickly waves of pain, he heard her hard demand. "All right, Savoie. You're going to tell me right now just what the hell you are."

Five

Max stood staring at her for a long moment, his eyes round with amazement and disbelief. She watched understanding dawn like a dark new day.

"Ah, hell," he whispered, almost too softly for her to hear.

And then he was a blur of motion.

He was fast, so fast, whirling, racing for her door, apparently planning to go right through it. She hit him like a linebacker in Bourbon French perfume and heels, driving him to his knees. He had no way to break his fall except with his face.

Shaking it off, he was instantly rolling, throwing her off him while she struggled to loop an arm about his neck. His head lashed back, catching her in the chin, clacking her teeth together. She grabbed the chain linking his cuffs together, jerking them up, bringing him staggering to his feet, but when his head went down, those red tennis shoe-clad feet kicked up and over, doing a hands-free cartwheel. Once his Converses were under him he plowed into her, his shoulder knocking the wind from her with a pained *Oof*.

She was still between him and the door, a barrier he couldn't breach without doing her significant damage. Still not an option at this point. His hands were useless. He only had scant minutes to escape before the poison in his system brought him down hard. He made an instantaneous choice, darting through the living room, diving over the couch into a slick tumble down the hall while Porky and Baco scrambled around their cage in frantic circles, shrieking. As the only other available route, he ducked into her bedroom, slamming the door behind him.

Cee Cee straightened, rubbing her chest and wheezing for air. He was quick and he was clever, but now he was caught. There was no way out of her room. The windows had bolted wrought-iron security grills; it would take a wrecking ball to break through them. But now that she had him, what was she going to do with him? Did cuffing him and trapping him in her apartment make him less or more dangerous?

She heard him stumbling about and cringed at the sound of her lamp breaking, then hard thumps of impact. He was actually trying to force his way through the bars. *Could* he? And even if he could, there was a two-story fall. Her hand was on the knob, picturing him sprawled and broken on her narrow patch of yard. Then it was suddenly quiet.

He'd pushed something in front of the door. She put her shoulder into it, shoving hard to shift her dresser to one side, giving her just enough space to slip inside the dark room. She tried the wall switch, but the bulb had broken when the lamp hit the floor.

"Max? I've got a gun and it's carrying loads that you won't like. Don't do anything stupid."

"You mean don't do anything *else* stupid."

She followed the sound of his voice to the far side of the room, and edged in cautiously to snap on a small bedside lamp. Its twenty-watt bulb barely reached across the queen-sized spread to where he sat in heavy shadow on the floor between the wall and the bed frame.

"I don't want to hurt you," she said.

"Too late."

She circled the foot of the bed. He'd burrowed back into a space just big enough to accommodate the breadth of his shoulders. With his cheek resting on updrawn knees and his back to the wall, his breathing coming in harsh, broken gulps, he didn't present an obvious threat. But Cee Cee could still see those cold, dead eyes in that severed head, and was cautious.

"I take it hoping for sex is out of the question," he said dryly.

"I want some answers, Max."

"When most people want to engage in a conversation, they sit down together on the couch, and start with casual chitchat. They don't start with handcuffs and poison and expect things to remain cordial." He raised his head slowly. His eyes glittered with that strange eerie brilliance against his sweat-slicked pallor.

"I wanted to make sure we understood each other."

"I think I'm getting the picture now."

As she settled on the edge of the bed, his stare never left hers. "I'm sorry. I wasn't sure I could trust you to behave."

"You'll never know now, will you?"

"Talk to me, Max."

"About what, Charlotte?"

"About how I stood right next to you when you took a bullet. About how I had my knife in your belly and now there is hardly a scratch to show for it. Explain that to me, Max."

"I'm a fast healer. And I have great skin."

"You said poison. Is that what silver does to you? It can kill you, but the bullet wound itself couldn't? Someone wanted you dead, Max."

"Sounds like you've got everything figured out." His smile was small and mocking as his features tightened in obvious distress. Was he as weak and shaky as he looked, or was that to lure her into lowering her guard?

"Is that what it's doing now? Will it kill you?"

"Would you be sorry if it did?"

"Who wants you dead, Max?"

"You, apparently. I didn't realize I was such a poor dinner companion."

"You're not." Her voice softened as unbidden

thoughts of the feel of his palm on her waist teased her memory.

"Maybe we could try it again sometime. Sometime when you don't want to kill me."

"There won't be another time, Max."

"Ah, well." His voice lowered into a deep, smoky ripple. "Thank you for the dress. You looked so beautiful, I forgot how to breathe."

For a moment, she was nearly seduced by the intensity in his eyes. She made her own hard and indifferent. "How does it work, Max?"

He just continued to stare up at her.

"You killed those men. You ripped them apart with just your hands. That's not possible, Max. Fangs and claws, that's what the coroner said. Explain that to me."

"I can't."

"You won't."

"I don't *know* how it works. It just does."

"Show me what you are that makes dangerous men wet themselves at just the thought of you. Show me what you become for Jimmy Legere."

His expression stiffened and his eyes chilled to pale, smooth jade. In a low, fierce tone, he said, "In your dreams, detective."

"Jimmy has to know," she mused. "Is that why he keeps you on such a short leash? All he has to do is snap his fingers, and you jump to become whatever creature you are beneath that civilized suit? What does he hold over you? What do you owe him?"

A stillness settled over him, calm, cold, and deep as the grave.

"Talk to me, Max."

"I'm not telling you anything. And even if I did, it wouldn't be admissible in court."

"No court is going to be judging you, Max. You know it. Who put the hit on you? Vantour? Petitjohn? Or was it Jimmy? How long before they start thinking that you might be a little too dangerous to control?"

A tiny flicker burned way back in his eyes, a pilot light that she would fan to full flame if she could.

"He's using you, Max. He's not thinking about you, only himself. He's trading off your loyalty, your love."

His voice was as slick as black ice. "And that makes him different from you how, detective?"

How indeed?

"What do you want from me, Charlotte? I'm not going to tell you anything you want to hear, so you might as well let me go."

"Back to Jimmy? Back to becoming his soulless killer?"

"It's all I have, detective. It's what I am. All I know how to be."

"Give him up, Max, before he turns on you," she urged. "I can protect you. Let me protect you."

His laugh was sudden and loud, springing out again to surprise her before dying a quick, terrible death as he growled, "And who's going to protect you from *me*? You have no idea what you're dealing with, no idea what I can do. I could tear off these cuffs and rip out your lying heart before it takes its next beat."

Alarm jumped in her throat, then was stilled by cool reasoning. "If you could, you already would have. But you can't, can you? You're not invincible, Max. I've found your weakness."

"Yes," he agreed tonelessly, "you have." He looked away from her, resting his forehead atop tented knees. He was shivering now, his breathing quick and uneven. And just as it had when she'd seen him in Hammond's cuffs, on the floor at the church, a pang of regret undercut her purpose.

It *wasn't* because he'd kissed her.

"I'll give you some time to think about it. When you get uncomfortable enough, you'll talk to me."

"If you're waiting for me to say something against Jimmy, I'll tell you now that I will sit here until I die. It shouldn't take long—maybe by morning. And how are you going to explain that, detective—a half-dressed dead man in handcuffs in your apartment? Or is that how you end all your dates?"

"Think about it, Max. You're a smart guy. You know there's no future with Jimmy Legere. You've got nothing to lose."

"Then I've got nothing to gain, do I?"

She closed the door quietly behind her and leaned back against it. How *would* she explain it to her coworkers, to a judge? *He's this monster, you see. He tears his victims to pieces with fangs and claws. No, I don't see fangs and claws, either, but he changes somehow. Really, he's not a man. He's not what you see at all.*

Dr. Forstrom would have her straitjacketed in a rubber room drinking Halcion cocktails by the next evening.

She went into the bathroom, changing into an NOPD sweatshirt and gym shorts. After scrubbing the makeup from her face, she went to fix coffee to prepare for a long night—and had to stop herself as she put out a second cup. Max Savoie wasn't here as her guest; he was a killer employed by killers. He wasn't a man at all, but something else entirely. Something out of the stories she'd heard as a child. Something that couldn't possibly exist, yet was handcuffed in her bedroom.

He didn't warrant the tears burning in her heart. He wasn't simply a charming, mysterious, exciting man whose kisses made her resistance melt. A man who looked so damned good in that dark gray Armani suit, in that dark blue shirt with its gray stripes. Colors that accented his eyes amazingly as he'd stared at her across the table. Those beautiful unblinking eyes, so calm on the surface, yet so deep and turbulent. He was not the man who could fill the lonely after-hours of her life with wit and warmth and hints that sex with him would be so glorious, she wouldn't ever want to leave his sheets.

He wasn't a good man. He wasn't a safe man. So

why did she wish so ardently that he could be *her* man?

What *was* he?

She moved restlessly into the living room, righting chairs, straightening furniture, putting a handful of timothy grass into the pig cage where Porky and Baco sat in frozen certainty that she was just fattening them up for the kill. They knew instinctively what Max was. A ruthless, vicious animal who acted without remorse, without pause.

She picked up his coat. Jimmy Legere must pay him well because he owned wonderful things. She stroked the fabric. Sumptuous, classic, elegant, just the way he'd looked when he came toward her to claim her as his dinner date. She lifted the garment up to her face so she could feel the material against her cheek and breathe in the scent of him on the silk lining. She'd wanted to lean against him while he was wearing it, to move with him on the dance floor pressed close, as close as she could get without being inside his clothes with him. Or without clothes entirely.

And that terrified her. Because it forced her to see the *real* reason he was here as her prisoner.

It wasn't because he was a murderer. It wasn't because she wanted to drag information out of him to convict Legere. It wasn't because she had to know what creature moved beneath his skin. It was because of the words he'd said on the foyer floor at the church.

If you care about me . . .

If you love me . . .

She threw his jacket on the couch and began to pace.

Why would he say that to her? How could he even conceive that it was possible? She was a cop, for God's sake. Her job was to hunt down men like him and put them away for life. How could he believe any relationship could exist between them beyond the satisfying adversarial one they enjoyed?

So beautiful, I forgot how to breathe.

Damn you, Max! How could you do this to me?

Who was the monster? Max Savoie, for being honest about who he was and what he did? Or Charlotte Caissie, for luring him in, abusing his trust, and torturing him because he was everything that frightened her in a male? Because she was so terrified of what she felt for him that she had to make him into something unlovable? Something as dark and fierce and unrecognizable as the man who had wooed her so stealthily, she wasn't aware of it until it was too late.

He wanted things from her that she couldn't give. Things that had nothing to do with who they were or what they did. Things she had never in her wildest nightmares ever thought she'd want to share.

She didn't want Max Savoie to care about her. She didn't want his attention, his touch, his devotion. She wanted their meetings stripped down to black and white, right and wrong—because that was safe; that she could handle. She wanted to be afraid of him, to push him into showing her not that he was different, but that he was the same. It wasn't the monster in him that frightened her—it was the man. She wanted him to prove that he would hurt her and betray her and shred that fragile trust she'd always, *always* felt when she was around him.

She stalked back to the bedroom, hearing the low, hoarse pulls of his breathing. Ruthlessly crushing any empathy, she walked around the foot of the bed. He'd tipped over onto the rug and was lying on his side, knees pulled up tight against his chest, shivering hard, bathed in sweat. His eyes were tightly closed. The area of shoulder where she'd stuck him with the silver hat pin was inflamed and bubbled like a hideous burn.

Because her immediate response was the desire to give comfort, she acted with ferocious disdain, grabbing him by the upper arms, shoving him back on his heels. He looked terrible, ashen and gaunt, as he gazed at her.

"Time's up, Max."

"Are you going to kill me now? You'd might as well."

She shook him, putting enough force behind it to snap his head on his neck, needing to bring that cold, hard focus back into his eyes. He slowly straightened to regard her, breath seething between his teeth, stare flat but keenly aware now.

"Show me, Max. Show me right now." She

crouched down, pushing her face up within inches of his, letting him see and feel the aggressive fury of her demand. "No more hiding behind that mask of humanity. Let me see what you *really* are."

She reached around him, jerking the silver pin from his back.

He made a soft sound of surprise before his eyes rolled back and he dropped forward until his head touched the floor. Then the muscles in his back and shoulders shifted and bunched, pumping up like a bodybuilder on steroids. The harsh rasp of his breath deepened to become a steady rumble. A growl.

"You want to see what I am, detective?"

There was nothing of Max Savoie in that gravelly murmur. His arms gave a powerful jerk, snapping the chain linking the cuffs. His hands came around to brace on the floor in front of him, splayed on either side of Charlotte's knees. His fingers stretched and grew; his nails thickened and curled into razor-sharp talons.

"Take a good look at the last thing you're ever going to see," he growled.

He pushed up with his forearms, head lifting until she could see his eyes. His pupils had shrunk to pin dots in a sea of molten bronze. She sat riveted by his stare as it brightened to an eerie phosphorescence. A low snarl of unbelievable menace vibrated up from a chest that expanded in bulk with every breath, his shoulders growing massive, muscles swelling until his neck had all but disappeared.

The angles of his face grew sharper, bolder, changing right before her astonished eyes. His jaw and cheekbones extended to form a pitbull-like muzzle. Heavy brows on a now prominent ridge and black hair thickened and lengthened. His five o'clock shadow became coarse and dark. His upper lip curled back from those elongated features, now more animal than human, to reveal a row of teeth right out of Little Red Riding Hood.

She shrieked in primal fear and scrambled backward as he lunged, looming over her, a fearsome, frightening being that was bestial, unnatural . . . and somehow still Max.

She froze, cowering, her heartbeats frantic. And then an odd jumble of emotions stirred. Fragmented memories. Half-realized feelings of relief, of safety. And her fear fell away before a sense of curious wonder.

She reached a tentative hand to touch the side of that misshapen face, her fingertips lightly following the ravening quiver of his jaw. Her words were a dreamy whisper.

"My God, Max. You're magnificent."

And familiar.

He blinked. The dark centers of his eyes swelled, cooling them to a clear pale green. He drew a short breath as the dimensions of his face reformed into recognizable contours. The hands he placed on either side of her head were *his* hands, still braceleted in metal.

And the sudden, hard kiss he pressed on her mouth transformed everything inside her. Her breath trembled against his parted lips for a long moment, then he eased back to regard her with typical inscrutability. "Thanks for dinner and the conversation."

Then he was up and over her and gone.

Cee Cee lay staring at the ceiling, tears rolling from the corners of her eyes.

She'd seen the monster in the man.

And it hadn't made a bit of difference.

Max bounded down the stairs, pulling on his shirt and jacket, refusing to think about what had just happened. About what she now knew. His heart was jackhammering; his senses were pulled in a dozen different directions.

Which was why he didn't notice them until they were upon him.

"Stand easy, Savoie."

He heard the revolver cock as it was shoved up under his chin. He stood easy. "What do you want?"

"Jimmy wants to see you."

At gunpoint? "All you had to do is ask."

The three of them were armed and nervous, which made them all the more dangerous. He could smell their fear of him and he was careful to give them no reason to act upon it. He got into the backseat of the Mercedes and sat quietly as they drove him out on River Road. He walked ahead of them to Jimmy's office, his shirt still untucked but buttoned.

Jimmy was in his chair, but he didn't look old and vulnerable. He looked fierce. And Max started to worry.

"Jimmy, where y'at?"

"I've been better. Where have you been?"

"Out to dinner."

"What's that you're wearing?"

He glanced at the broken cuffs. "Just having some fun with my girl."

"Your girlfriend. *Detective* Caissie?"

"Yes."

"Are you crazy? What are you thinking? What are you thinking *with*?"

"I'm thinking you never told me I couldn't have a personal life. I'm thinking I really like her, and she makes me feel—" Alive? Human? He let Jimmy fill in his own word. But maybe he shouldn't have, because maybe the word Jimmy came up with was disloyal.

"What else have you been doing?"

"I don't understand." He looked from Jimmy's angry glare to Francis Petitjohn, who slid in behind his three thugs. "What's going on?"

"You tell me. You tell me why you took it upon yourself to start a goddamn war." Jimmy flung something at Max's feet.

Max looked down, at first confused, then filled with an icy clarity.

Thumbs.

Six

I'M GUESSING THIS is Vic Vantour. Where's the rest of him?" he asked.

"You tell me, Max. These arrived overnight express. Probably all of him that would fit in the saver envelope."

"I don't know, Jimmy. He had all ten digits when I saw him down at the docks."

"His men have been looking for him since that meeting. Since you and Paulie went your separate ways. If word gets out that we have part of him here, I don't need to spell out for you what will happen, do I?"

"I know how to spell, Jimmy."

Petitjohn looked to his cousin. "They're going to know it was him, Jimmy. They're going to want something from us. What are we going to give them?" *Who* was his unspoken demand. Who was going to be sacrificed to keep peace between their families?

Legere gave Max a long, hard look. Max returned it evenly, never blinking, never sweating, totally motionless. The old man sighed in aggravation. "As long as Vantour doesn't surface, they're just guessing at best. Once we know how he was killed—*if* he was killed—then we'll know how to deal with it."

"And if other parts of him are missing? Like his heart?" T-John prodded.

"I said we'd deal with it!" Jimmy roared. He took a shaky breath, then waved them off. "Look for the son of bitch. Do it quietly. Max, a word."

Max stood where he was until the others had gone, then he spoke plainly, without emphasis or emotion. "I didn't do this. I had no reason to. Either you believe me or you don't. Which is it?"

A long, weary sigh. "I believe you, Max. You've never lied to me before."

But was Jimmy lying to him now? Max couldn't tell, and that uncertainty was worse than any outright accusation. Doubt was an ugly thing, gnawing away at his sense of safety, making him wonder why Jimmy had sent armed men to bring him home when he would have returned just as quickly to the usual call. And that made him think again of the assassin at the church, an assassin who knew what kind of bullet to use to bring him down. He chose his words carefully. "If you have to give me up to satisfy them, I'll understand."

"No one's giving you up. Come here."

Max crossed to his chair, hunkering down on the balls of his feet, hands resting easy on Jimmy's knees, his stare direct and open.

"Haven't I always protected you, Max? I made a

promise to you. Did you think I was going to break it? Over the likes of Vantour and his lot? What's going on with you, boy? Why would you be thinking such things? Are you unhappy here?"

"You've always been good to me. I have no reason to want to leave." His tone quieted. "This is my home. I owe you everything."

"This woman, this detective—is she going to get between us?"

"We don't mix business with personal." He spoke the lie as smoothly as all the truths spoken before it.

"If she becomes a problem, will you handle it, Max?"

"Don't ask me to, Jimmy."

"Are you saying no?"

"I'm saying don't ask me to."

Clearly unsatisfied with that answer, the old man still put his hands over Max's to press lightly. "Don't forget where your loyalties lie, boy. Don't forget who's taken care of you. Don't forget what's on the other side of that wall."

"I won't, Jimmy." And the uneasiness that always crept into his eyes when he was reminded of his past was there, comforting Legere that all was as it should be.

"Go get cleaned up. I'll have someone bring up some metal shears." He nodded to the handcuffs. "That's not a good look for you, son."

"That's okay. I can take care of it."

And as he would do once in a while, when his

mood was pensive or disturbed, Max bent down, letting his cheek rest on one of the gnarled hands in a gesture both submissive and trusting. But this time he felt far from comforted by the weight of the old man's other hand on his head. He shut his eyes tightly, feeling Charlotte Caissie's slight tug on the leash of his loyalty.

"GOOD MORNING, DETECTIVE Caissie. Some coffee and beignets? I have them delivered from Café du Monde while they're still hot."

"No thank you, Mr. Legere."

"Mr. Legere? So formal."

"This isn't a social call."

It took Max five seconds to appear behind Jimmy Legere's chair on the front porch. No charming manners and fancy suit this morning. He wore faded jeans stuffed into the tops of half-laced muddy work boots and his long raincoat over a tee shirt. His cheeks were dark with unshaven stubble. His hair stood at wayward angles, spiky with sweat as if he'd been engaged in heavy labor. His rough, earthy look growled with a dangerous male sensuality that had Cee Cee's pulse kicking up a notch. But his gaze was crisp and cool, inanimate as he took in her appearance.

She was as fresh as he was rumpled, wearing a white cotton shirt tucked into skinny black jeans and a man's brocade vest. His gray silk tie was knotted loosely around her neck and secured by the silver stick pin he recognized with a slight narrowing of his eyes.

"Max, pour Detective Caissie some coffee. It's just the thing to cut this muggy heat."

He filled a cup without comment, never taking his eyes off her. When she reached for the saucer he caught her fingers with his other hand, lifting them to press a surprising kiss on her knuckles. Then he passed her the cup, all without a flicker of expression.

Aware of Legere watching the exchange, she didn't react. Wondering what Max was up to with that unexpected display, she took a sip of coffee before getting straight to business.

"Word has it that Vic Vantour is missing. Any insight on that, Jimmy?"

"None, detective. Mr. Vantour and I had some business dealings together and a fairly good relationship, but I can't say that we ever socialized. You must suspect foul play or you wouldn't be here."

"Just following leads that somehow always lead to your door. Why is that, do you suppose?"

"I'm a powerful man. Power attracts speculation and suspicion. I knew your daddy, detective. He was a good cop. A tough cop. I understand you've followed in his footsteps."

Cee Cee stiffened slightly but her voice remained conversational. "My father was killed by some powerful, cowardly rat bastard who blew the top of his head into my red beans and rice as we ate our Sunday supper. Don't tell me what my father was."

Legere regarded her for a moment, his expression intrigued, even amused. Then he touched the back of Max's hand. "Max, did you take care of that matter we discussed?"

"Yes."

"You're a good boy, Max."

"Happy to do it for you, Jimmy." Though he addressed his boss, his stare was fixed on Cee Cee.

"Go get yourself cleaned up and put a civilized face on you. You know I don't like my people going about untidy."

"Sorry, Jimmy. I'll take care of it." But he didn't move.

"Max. Now."

The unblinking gaze flashed between Cee Cee and his employer, reluctance subtly shading his expression before he repeated, "I'll take care of it."

After he'd gone into the house, Jimmy Legere waved his hand to a seat at the wicker table beside him. "Join me, Ms. Caissie. We need to get better acquainted."

"I know all I need to know about you."

"But you don't know all you need to know about Max. Sit down."

She sat.

"You have him well trained," she observed dispassionately. "Does he roll over and play dead, too?"

The old man got right to it. "Max tells me you're involved."

She kept her features from betraying any surprise. "How ungallant of him to kiss and tell."

"You don't see a conflict of interest there, detective, seeing as how Max is what he is and you are what you are?"

"What we are is none of your business."

"Oh, you'd be wrong there, *cher*. Max is more than my employee. He's my family. So what involves him, involves me. Do you understand my meaning?"

"It means holidays might get complicated."

"Complicated. Yes. Has Max told you how he came to live here?"

Max had told her absolutely nothing about himself. In all the years she'd known him, with all their verbal parries, he never got around to it. He was a complete mystery to her. And to everyone else.

Jimmy took her silence for a negative. "He and his mama were swamp folk. Ignorant, superstitious people with their strange ways of looking at life. She got to thinking she'd like him to have a better one, so she moved them to a poor little shanty town where she started plying the oldest profession to buy him shoes. She told him the measure of a man was in his shoes. And one day, one of her customers had a disagreement with her; I don't know what about. He took her and Max out into the swamps and shot her, but for some reason Max was spared. He was four, maybe five years old."

Cee Cee remained still, her heart weeping for Max.

"Some of my associates and I happened to be out in the neighborhood taking care of some business."

Probably out disposing of a body themselves, she thought.

"We come across this boy and his dead mama. I don't know how long he'd been out there—maybe two or three weeks. You see, he wasn't big enough to drag her out, but he had too much heart to leave her there alone. So he stayed with her to keep the predators off. Just a child, out there all alone in that dark, dangerous place. Imagine that, detective."

Her eyes glittered with unshed tears.

"It was the stink we noticed, first. I don't know how he'd stayed alive. He was half crazy with fear and grief, sick from bad water, nearly starved, torn up from whatever he had to fight off to keep his mama safe. Just this filthy, terrified little kid—the deadliest creature I'd ever seen before or since. He was on us before we even knew what hit us. My associates wanted to put him down right then, but there was something about that boy and those fearless protective instincts."

Jimmy shook his head, still marveling over it. "I put my hand down to him. I told him to come with me. That I'd see his mama was taken care of, that I'd take care of him and keep him safe. When he took my hand, he gave me everything he was and everything he would be. I took him home with me, saw his mama buried properly, fed him, clothed him, educated him, and loved him like he was my own."

"And made him into a killer."

"Oh, my dear detective, I had nothing do with that. Whatever horrors he went through to survive out there in the swamps made him fierce and grateful. A powerful combination. If I said to him, "I want your right arm," he would tear it off without hesitation and say, "Happy to do it for you, Jimmy.""

"And if you unsnap his leash and say 'kill', he does that for you, too."

Legere didn't answer.

"Did you send him to kill Vantour?"

"No."

"Would he, if you had asked?"

"Without question."

"Gautreaux and Surette?"

"No. Max is a very valuable resource. I would never jeopardize him carelessly."

"How lovingly paternal of you."

"Sneer at me if you like, Ms. Caissie, but the truth of the matter is, Max has one master: me. No matter how lovely you are, how charming, how tempting, Max is not going to choose you.

"I understand him. I keep him safe from a world that would not be so forgiving of what he is, through no fault of his own. I wanted you to know these things to spare you any future heartache."

"How considerate of you to think of my feelings, but you needn't have concerned yourself. What Max and I have between us is business. If I come for him, it will be to take him to jail, not to my bed. And if I decide I want him for any other reason . . ." She paused for effect. "You won't get in my way."

Jimmy gave a cold chuckle and smiled. "Very sure of yourself, aren't you, my dear?" Then the smile was gone. "You're playing a very dangerous game—one that will hurt him and destroy you."

"Thanks for the warning."

She glanced over his shoulder to see Max framed in the doorway. He'd changed into an expensive dark suit with a stark white shirt. And bright red tennis shoes. For a moment, his gaze was as naked as his cleanly shaven face.

Then the impassive mask settled into place. "I'll walk Detective Caissie to her car."

Jimmy Legere gave her a nod. "Always a pleasure, detective."

"I look forward to visiting you in prison."

As Max walked silently beside her, Cee Cee wondered how much of their conversation he had heard. His brows were leveled into a formidable line and she could have pounded out horseshoes on the surface of his hard jaw. She'd rarely seen any emotion on his face.

"Max—"

"You shouldn't go making such bold claims when you don't know if you can back them up."

He was angry. She tried to make less of it. "I was just trying to provoke him."

"Well, I find myself plenty provoked, too. I may

trot at your high heels and sniff at your skirt, but don't think for one minute that I'll leave my yard and come running if you whistle. Because I know chances are, you'll be coaxing me to dash right out in front of a truck. I'm not stupid, Charlotte. So don't confuse pulling on a leash with wanting to be off it. I know where I belong."

"Especially when the first thing he taught you was heel. You're a coward, Savoie."

"If you say so, detective."

As he opened the door to her car, she met his unreadable stare, first in challenge, then with a gradual softening because of all the things she'd learned about his past.

Her empathy immediately knocked him back on the defensive. "Don't pity me," he growled. "Don't you dare feel sorry for me."

"It's not pity, Max," she assured him quietly. "It's . . . I don't know what it is." She didn't have a name for the emotions crowding up to burn the back of her throat like a spicy meal. She reached out, cupping the back of his head to hold him in place, then leaned forward to touch a light kiss to his cheek. His skin was smooth and warm, smelling of shaving soap, tasting of unspoken dreams.

He stood rigid, unmoving, not even breathing. Slowly, because she knew Jimmy Legere was watching them from the house, she flicked up her middle finger behind Max's head.

Just then the sultry heavens tore loose, drenching them in seconds with hot, pelting rain. Max shrugged out of his jacket and tented it over her head. He waited in the downpour while she dragged up the convertible top and snapped it in place. When she attempted to return his coat, he waved her off.

"Keep it. When you have enough of my clothes at your place, I'll have to start staying overnight so I can get dressed."

"Dream on, Savoie."

"Every night, detective."

He turned and strode up to the house, ignoring the desire to look around to follow the car as it wound toward the road. But he didn't think he could ever stand watching her leave him.

Jimmy still sat on the porch, finishing up the last of his eggs Benedict.

"She's an unmannerly creature, your detective," was his mild comment.

His detective. Who'd come out here to do more than ask about Vic Vantour. She'd wanted to get another look at him, to puzzle over what had happened between them. To fret over what to do next.

He was wondering the same things.

His cheek still tingled from the brush of her lips.

He should have gone right into the house without comment, but something about Jimmy's attitude provoked him just as much as Charlotte's confident goading. He didn't like that they were jabbing at each other with him in the middle. And even more, he disliked the tug-of-war going on inside him as they carelessly pulled on his affections as if he didn't matter.

Max paused beside the table, his features closed down tight, displeasure roughening his voice. "If I want her to know any of the particulars about my past, I'll tell her myself. That's my business and you'll stay out of it."

Before Jimmy could placate him with an apology, Max disappeared into the house, the door closing quietly behind him.

Jimmy frowned. This was the first time Max had spoken to him with even the slightest edge of warning. As if man to man, on equal ground.

It was the woman, of course. Just because Jimmy had never married didn't mean he didn't understand and have a healthy respect for the "weaker" sex. There was nothing weak about a woman. Not when she held a man's foolish hormones in her cold, greedy hands. Even the smartest, shrewdest, most capable male could be reduced to a foolish puppet with one calculating twist. He'd seen it done by his own mother and sister. Clever females, diabolical and treacherous. Sorrow lanced through his heart when he thought of his cousin, led into betrayal by sweet words whispered in his ear. Choosing lust over love of family had been a very bad move on his part. His last.

Jimmy crumpled his newspaper and tossed it to the floorboards. If that skirt with a badge and impressive tits thought she was going to lead Max down the same self-destructive path to ruin, she was sorely mistaken. Max may not be human but he was still a vulnerable male of his own species, and she was cunningly working him up into a mindless, panting frenzy.

What she didn't understand was that Max Savoie was his, bought and paid for. He hadn't spent so much valuable time and effort to tame and teach and train a dangerous wild thing into an efficient, deadly weapon just to have her distract him from his duty.

Don't ask me to.

Temper simmered as Jimmy recalled those bold words. How dare Max put conditions on his loyalty? Standing on hind legs didn't make Savoie into a man: He was an animal, an extremely valuable creature of intelligence and talent.

But if Max was confused about what he was, it was as much Jimmy's fault as the detective's. He'd allowed himself to grow fond of his prized possession, as proud and protective as a father of what he'd nurtured and groomed over the years. He'd spoiled Max with love, using that to control him instead of harsh discipline. But loving one's pets didn't mean an undeserved bite would be forgiven. Or that they'd be allowed to break loose and run free after the scent of a female without being punished upon return.

Max would have to learn that, since Detective

Charlotte Caissie was rapidly becoming a force to be dealt with.

"STILL OPEN FOR business?"

Sister Catherine stopped in surprise, recognizing the voice before she identified the figure slumped in one of the rear pews.

"My business or your business?"

"Yours this time. I'm off the clock."

Mary Kate had never seen that particular phenomenon before, but there was something in Cee Cee's expression—a worry, a weariness—that made her sit in the pew ahead of her. "Meter's running. Go ahead."

"Remember when we were little girls, and Lucy Martel used to scare us with her stories when we were supposed to be sleeping?"

Mary Kate smiled. "The bogeyman. Keeping an eye open all night was the reason I was always falling asleep during catechism class."

"*Te-taille, couche mal, Madame Grand Doigt,* and *fille folle,* coming to chew off the toes or smother bad little children at night. They seemed so real. The possibility that you might open your eyes and find them there in the room made your heart race and your hands sweat. And if you turned your head real fast, you could almost catch sight of them there in the corners."

Mary Kate frowned in concern. "Lottie, are you all right?"

"What if some of those stories were actually true? I mean, where do stories come from? From fact? From some splinter of fact? Demons, monsters—are they something made up to frighten us into good behavior, or are they warnings that such things can and do exist?"

Mary Kate grew very still. She knew Cee Cee expected her to laugh or launch into some philosophical tangent. Instead, she slipped her hand over her friend's and squeezed tightly.

"Mary Kate, I've seen something that shouldn't exist, not in our world. I can't explain it. I can't understand it. I think I must be losing my mind."

"Are you talking about Max Savoie?" Mary Kate asked gently.

As if shocked to the soul, Cee Cee just stared at her for a moment. Then she whispered, "What do you know about Max?"

"Things it's time you knew." She stood. "I'll put on the tea. And I think Father Furness's whiskey would probably be permissible."

Seven

THEY WERE TWO best friends, complete opposites. Day and night. Dark and light. Mary Kate Malone was a cheerleader, a student council representative, a fund raiser, a club joiner. She was blonde, bouncy, and a bit bubble-headed. Everyone loved her. Her one goal going into her senior year was to get into the basketball shorts of Terry McFee.

Charlotte Caissie was the other side of that coin. Tall and intimidating, she would have been Goth if Goth had been in fashion. While Mary Kate craved involvement, she sought solitude. She wasn't a joiner; she was a watcher. She didn't want to be like everyone else. She was proud of her uniqueness, calling herself a daughter of the world. A Creole, she was French, Spanish, and Haitian, with all their dark passions. And she thought Terry McFee was an idiot. She had the better hook shot.

Unlikely friends, they were joined together living under the roof of St. Bartholomew's.

Mary Kate's parents had been killed by a drunk driver during Mardi Gras when she was seven. St. Bart's opened its door to take her in. Charlotte's mother was an alcoholic living someplace in California, her father an undercover cop. While he was prowling the underbelly of New Orleans to bring down organized crime, Charlotte stayed at St. Bart's, warmed by the knowledge that her father loved her. That he was a good cop. Too good.

Just seventeen, she and Mary Kate were on their way home from a basketball game, walking as if nothing could ever harm them. Then a delivery truck pulled over to the curb, grabbed them up and, over the next four days, shattered their innocence forever.

Remembrance came back to Charlotte, bringing the taste of blood and kerosene from the rag they'd stuffed into her mouth. Then the terrible fear at being snatched off the street and locked away in the care of those animals. They'd tried to make her beg on the phone, to beg her father not to testify, but they couldn't force a sound from her. Not then. Not later. Because she'd believed he'd come for her. She'd believed all she had to do was stay strong, be brave, protect Mary Kate, and he'd come charging to her rescue.

But he hadn't.

"Ancient history," Charlotte murmured into her cup of tea. "What does this have to do with Max Savoie?"

"He was there, that last day. Just for a minute, but I saw him. I called out to him for help."

Charlotte gripped her cup, her hands shaking.

"He saw us and he did nothing?" A host of emotions fisted about her heart. Disbelief, shock, fury.

A smile touched Mary Kate's scarred face. "Not then. But he came back later." Her smile grew cold and savage. "And then he took care of everything."

Don't be afraid. They won't ever hurt you again. I took care of them for you.

He would have been around twenty then, already a solid fixture in Legere's world. But she hadn't met him until several years later. Until after she joined the force and became part of her father's vigorous campaign against crime. She remembered it so clearly. She'd heard of him, the sleek, silent killer who carried out Legere's commands with terrifying and deadly efficiency. Seasoned members of her squad had actually trembled and crossed themselves when he'd been brought into the station in handcuffs on one of many charges never proven. Curiosity had her craning her neck for a look at him and she remembered thinking, *Why, he's not much older than I am.*

She remembered his calm, graceful stride, the way he carried himself so fearlessly through a bristling crowd who would have shot him dead just to claim they'd done so. Because he scared them. *He doesn't look so scary,* she'd thought as their eyes met for the first time. His beautiful pale green eyes in that harshly sculpted face met and held hers, and a shock zapped her like a fork in a light socket.

A shock of recognition for someone she'd never seen before . . .

Not in his human form.

"You told me you didn't remember," she accused her friend, her tone agitated. "You said you never saw who pulled us out of there just ahead of the flames. You lied to me, Mary Kate. Why?"

"Because I wanted to do something for *you*. After all you went through trying to protect me, this was one burden I could carry for you."

Charlotte's voice trembled. "You saw what he did to them? How he did it?"

"He did what I would have done if I'd been strong enough. He did what they deserved to have done to them. He butchered them like the animals they were, and then I helped him burn the bodies."

So they couldn't be recognized. So they wouldn't lead back to his boss. Or to him as their killer. Protecting all three of them in that quick, clever move.

He'd known all along what had been done to them, to her. He'd known why his touch, any man's touch, would frighten her. So he'd kept his distance, his manner easy and nonthreatening. He'd understood why she covered her weakness with a wrap of barbed-wire temper, so he'd snipped his way carefully through each strand. Knowing helplessness would bring panic, he'd rescued her, then released her when she asked him to. Her soul shuddered. Her emotions splintered.

"He carried you to the hospital in his arms and wanted to wait to see if you'd be all right, but I convinced him to go, that it wouldn't be safe for him.

Max and I have become friends of a sort over the years, because we shared you."

It was too much to take in all at once.

"But why would he risk so much for the two of us? Why, Mary Kate?"

"He's never told me."

"What brings him back *here*? He said it was to cleanse his soul. Is that what you do for him? He comes to you with his hands all bloodied, and you forgive him?"

"I would if he asked, but that's not what he asks for. And no, I won't tell you what it is. That's between him and God, and only he can tell you."

Each fact only added to her distress. "How does he do it? How does he change what he is? How is it possible?"

"It's miraculous, Lottie. He was an answer to prayer."

"Nonsense. Max Savoie is more demon than angel."

"Is he? You don't know him very well, do you?"

Now Max Savoie was a saint, and her saintly friend was out for bloody retribution? Charlotte didn't understand . . . and then she understood all too well.

"*You* sent him out to kill Gautreaux and Surette. Mary Kate, tell me you didn't!"

Her gaze was cool and unrepentant. "After listening to that poor woman talking about all she'd gone through, tell me *you* didn't want them dead."

Charlotte drew a tortured breath. "That's not my decision to make. It's not yours. It's not Max's. That's why we have laws."

"The law wouldn't do anything, Lottie. The law turned its back on her, just as it would have turned its back on us. It never punishes the true monsters in this world."

"So you ask Max to do it for you?" She moaned softly, covering her face with her hands. It was one thing for Jimmy Legere to direct Max's unique talents. But Mary Kate . . . Sister Catherine . . . "Why does he do it? What's in it for him? Why would he care about these people he doesn't know?"

"Neither of us can condone the harming of innocents. You know my reason. He's never told me his."

But Charlotte knew. It was because of a small boy out in the swamps protecting his dead mother. A mother who'd allowed herself to become a victim so he could have shoes.

But knowing the reasons didn't excuse his actions. Or excuse what she herself had done to protect him. As she now would protect both Max and Mary Kate. The weight of those obligations hung heavily on her soul, and she wondered how her friend didn't buckle under the burden.

"How many of these little favors has Max done for you?" When Mary Kate wouldn't answer, Charlotte rested her head on her arms, too sick at heart to think of how to handle the information. Then she lurched to her feet and slid out of the chair. "I have to go."

SHE SLIPPED INTO her apartment without turning on the light. She needed the shadows to hide from all the shocking truths she'd learned.

Inside those robes, behind the rosary and gentle smile, Mary Kate—Sister Catherine—was as blood-thirsty as Jimmy Legere, both of them using Max to dispense their own personal justice without giving him a thought.

How could her best friend expect her to deal with such knowledge? The code she honored called upon her to do the right thing, but how could arresting a nun be the right thing? How could jailing Max Savoie for stepping between her and horror at the hands of brutal men, not once but twice, be considered justice? Yet how could she excuse either of them, even if she understood so painfully and personally why they did what they'd done? When a primitive part of herself had so often wanted to do exactly the same thing? But that didn't make it right, legally or morally. What the hell was she supposed to do? By doing nothing, she was condoning murder. By saying nothing, she was equally guilty.

She picked up Max's jacket, crushing the elegant folds to her chest.

She'd had a concussion, a broken arm, and internal bleeding. Her body had slipped into shock; her mind, she'd assumed, into delirium. How else to explain the face of her rescuer? A beast with flaming eyes and dripping fangs, right out of a child's nightmares. Yet oddly, there was no fear associated with that horrific vision.

Don't be afraid. They won't ever hurt you again. I took care of them for you.

Relief, safety, gratitude—those were the emotions that came swirling around her even now as she buried her face in Max's coat. It was his scent that clung to the fabric of the jacket, to her remembered dream. It was the low, firm assurance of his words.

It was the shoes.

She picked up the phone and dialed.

"Max Savoie, please. Tell him it's Charlotte."

A three-second pause, then the deep, cool rumble of his voice.

"This is a surprise."

"I need to talk to you."

"Where are you?"

"At my apartment."

"Will this conversation involve poison and torture?"

"Max, I need to see you."

"Some incentive, detective. Will it involve anatomy?" His tone roughened slightly.

"Max . . . please."

He paused. "Twenty minutes."

HE WAS AT her door in eighteen.

He regarded her warily from the stair landing. His dark hair, eyelashes, and brown leather jacket were beaded with early evening drizzle. His words were cautious, concerned. "You sounded strange on the phone. Is everything all right?"

"Come in, Max. Don't look so suspicious. I'm not going to try anything."

A ghost of a smile. "Should I be relieved or disappointed?" He entered just enough for the door to close behind him. "What did you want to talk about, Charlotte?"

She moved away from him, all jerky motion and restless energy as she paced and circled until finally facing him from across her crowded living room. Her gaze searched his features intently, as if trying to find something there. Apprehension began to quiver in his belly. This wasn't the calm, capable woman who always confronted him with her indomitable spirit and words as direct as a bolt from a crossbow.

"Charlotte, what was it you wanted?"

She was staring at his feet.

"Do I have someone on my shoes?"

Her eyes misted up, and her words were a faraway whisper. "I remember thinking I didn't have to be scared of a monster wearing red tennis shoes."

Silence. Then a quiet, "When were you thinking this?"

"Twelve years ago."

He went completely still.

Her features worked with anguish, then steadied. "Why didn't you ever say anything to me, Max?"

"I figured anything you didn't remember was a blessing."

Her expression darkened with complex emotions, but her voice was low and tough. "Did you know what they were doing? What they had planned?"

"Not until I stumbled onto it. No."

The tears on her face startled a bittersweet panic within him as he remained motionless, a room away from all her pain.

"Did you know about my father? Were you in on that plan to kill him?"

"No."

"Would you if he'd asked you?"

"He didn't ask me."

"That wasn't the question."

"He didn't ask me."

He watched the horror, the fury, the fear well up inside her. And he braced himself, in dread and a terrible resignation, for her one question.

"Why, Max? Why did you come back?"

It wasn't the question he expected, and for a moment, he had no response.

"Why? Why didn't you just walk away?"

He explained as best he could the conflicting feelings tightening inside him even now. "Because she was crying." Then his voice dropped to a husky register. "And you were so brave."

She came toward him then. He held his ground as long as he could while a nervous alarm spiked through him. Then he tried to retreat, reaching for the knob as she backed him up against the door. Her hand slipped over his, closing around it. He stood frozen as her other hand lifted, as her fingertips grazed along the angle of his jaw. His eyes grew huge.

"It wasn't my father," she began in a rough voice. "It wasn't the doctors in the ER. It wasn't the detectives or the shrinks who made me feel safe. It was *you*. It's your face I remember—your other magnificent face. You were my hero, Max. You saved me."

She leaned into him, her head on his shoulder, her soft breath on his neck. He closed his eyes, breathing her in until all his senses were shivering. "Don't try to make me more than I am, Charlotte."

Her fingertips traced the curve of his ear. "Stop pretending to be less than you are."

He jerked his head away from the touch that scrambled his ability to reason, to react. "I'm not heroic. I'm not one of your good, decent, hard-working heroes."

It was then she understood what Mary Kate was trying to tell her. And that truth freed her conscience. "Those good, decent, hard-working heroes did nothing, Max. *You* did. You stepped in when you didn't have to, and you saved us."

"No. I didn't. I was too late. I didn't know. Charlotte, I couldn't—"

Her fingers touched his mouth, silencing him.

"That's twice you've been there for me, and neither time I've thanked you."

He swallowed hard, unable to speak.

"Thank you, Max."

She sighed and burrowed in closer, closer to the frantic beat of his heart. The feel of her was heaven. His hand came up slowly, settling to rest lightly between strong, capable shoulders that for a moment sagged with the weight of past demons.

With his heart so achingly full, it would be a tremendous relief to release the burden he'd carried for so long with those three, powerful words. But he held them back, not trusting himself. Not trusting her with them.

"I'm so tired, Max. So tired of carrying everything alone. Stay with me tonight. With you here, maybe I'll be able to let the shadows go and get some rest."

His fingers began a firm massage of the tight muscles in her neck. The sound she made was liquid contentment as his mouth moved lightly along her brow. "If I stay," he warned gruffly, "I can't promise you'll be resting."

Silence.

Then her head lifted and her stare locked into his. "That might be all right, too."

Everything he'd ever desired was in that soft *carte blanche*. He'd be crazy not to act on it, not to satisfy all those restless, urgent fantasies that only she could fulfill. Not to take with desperate need all the things he wanted from her.

Wanted her to *give* to him. Not just allow him to take from her.

He took a shaky step back. "What do you want from me, Charlotte?"

"I don't know, Max. I'm not thinking straight right now." Her hands stroked up and down the front of his jacket, rubbing his response to her into a dangerous confusion. Then she stopped and he was able to breathe. "I just want your shoulder—if the offer's still open."

A small smile. "Is that all?"

A small smile in return. "For now."

Mentally beating his head against the wall, he heard himself say, "Okay."

She led him by the hand to the couch, her expression so absurdly grateful that he felt like something disgusting she should be scraping off the bottom of her shoe. When she reached over to turn down the light, he shrugged out of his jacket and hung it over the back of a chair to dry.

"Nice coat."

When he saw her admiring glance, he scowled. "I'm not leaving it here."

"I just said it was nice."

"It was a gift."

"Oh." A lot of thorns prickled around that little word.

"From Jimmy. I've never really bought anything for myself."

Bringing up Jimmy Legere returned a degree of

her tangy spirit. She snorted, regarding him through chiding eyes. "Next you're going to tell me he only pays you minimum wage."

"He doesn't pay me anything at all."

She stared at him, drawing harsh conclusions as she frowned. "So he owns you lock, stock, and wardrobe."

"No, of course not. I can have anything I want. I just don't want much. Except once I wanted to take this maddening woman out to dinner, and she ended up trying to poison and torture me. I'm not very good at investing my money wisely."

"Don't worry about your coat," she told him archly. "I don't want anything of Jimmy Legere's."

"What about me?"

Alarmed at where the conversation was leading, she tried to lighten the tone with a gentle tease. "I never said I wanted you, Max."

He took her comment unblinkingly, as if it weren't a sledge between the eyes.

Cee Cee waited for his usual sharp and sassy rejoinder. His unexpected silence stretched out uncomfortably between them. Finally, still tightly shuttered behind an impassive stare, he plumped several pillows against the arm of the couch and sat down. He patted the seat beside him and waited expressionlessly for her to join him. When she settled on the cushion, he angled slightly toward her and patted his shoulder. She settled into that offered comfort without reservation, tucking her feet up, her eyes closing on a sigh. They sat like that for a moment until Max began to shift restlessly, finally toeing off his shoes. Moving Cee Cee away from him long enough to twist on the seat, he slid one leg behind her, then leaned back against the arm of the couch, drawing her between his knees to stretch along the lean length of him.

"How's that?" he whispered into her hair.

"Nice," she murmured, snuggling into the circle of his arms, nearly asleep on the gust of her first sigh.

He lay still, barely breathing until he was sure she was slumbering deeply. Then he let the tension in his muscles unknot, and let himself explore her with his heightened senses. One denim-clad thigh rode his hip. An arm curved about his ribs, the other curled behind the back of his neck, her knuckles folded beneath his chin. She wasn't light, but he liked the firm, muscled feel of her contrasting so deliciously with the soft cushion of breasts pushing against him with every gentle inhalation. He closed his eyes and breathed deep, drawing in the unique fragrance of her.

She wore perfume from Bourbon French perfumery on Jackson Square. He'd smelled it when walking past, and located the rich tones in one of the smoked glass bottles. *Voodoo Love.* He'd smiled, wondering if she'd put a spell on him. That would explain the way logic melted away the moment the scent of her tickled up his nose. It was more than the perfume though that was thickly sensual and exotic. It was the way the liquid warmed and awakened with her skin chemistry. The way it blended with her sultry female heat. Intoxicating pheromones that wound him up into a tight coil of yearning and near madness.

But whatever he might feel for her was not returned. How many more times did she have to tell him that brutal truth, in actions and words, before he believed her?

He nuzzled her soft hair.

At least one more time.

The urge to move his hands from where they rested safely on knee and shoulder began to tempt his resolve, so he let his senses stretch out beyond her to distract him from her closeness and availability. He heard the quick patter of heartbeats. Her two rodent pets, frozen with the certainty of impending doom. There was a slight drip at her bathroom faucet. Her bed was freshly made, laced with some floral-scented dryer sheets. There were Chinese take-out containers in her trash—moo shu pork. It was a wonder her guinea pigs weren't watching her more closely. His Armani jacket was in her closet. Did that mean she wasn't planning to return it? He smiled and let his radius expand outside her apartment.

The couple downstairs had three cats. He worked around oil and automobiles. She was an artist. They'd just finished making love, while their barbecued ribs grew cold on the table and the wine warmed in their glasses. They were murmuring things he didn't think they'd want him to hear, so he turned his attention to the street. To a car parked on the far side. The occupant was a man, drinking hot coffee and carrying a gun. He smelled like fast food and gym clothes. A cop.

Max rolled out from under Cee Cee without causing her to stir. He padded to the balcony in his socks and leaned out, just able to see the rear bumper of the voyeur's vehicle. In a quick movement, he vaulted over the wrought-iron rail and dropped to all fours into the wet grass below.

Alain Babineau checked his watch, then rubbed at his eyes. He sat up straight, blinking, wondering if he'd actually seen something rush up toward his driver's window. He heard a light thump on his roof. By the time he followed the sound up and over, he was staring at Max Savoie in his passenger seat. He jumped, spilling his coffee into his lap, cursing as he tried to blot it up with a handful of paper napkins.

"Good evening, detective. It's a lot more comfortable upstairs than down here spying through the windows."

"I wasn't—oh, hell. Yes, I was."

An awful thought roughened Max's voice as he studied the boyishly handsome man who had the same calculating eyes as his partner and a shiny gold ring on his left hand. "Did Charlotte ask you to watch out for her?"

"God, no. She'd bust my butt if she knew I was out here."

Relieved, Max still wasn't through intimidating him. "Then why are you out here?"

"Because you were up there. If our roles were reversed and she was your partner, and I was a cold-hearted bastard with blood on my hands alone with her in the dark, what would you be doing?"

Max smiled slightly. "I'd either be calling for a lot of backup, or I'd trust her and go home to my wife. You've got about two seconds to decide which one you're going to do."

"She's important to me."

"And I'm not going to hurt her."

Babineau started the car. "I'm more worried about your friends."

"They're not going to be messing with her."

"Yeah? I followed them here." Babineau shone his spotlight out the window, letting it dazzle off the windshield of a big black Olds parked a block down. The car immediately roared to life and executed a quick U-turn disappearing act. "Anyone you know?"

Max didn't answer, thinking of those photographs from the station steps. He'd had Pete, Jimmy's driver, drop him off near the Quarter and he'd walked the rest of the way. Why was Jimmy having him followed? And why was Babineau tailing his observers?

"She likes you, Savoie. I don't know why, but she

does. It could do some serious damage to her career, the two of you together like this."

"We're not together."

Babineau sighed. "Right. Get out of my car. I'm going home. I suggest you do the same."

Max waited until the car was out of sight before jogging back across the street. He stood beneath the balcony, crouched, then sprang easily up and over the rail. As he reentered the dim living room, he sensed movement. Then he felt a pistol barrel tap under his chin.

"Who were you talking to?"

"Your partner."

The pistol lowered as Cee Cee swore fiercely. "What's he doing here?"

"Both of you have some serious trust issues. He's worried about the company you keep. I told him he had nothing to concern himself over, that I was just leaving." Hard to do when she was standing next to him warmed by sleep, with the scent of him all over her.

"You misinformed him. You're not leaving. Not yet."

"Why not?"

"I never said I wanted you, Max. But I do."

Eight

MAX STOOD AS frozen as her little rodent friends, his heart beating just as fast, his mind just as paralyzed. When her palm cupped the side of his face, a fierce tremor raced through him. And his eyes narrowed suspiciously.

"What do you want me for? Your bodyguard? Your best friend? Your snitch? You're going to have to spell it out for me, Charlotte."

"You make me sound very manipulative." She continued to touch him, her fingertips outlining his face. He struggled not to turn into her palm, to suck on her fingers.

"Why is that, I wonder? Could be you've stuck it to me one too many times?"

"And now that I'm asking you to stick it to *me,* you're saying no?"

Instead of answering, he asked his own question. "Why did you kiss me, Charlotte? When you brought me here the other night, why did you kiss me? You didn't have to."

"No," she agreed softly, "I didn't have to. I wanted to."

"Why?"

"Because when you kissed me for the first time at my car, I didn't know how to react to it. I was too upset to think, to feel."

He went very still, his breath stopping as she traced the shape of his mouth.

"Max, you've been chasing after me for years. Didn't *you* ever think of what you'd do if you caught me?"

"You'd be surprised how little I think of anything else, detective."

Cee Cee let that go for the moment. "I asked you here that night to break your trust. I wanted to hurt you and drive you away."

"Why?"

"Because you scared me, Max—and dammit, I don't scare easily." Her fisted hands struck his chest in frustration, then gripped his shirt, kneading the fabric in agitation until his hands slipped over them to hold them tightly.

"What did I ever do to make you afraid of me?" He sounded so genuinely upset that she laughed a bit frantically.

"Nothing. You didn't do anything. I'm not afraid of you; I never have been. That's what scares me: You are the last person in the world I should feel safe with. I don't *want* to like you so much. I don't want to look forward to being irritated by you. I don't want to see you in handcuffs and lie to my superiors, my coworkers, my friends, to get you out of them. You're a criminal, and I'm supposed to want to put you away for life. But all I can think of is how miserable I'd be without you." She grabbed a shaky breath while Max stared at her through wide, unblinking eyes.

"I wear your clothes because they make me feel like you're wrapped around me. When you touched me, I couldn't think of anything but how much I wanted you to keep on touching me. I kissed you because I couldn't stand not knowing how it would feel to kiss you back, and I didn't know if I'd ever get another chance. I don't care who you are. I don't care what you are. And that scares me, because I *should* care. When I woke alone just now and you were gone, all I could think was that I might never have another chance to be with you. I want that chance, Max—and I don't care what it costs me."

He gripped her face between his hands and pulled her up to the hard, hungry crush of his mouth.

There was nothing gentle about him. His hold on her was firm, controlling. His kiss bruised and demanded. The unyielding plane of his body offered no comfort.

And she didn't want any. She wanted a toe-to-toe, hip-to-hip, lip and tongue confrontation. She wanted to be bruised and mashed and wrestled in rough passion. She wanted to let go of the fear that blocked all natural reactions to a man's touch. And she found no barriers in Max's arms.

Their hands were all over each other, touching,

groping, tugging, and stroking, hurried and awkward. She panted wildly as his mouth tore away from hers to move greedily down the offered arch of her throat. Urging him to rush because she was afraid she'd freeze up if the momentum slowed from avalanche intensity.

She unbuckled her jeans and wiggled them down, stepped out, and kicked them away. Then she jerked his shirttails free, rubbing her palms up and down his hard flat stomach, the feel of him exciting. He made a raw sound at that first cool touch. Then, hands shaking, she was undoing his belt, his fly, fumbling until he reached down to assist her.

Her arms whipped around his neck as she cried, "Now—hurry! I want you now." Desperate to have him, desperate to know if it could be different with him.

His hands clamped onto the backs of her thighs, lifting her off the floor. He hadn't meant to be so abrupt, but he was on fire and she wasn't helping matters, chewing and licking his ear, driving him mad with the hot pulse of her breath shivering all the way to his animal soul. He was desperate to have her, desperate to know if fact could rival fantasy.

He'd imaged this moment until he feared he'd explode with tension from just a whiff of her perfume. He'd dreamed of having her, taking her, mating with her in every way and place his fevered mind could come up with. In his bed, in hers, in the impossibly cramped front seat of her car. From behind while she was splayed face down across her desk, beneath him on the hard, narrow beds in lockup. On his lap in the big leather chair in Jimmy's office. Rolling naked with him on the groomed grasses of Jackson Square. But none of those raw, explicit imaginings compared to this.

Her body was hot and damp for him, her scent all potent, alluring female. He wanted to sniff her, taste her, devour her, claim her. He'd planned to be gentle, to ease into intimacy so as not to remind her of what had been stolen from her by force. He'd meant to temper his growling passion with care. But the feel of her silky thighs sliding over his hips, opening his way to all her wondrous secrets, the sound of her husky voice urging him on—he couldn't wait.

He crushed her to him, burying his face in the valley of her breasts, drawing the fragrance of her skin through the fabric of her shirt, hearing her heart beat with the primitive lure of fertility drums. Her ready dampness scorched against his belly.

He angled her hips, holding her poised for a moment beyond madness, then sheathed himself with her tight, wet heat in one mind-blanking instant.

His eyes closed.

His breathing stopped as a long shudder rolled through him.

Ah . . . yes.

If lightning struck him now and burnt him to a cinder, he wouldn't have the slightest regret.

This was what it was like to belong to another. To be part of someone else. To not be alone. This scalding, comforting, completing union of body and spirit. He wanted to laugh out loud with the surprising joy of it, but was afraid he'd start to weep. He felt like throwing back his head to howl, to express the amazing bliss. He'd never felt so powerful. So free. But all he could do was whisper her name.

"*Charlotte.*"

Then his awareness expanded to where her fingers jabbed into his shoulder blades. Her supple body had stiffened at the shocking force of his entry. He didn't move as that hot, huge part of him throbbed impatiently at the door of her frantically guarded memories. Now, he thought with a terrible sense of shame and loss, now she would say "No" and "Stop," and he would have to comply. And he would kiss her calm, if she let him, and then he'd go home.

He gentled his grip on her and started to lift her off him, when her knees locked tight at his waist. Her face was pressed against his neck. He heard her quick, harsh breaths slow and deepen, felt her inhale, felt her nuzzle and taste his skin. She said his name, a low, throaty welcome as her arms and legs twined about him. And she began to move on him, letting the hard, slick feel of him soothe her fears and rub her passions raw.

"*Max.*"

Then there was nothing but sensation. Hot-edged

friction carried on a steady tide. Fierce and pounding, undercutting Cee Cee's control until she hung onto him as her world was swept away. *This* was what the guys spoke of in the locker room with sly winks and ribald innuendo, when they bragged of reducing the women they bedded into wailing, clawing, screaming she-demons. She'd snorted in disgust, sure they were building themselves up with macho exaggeration, trying to impress her and each other with their tales of conquest and impossible sexual feats.

Yet here she was, filled to bursting with Max, taking him inside her when she wasn't even sure what exactly he was—man or beast. Letting him take her on a sensory ride with the top down and the wind howling. Nothing mattered except what was building, massing upon her nerve endings. A strange, wild tightening shot through her thighs, clenched at her belly, squeezed her breath out in short, harsh spurts until—

"How long?"

She fought to pull her thoughts from the realm of exquisite madness. "*What?*"

"How long do we have?" His breathing was only slightly steadier as he held her pinned against his chest. The incredible Mt. Everest climb stopped.

With a moan of objection, she panted, "I have to meet my partner in the morning at seven. Max, what are you are *doing?*"

"We've got plenty of time. No rush."

He was carrying her, not to the bedroom but to the couch. She did groan aloud then. "Max, I'm not in the mood for conversation."

"I don't want to talk to you. I want to *enjoy* you."

The way he said it provoked a long, voluptuous shiver of anticipation. He sat down with her straddling his lap. His hands topped her thighs, holding her still while he pulsed far up inside her.

"Okay?" he asked her with a strange sort of quiet, considering what they were in the middle of.

"Okay?" she repeated blankly, then smiled with wanton satisfaction. "A whole helluva lot better than okay. On a scale of one to ten, forty-seven. My God, I'm outstanding. How 'boutchu?"

"Outstanding," he agreed softly.

In the darkness of the room, with only light from the next building spilling in through the open slider, his face was all strong shadows, like a bold Frank Miller pen and ink drawing with only his eyes gleaming in color. Harsh lines, fierce angles, dangerous contours.

"Max?" Her hands moved restlessly over his shoulders, shifting soft fabric over a hard terrain of bone and muscle. A breathtaking landscape that she briefly wondered how many others he'd allowed to scale. A growly irritation roused at the thought because part of her already started to think of him as hers. And she was hot, itching, and hungry to claim him. "A gentleman doesn't make a lady wait."

"As you said, I'm no gentleman." He watched her expression slide from luscious pleasure to edgier annoyance as he continued to hold her motionless.

She tried to lift up, to get the hot momentum going again, but he held her firmly in place. She cursed him colorfully and demanded, "Finish what you started."

"I love it when you talk dirty."

She glared down into the infuriating face of his calm. She didn't want him calm. She wanted him wild for her again, as desperate as she was. Why wasn't he?

"Kind of like torture, isn't it, Charlotte?" he goaded softly. "Kinda like inviting a man up to your place, getting him all hot and bothered with your kisses, getting his mind spinning with thoughts of sex, and then stabbing him in the back. Sucks, doesn't it?"

Not in the mood for games, she snarled, "Give me what I want, Savoie."

His hands lifted, raising up above his head in a mock gesture of surrender. "Take it from me."

She released a shaky breath, trying to decide between strangling him with her hands or choking him with her tongue down his throat. Choosing the latter, she groaned with satisfaction at making the right choice.

He was pleasure incarnate, inviting her to partake as fully and deeply as she dared.

His hair was black rumpled silk sliding through her fingers, a sleek contrast to the rough texture of his jaw and cheeks. His mouth was a wicked path to all things dark and dangerous, and she took from it with fierce determination. She began a slow rocking with her hips as she worked her way down his shirt buttons, pushing the material aside, bending to taste his warm skin, her fingers tunneling through the crisp mat of hair. The easy rocking became small, tempting lifts, just an inch or two up and down, slow and controlled, teasing their nerve endings into a heightened state of awareness.

His arms rested above his head, overlapped at the wrists as if he were her prisoner. That wouldn't do. She caught his hands, fitting his palms to the taut curve of her thighs, moving them in the same taunting rhythm. His eyes never closed, not when she kissed him, not as she rode him at an ever-quickening pace. He watched her, transfixed, charting every new discovery that bloomed in her expression until she was flushed and sleek with perspiration. Her breath hitched, her body shuddering like her sleek sports car shifting into overdrive. Her movements quickened and tightened with purpose.

She seized his hand and guided it urgently to the wet heat of her body, showing him the rhythm she craved. She sighed raggedly as he pursued it, so that he stroked her, inside and out. Hard and smooth within the walls of her frantically clutching body; his thumb massaging and igniting her.

Her hands clenched in his hair as she pulled back his head to take his mouth with a rough insistence, feeding off his lips, swallowing his breath until she couldn't seem to catch hers. Then she spun out of control, smashing through the last guardrail of her restraints to hurtle off the cliff, his name spilling from her in reckless wonder, in triumph, and finally on a breathy sigh. "Max. Max! Oh, baby."

With a final, glorious spasm she collapsed upon him, spent and trembling, beyond conscious thought. He simply held her because she had no strength of her own. Finally, after she was able to sit up to meet the smoldering heat of his gaze, to return the sudden flash of his smile, she laughed with shaky delight.

"I need oxygen. That was . . . wow." She grinned; she couldn't help it. And she couldn't resist helping herself to the feel of his cheekbones beneath her fingertips, to the taste of his mouth. She whispered, "I knew it would be like this with you. I knew it. Good God, Savoie, you are so hot." She snuggled against his shoulder with a sigh, boneless, vulnerable, content. She felt his hands in her hair, his kiss on her brow. Then she heard his low murmur against her ear.

"Charlotte, I've never wanted anything as much as I want you. So brave. So beautiful. You have nothing to fear from me. Can I have you now?"

Her voice was weary with exhausted pleasure. "I'm all yours, Max. All yours."

"Thank you, *sha*."

She dozed in his arms, afloat in a heavy lethargy that suddenly became her cool sheets beneath her bare skin. She smiled, not opening her eyes as Max lifted her foot, then laughed softly as his tongue danced lightly across her toes. His hands moved up her leg with firm, kneading motions that had her purring softly in encouragement. He kissed her knee, her hip. His teeth nipped gently at the curve of her waist. She felt his warm breath blow on the sensitive skin between her breasts, where her shirt veed open, then the slow rasp of his tongue drawing an exquisite line up to the curve of her neck, quickening that wondrous thrill of need all over again. When his lips brushed whisper soft against hers, she opened her eyes to gaze up at him in drowsy bemusement.

"Max." Her fingertips threaded back through his hair. "How could I help but fall in love with you?"

That eerie stillness settled over him. Finally he said, "I don't know." Softer still, "Are you?"

She touched his lips. "I am incredibly fond of you at the moment."

He sucked at her fingers, biting them, kissing them while his solemn stare never flickered. She knew it wasn't what he wanted to hear, but it was all she could give him for now. Maybe ever. She'd come a long way in one evening, but she couldn't lower the barriers that one last notch. She was too uncertain of herself.

"I want to be with you, Max. I want you. I love making love with you. Is that enough for tonight?"

She drew him down to her, kissing him sweetly until he responded, reluctantly, then with an aggressive longing that stirred her all the way down to her well-licked toes.

"No . . . but I'll learn to live with the disappointment."

She sat up as he sat back. She peeled off her shirt and the one he was still wearing, adoring his bared arms and shoulders roughly with her palms, the broad expanse of his chest with her wet kisses until he followed her back down to those scented sheets. She held his face between her hands and smiled at him, her eyes full of daring challenge.

"Make me love you, Savoie."

He smiled back, a slow baring of his teeth. "I will, Charlotte."

And as he had her moaning, straining, writhing beneath him until the encroaching dawn pushed back the moon shadows, she had to bite her lips to keep from telling him exactly what he wanted to hear.

HER ALARM BUZZED, dragging her out of a near coma of fatigue. Cee Cee slapped it off her night-stand, then rolled over to confront a sleeping and very naked Max Savoie. He was stretched out on his stomach, his face turned toward her. Her gaze trailed over him in a hot, hungering sweep. Damn he was gorgeous, with his mussed black hair and whisker-shaded cheeks softened by the long slant of his closed eyes. And that lean, sleekly muscled frame she was now so intimately familiar with. And the tight, sweet curve of his butt that just begged for the squeeze of her hand. Even his bare feet choked her up with all sorts of emotions. While she was wondering wildly what to do with him, his eyes opened.

Against the mossy color of her sheets, his stare was a beautiful pale green. Her heart shuddered in panic.

"Heya," he muttered, his sleepy voice a low musical rumble. "You look like you can't decide whether to toss me out or have another go-round with me."

Her smile wobbled. "I'm afraid it's the heave-ho. I've got to go to work and I'm late. I'll have to grab a shower at the station."

"Just treat me the way you would any of your other overnight guests."

"I've never had—that is, I've never asked . . . You're my first overnight guest."

"Oh," was all he said, but there was a smirky, self-satisfied look on his face as he rolled onto his back.

Her gaze devoured the sight of him. Though he might appear relaxed, he was all strength and tense readiness, right down to the rock-hard erection rising tight against his belly almost to his navel. The tempting, slightly terrifying sight forced her to leap off the bed before she jumped his bones. "Get out of here, Max," she told him grumpily as she ducked into the bathroom.

She was brushing her teeth furiously when he

appeared behind her to press a kiss at the nape of her neck. Heat shot through her in immediate response. His arms circled her briefly, his hands rubbing up the insides of her thighs, reestablishing his claim of her body. Before she could smack his bold touch away, he was gone. She hurried into the living room, toothbrush still in her mouth. He was on her balcony, dressed and about to walk away from all they'd shared. And she wanted him back.

"Max," she called through a mouthful of toothpaste.

A slight smile curved his lips. "Thanks for the hospitality, Charlotte."

"I'll see around, Savoie."

"Yes, you will."

Before she could take a step forward, he took a light hop up onto the railing and stepped off. When she remembered she was on the second floor, she rushed over to the rail but he'd already disappeared. She turned back with a sigh, and the first thing she saw was what he'd left behind.

"NICE JACKET. Is that real leather?"

"Hands off." Cee Cee shut her locker, then stroked the buttery-soft sleeve herself. "It is nice, isn't it?"

"Did you get a bump in pay grade to support this lavish new wardrobe? One might say you're beginning to resemble a certain smartly dressed mob enforcer."

"Is that what *you're* saying, Babineau?" She squared off with him in the aisle. "Anything else you want to say to me that is even remotely your business?"

Her partner sighed, raking a hand through his hair. "I'm worried, is all. You're not being careful."

"I'm always careful. What are you talking about?"

"Not in this. Not with him. What's with this guy, Ceece? You know what he is. You know what he does. What's the big attraction?"

"He's great in bed, all right? He's the best in the sack I've ever had. Is that what you wanted to hear? Do you need any other pornographic details, or can your nasty little mind fill in the blanks?" She whirled away and stalked the length of the locker row with Babineau a step behind her.

"I don't care if you're doing the horizontal mambo with him. About time you're doing it with someone." That was muttered under his breath, but she drew up short and faced him furiously. He didn't flinch away from her cold stare. "A better choice would be an accountant or a hotel pool boy. Even a cop, for God's sake—anything but a criminal. But you're right. Who you're dancing with after hours is none of my business. I don't care."

"So why were you staked outside my apartment, if it's no big deal?"

"Cee Cee, this guy is bad news. If you want to fuck him, fuck him. But don't fall for him."

Suddenly all the tension and turmoil inside her exploded. "I am not in love with Max Savoie!"

Heads turned throughout the locker room, and cursing, she strode out into the crowded mill of their workplace. One look at her, and a path was made by perps and coworkers alike. She burst out into the morning heat to grab a saving breath.

Babineau gripped her elbow, but immediately let her go when she flinched away. His tone low and intense, he said, "Ceece, you don't know this guy. You don't know what he is."

She snarled, "I know exactly what he is. He's my way to Legere. That smug bastard killed my father, and I'm going to get him. I don't care who I have to sleep with. Savoie can get me in close. He can give me Legere."

"Cee Cee, you're dreaming. He'll never give up Legere."

"Yes, he will. He'll do it for me."

"Yeah? Do you know how he made his bones for Jimmy Legere? You ever hear that nasty little detail of his criminal résumé?"

She stood seething, not wanting to listen but needing to hear. "No."

"He'd been hanging around Jimmy's heels for years, just some kid from who knows where, never speaking, never getting in the way. They used to call him Legere's little lap dog until he was about twelve, maybe fourteen. Jimmy was having some labor trouble with a tough and smart union steward by the name of Fevre. They had a dockside meet—Fevre and half a dozen of his armed goons—and Jimmy shows up with just the kid. Fevre starts throwing muscle around and thinks to put the squeeze on Legere by having his toughs rough up the boy. Legere says something like, 'Take care of them, Max,' and he says, 'Whatever you want, Jimmy,' and Legere just leaves him there in a room with them, supposedly to be pounded into paste. Well, about five minutes goes by and Fevre starts to wonder why Legere doesn't seem concerned. Then the kid comes walking out of the room, soaked with blood from head to toe—none of it his. And he says cool as can be, 'I took care of it, Jimmy.' Fevre goes to look inside, and you'll never guess what he sees."

Cee Cee had a pretty good idea.

"His men were dead. Slaughtered, butchered. Rumor has it he'd eaten their hearts. Legere's little lap dog was a goddamned pit bull."

The uncanny comparison made her shudder. She closed her eyes against the image of his savage beast face, but then all she could see were the dead eyes glazed with horror from that head in the alley. The sounds of those screams flooded her ears as Babineau continued.

"So imagine what he is now. He's a stone-cold psycho, Cee Cee. Stay away from him."

"I know what I'm doing, Alain," she managed steadily.

"I hope so."

She swallowed, everything inside her beginning to shake. "I've got to go back for something. I'll meet you at the car."

Without waiting for his reply, she jogged back up the walk and slipped into the cool of the building. Her face flushed hot as she staggered into the ladies' room and dropped to her knees inside the first stall, her head spinning, her stomach emptying in huge, wracking spasms. Then she washed her face in cold water, not looking at her reflection.

And as she left the bathroom, she stuffed the leather coat into the trash.

Nine

JIMMY LEGERE WAS worried.

He'd been trying to read his *Wall Street Journal* for the past half hour, but his attention kept straying across the room to where Max Savoie was stretched out on his leather sofa, napping bonelessly. The edge, the constant underlying alertness was missing this morning, and Jimmy was very afraid he knew why.

Max and Detective Caissie were having sex.

Max wouldn't come out and tell him and Jimmy couldn't ask. When Max came sauntering in at quarter to seven this morning wearing rumpled clothes from the day before and a rather silly little smile, he answered Jimmy's question of had he been out all night with a calm, "Yes, I have." And when Jimmy asked if there was something Max should tell him, Max regarded him with an unblinking stare and told him no, nothing. And Jimmy had to let it go, or let *him* go. And he didn't like it.

Caissie's father had been a provoking irritant. He wouldn't be bribed, he couldn't be scared, he couldn't be broken. His daughter was made in that same mold: tough, merciless, and motivated. And Max, for all his ferocious loyalty and shrewd intelligence, was sometimes as naive as a child when it came to emotions.

Jimmy wanted to dismiss it as hormones but he knew better. He'd always taken his own ease with the professionals on Bourbon Street, preferring a cold cash transfer to any other type of entanglement. From the time Max was old enough to express an awkward curiosity, he'd offered to pay for whichever woman caught Max's fancy. None did. He'd shied away at first, upset and horrified by the idea, probably because of his mother's past. By the time he was out of his teens, he was clearly indifferent to temptations of the flesh. Jimmy just figured he wasn't interested in human females. Until Charlotte Caissie started twitching her short skirt in his direction.

Jimmy didn't know what it was about her. Until Max picked up her scent, he paid scant attention to what went on around him. Like a well-trained attack dog, he waited silently and still with infinite patience for that command that would set free that coil of lethal power. He didn't speak to the household staff unless they asked him a question, and mostly they made a point of steering clear of him. He had no comments, no opinions to express when they were taking care of business. But Jimmy never mistook saying nothing for having nothing going on behind those unblinking eyes. Max had an unbelievably sharp mind, with a tremendous ability to learn by imitation and through devouring the massive library of books in the back wing. At eleven one night he'd pick up a Larousse dictionary, and by breakfast the next day he was speaking French. Fluently. When he asked the occasional question, it was clipped, concise, and amazingly provoking.

Max Savoie was no dumb beast. He just had no experience or interest in interacting with people. It was probably part of the fear impressed upon him by his mother. That wariness that had him crouching beside Jimmy's chair beneath his hand as a child, then standing in the shadows behind it as an adult. Content in his place—until Charlotte Caissie.

The second he saw her, he was a dog sensing a female in heat, gait stiff and nostrils quivering. He first sought her out just to gaze at her, then finally for conversation in a way he'd never done with any other. He smiled. And laughed. Both were so out of character, Jimmy was bemused. And alarmed. His tough, stoic killing machine was infatuated with a policewoman. And now he was pumping her to the point of exhaustion. How long before she was pumping him just as vigorously for information?

Jimmy had protected him too much, had kept him sheltered from life's cruelties, figuring he'd seen enough of them at such a tender age. He was smart but he was innocent of the sour taste of betrayal. Charlotte Caissie was using him, but Max would never believe it if he just told him that straight up.

He'd have to learn the hard way, and life's lessons never came without some pain.

So it was hurt him now or kill him later. What choice did he have?

Dangerous times were coming. Something deadly was shifting on the current of the Mississippi. The business with Vantour, for starters. And the other business he meant to take care of today. He had to know Max was still his to command.

"Max."

He'd been sound asleep and Jimmy didn't speak above a whisper, but Max was on his feet in an instant. Jimmy felt a stir of pride, looking at him. Polished, elegantly groomed and clothed, all but those wretched sneakers he insisted on wearing. Like a finely crafted weapon, Max was sleek and deadly in the right hands. *His* hands.

"Have Pete bring the car around."

"Whatever you want, Jimmy." Quick, unquestioning, obedient.

What could Detective Caissie turn him into if she found out the truth and told him?

"Max?"

He turned, brows lifted in question. "What is it, Jimmy?"

"Nothing. Nothing, boy. Get the car."

As Max strode down the hall, heading toward the garage side of the big house, he passed an open door. A sudden, and recognizable odor brought him up short. Cologne. Cheap, fruity, and unpleasant.

He backpedaled a few steps and looked inside, seeing two men playing cards. He knew who they were by sight but not name. And he knew what they were.

They looked up when he entered, their bright, beady eyes suddenly wide with alarm, reminding him of Charlotte's little rodents.

"Mr. Savoie," one of them mumbled. "Do something for you?"

"Who gave the order?" he asked, low and firm.

"T-John for Mr. Legere."

They were weasly little creatures, with no sense of honor or loyalty.

Max leaned down, placing his hands on the tabletop, fingers splayed wide. A deep rumble came up from the back of his throat and both men trembled at the growl.

"You will not go near Detective Caissie. Is that understood?"

His hands curled, tearing vicious grooves through cloth and wood. Both heads jiggled like bobble-headed dolls.

"And if I ever get wind of you following me again, I will scoop out your eyes and spread them on my toast for breakfast. Is *that* understood?"

The light caught his gaze, reflecting back something that was far from human. The sweat of fear and another pungent stink filled the room as the men said weakly, "Yes, Mr. Savoie."

They were both crossing themselves when he turned his back and walked out of the room.

But the uneasiness stayed with him.

As Max rode in the back of the big town car beside Jimmy Legere, his thoughts churned anxiously. Why was Jimmy having him watched? Because of Vantour? Jimmy said he believed him when he swore he didn't kill the rival boss. Why, then, hadn't he asked to see the body Max had found dumped and bagged, minus thumbs, in a dockside trash bin? Why hadn't he insisted on proof of the cause of death, a savage wound to the throat, unless he feared what he might see? Unless he was afraid the evidence would come full circle back to Max?

He'd been very specific: Find the body, take him out in the swamps, and scatter him. A bad feeling had stayed with Max as he did as told. Vantour would never be found. But Max would never be cleared of suspicion, either. Intentionally? Was Jimmy using that hint of the unknown to put fear in his opponents? So Max could be sacrificed as a scapegoat later?

Someone had killed Vantour and had done so to cast doubt upon his loyalty. Someone had fired a bullet made of silver, hoping to kill him on the steps of St. Bart's. Who was whispering in Jimmy's ear— and why was he listening?

Max stared straight ahead like a radar picking up everything around them, while his heartbeat quickened.

Would Jimmy have reason to want him dead? Why was he sensing fear where there had never been anything but love?

Then he saw their destination. St. Bartholomew's.

The driver got Jimmy situated in his wheelchair while Max stood behind him, aware of everything and everyone around them. He pushed the chair up the side ramp and down the middle aisle, not asking any of the questions that worked behind his stoic face. Not yet. But soon.

"Mr. Legere. This is a surprise. I thought you attended a parish church in the Garden District."

"Good morning, Sister. Am I not welcome then?"

Mary Kate smiled benevolently. "All are welcome here."

"I think you know Max."

Her gaze lifted, betraying nothing. "Mr. Savoie. I'm afraid you just missed Father Furness, Mr. Legere."

"Actually, I'm here to talk to you, Sister Catherine. Might we speak somewhere privately?"

"Of course." She gestured to a quiet corner. "We won't be overheard there."

"Max, you wait here."

He frowned slightly, but stepped aside to let Mary Kate push the chair away. And then he wasn't thinking about Jimmy and what he might want to discuss with the nun. His senses were tingling all over.

He breathed in slowly and let recognition shiver through him. Without looking around, he could feel Charlotte skimming the perimeter of the main sanctuary, keeping to the heavy shadows beneath the upper balcony. She didn't approach him or speak to him, and he wondered why. Then he had to *know* why.

She was so intent upon being stealthy that when he touched her shoulder, he had to jump back to avoid her defensive swing. Her eyes flashed, black and bold. Afraid.

"A little overly caffeinated this morning, detective?"

"Holy geez, you about scared my hair back to its natural color."

He blinked. "You dye your hair?"

"What do you want, Max?" She sounded cross and breathless. And something else. He wasn't sure what, but it wasn't good.

"It would be in rather bad taste to say what I want, considering where we are. I didn't think I'd be seeing you again so soon." He stepped in close, his hip bumping hers, their shoulders brushing as his hand slipped up the back of her shirt to stroke warm skin.

She flinched away. "I'm not here for you. I'm meeting Mary Kate for lunch."

He leaned in again and his tongue rimmed her ear wetly. She jerked back so fast, he almost ended up hooked on her earring like a bass.

"Stop it, Max."

"You wouldn't be so tired and grumpy now if you'd said that to me at about two this morning."

She started walking briskly along the rows of pews with him circling around her, nearly tangling them in each other's strides. When she halted in exasperation, his hands were on her, touching her hair, her cheek, her elbow, her breast, her waist, until she gripped his wrists to hold him at bay.

"What do you want, Max?"

She'd hoped her irritation would discourage him, but she should have realized just the sight of him would rev up her emotions into desire. That the slightest brush of his fingertips would have her will crumbling. She couldn't afford to be weak, not now. But he had no intention of letting her slip away.

"What do I want? A kiss good morning. I would have asked earlier but you would have poked my tonsils out with your toothbrush. Just one. Real quick. Please. Then I'll go away."

"One. Quick."

She should have been warned by the way his eyelids lowered, by the way he moved in so slowly. His mouth settled over hers, sliding to reacquaint itself with her every contour, inside and out. He fenced lightly with her tongue until she was leaning into him, then pursued her more aggressively when she tried to pull away.

"Max, just one," she gasped.

He was sucking her lower lip, his breath quick and light. "Same one. Almost finished." And he slanted hard, twisting her head back until she made a soft sound of surrender. Then one, two, three fast snatches. "Curtain calls," he murmured, then plunged his tongue deep. Finally, breathing huskily, he whispered, "Standing ovation."

She released his hands so she could cup his face in her palms. "What am I going to do with you, Max?"

"A couple of suggestions have come up." He rubbed against her with an explicit preview of coming attractions.

She pushed him back, the sternness returning to her tone. "Stop."

"I wasn't going to throw you down on the kneeling rail. Tell me when and where."

"No."

"No?" She started walking and he followed. "What do you mean? No, you don't want to tell me? Or no, you don't want me?"

She pulled up so sharply, he bumped into her. And his hands were immediately under her shirt. She squirmed away. "Max, stop. Give me some time to think. Some time to breathe. *Please.*"

His hands dropped to his sides and he took a step back. "All right. I'll behave." Then his voice lowered. "Charlotte, what's wrong? Have I done something wrong? Tell me."

"Nothing's . . . wrong." Her thoughts were fragmented. What could she tell him? She wasn't ready to confront him after what Babineau had told her. She couldn't just make up some complaint, some reason for her distance. If it wasn't the truth, he'd know. It didn't have to be *the* truth, only *a* truth. She scrambled to pick one, any one. After all, there were enough things about him that upset her to the point of ripping out her own fingernails.

"What? Tell me."

She blushed, reddening to the roots of her hair. "It's just that in all the times we . . . in all the times you made me . . . the many, many wonderful times . . ."

He smiled, rather pleased, urging her to continue with a lift of his brows.

"In all those times, you never once . . . finished. Why?"

The smug smile vanished. "I thought ladies liked a fella with stamina." His tone was flippant, his gaze evasive.

"Stamina's one thing. But you've got to be backed up like my kitchen sink. Why? If you were worried about protection, all you had to do was say something."

"I've had all my shots, detective." He edged back a bit farther, looking uncomfortable, even angry, and everywhere but in her eyes. "It's not that. It's just that I choose to save that one thing to share with someone who cares for me."

He'd walked halfway to the front of the church before her surprise snapped and she hurried after him. She gripped his elbow, spinning him to face her, unsure of why she was so upset, so . . . insulted.

"I care about you."

He shook his head and laughed softly. "But you

don't love me, Charlotte. Why are you making this a big thing? Why would it matter to you? You got what you wanted from me."

She couldn't think of how to answer that. Yes, she had. She had absolutely no complaints. Which was why she was trying to come up with an acceptable reason to throw him down between the pews and have him all over again, in spite of the fact she was so raw she could hardly walk. In spite of the fact that he had eaten the hearts of Legere's enemies, and she was probably going to be forced to eventually take him down in a way neither of them would enjoy.

His fingers stabbed back through his hair distractedly. "I do have some self-control, some choices. I'm not an animal, detective. I don't have to give everything that means something to me away, and have nothing left for myself." He stared up at the ceiling, his breaths shaking. Then, realizing he was overreacting, he took in a slow, deep breath.

"Max, what's wrong?"

"Nothing. Maybe I need to start drinking coffee." He shrugged off the concern in her voice and was instantly himself again. He nodded toward the far side of the church as a convenient distraction. "I wonder what they're talking about."

Cee Cee glanced over. "Probably not sex." His laugh jumped out of his tightly boxed emotions, and the tension relaxed between them. It felt good to rest her head against his shoulder for just a moment. Just long enough for the stabilizing sense of warmth and safety to return. She didn't want to fight with Max. She didn't want to see those awful images her partner planted in her mind.

Everything for nothing. He could be describing her life, as well.

She pressed her hand to his cheek, her heart taking a little leap when he nudged into her palm. "You can trust me, Max. If you're in trouble, you can come to me."

His chuckle vibrated beneath her. "Come into my parlor. I'll be waiting with kisses and handcuffs. Thank you, Charlotte. I'm fine."

But he wasn't. She watched his gaze shift cautiously over to Jimmy Legere, and worried about what he wasn't telling her.

"SISTER CATHERINE, YOU have become a noticeable pain in my backside."

Mary Kate smiled at the old man, maintaining her air of serenity with some difficulty. "I assure you, that's never been my intention."

"Oh, I doubt that very much. I think you go out of your way to annoy me and you delight in my aggravation. Shame on you, Sister, hiding such ill will behind God's mantle of forgiveness."

"Let Him forgive you, Legere. I never will."

He laughed at the sudden flash of fury in her eyes. "Ah, Ms. Malone. How nice to finally meet the real you."

"Sister Catherine *is* the real me. I'm just not terribly good with "turn the other cheek" where you're concerned. Last time I did that, my jaw was almost broken."

"The world is a cruel place, Sister. You should stay where you belong."

"Are you threatening me, Mr. Legere? In church?"

"Did that sound like a threat? Let me clarify myself. I know you use the resources of this church to meddle in my affairs. You counsel those who've foolishly gone in over their heads with the various vices I make available. I shrug it off as a business loss. You interfere with my professional girls, making them think they're being exploited, that they have the right to walk on that high road you expound upon. Perhaps they do. But you have done one thing that I will not forgive or overlook. Do you know what that is?"

Before she could stop herself she glanced across the sanctuary, where she was surprised to see Max and Charlotte in intense conversation.

Jimmy noticed and his displeasure grew. "Yes. Max. I don't know what hold you have over him, Ms. Malone, but you will let him go."

"I have no hold over him. Unlike you, I've always let him make up his own mind. He's never done anything that would go against you. He's always refused to cross that line."

"I appreciate your telling me that. Nevertheless,

you are using his particular talents foolishly, brazenly, hoping to make an example that others will respect and fear."

"Much the same way you do."

A tight smile. "Exactly. But he belongs to me, Sister. He's my property. And you are trespassing."

"You can't own a human being."

"You are wrong there, my dear. He may walk upright when it suits him, but there's nothing human about Max. Don't ever forget that. Don't ever expect him to behave or react as one. He's a dangerous and unnatural creature bred for only one thing: violence. That's what he does. That's all he is. He has no emotions, no conscience, no soul. You are not going to save him with empty promises that he can live as you and I do out here in this world. Giving him that kind of false hope will end ugly, because you can't change what he is. You can't put something inside him that doesn't exist."

"You're wrong," she told him with quiet force. She saw Benjamin Spratt wheeling his mop bucket across the front of the sanctuary and waited until he was on the far side. "Max is not an animal."

Legere laughed. "That's exactly what he is. And he belongs to me. He knows it and he doesn't want to change it. I protect Max. I would never, ever let him come to any harm by being exposed for what he is. He is very dear to me, and that's why your influence and that of Detective Caissie will stop now, before you confuse him into doing something I can't forgive. And if you see a threat in *those* words, Sister, you would not be mistaken."

"What can you threaten me with? I have nothing."

"Nothing but your pride and your friendship with Charlotte Caissie."

Mary Kate's gaze darted to her friend, who was cozied up against Max Savoie in a rather telling pose. "You wouldn't dare harm her."

"She's a policewoman in a very dangerous line of work."

"You harm her and *I'll* expose your little pet for what he is."

Jimmy's smile didn't falter. "There, you see, is the difference between us. You want to use him and I love him. This is how we're going to handle this awkward situation. You will talk to your detective friend and dissuade her from this nonsense with Max. You will let her know in no uncertain terms that if she doesn't discourage him and give up her rather determined crusade against me, you and all your annoying little projects will suffer for it. You remember how it was to suffer for the stubbornness of a Caissie, don't you?"

Her hand rose to her scarred cheek as fear shadowed her gaze.

"I'll give you until this evening to think it over. You are a smart girl, a brave girl, or you wouldn't be here today. God doesn't need another dead martyr on His hands. I'm sure you'll make the wise decision and save yourself a lot of unpleasantness." He raised his voice. "Max."

He came at a lope, wiping Charlotte Caissie's lipstick from his mouth with his hand, then fell in behind the wheelchair at perfect motionless attention.

"Always a pleasure, Sister," Jimmy said pleasantly. "I admire the good work you do here. A shame if you couldn't continue it."

Max's gaze flickered to hers but found no answer.

CEE CEE HELD on to her frustration when Max responded instantly to Legere's call. If only there were some way to break him free of his dependence, to keep him safely out of the way when she bulldozed down the empire Legere had built on her father's blood.

"You'd best let him go, Miss Lottie."

She gave a start, not realizing Benjamin Spratt was behind her. Since everyone suddenly seemed intent upon shoving their opinions of Max in her face, she asked a bit testily, "Why's that, Ben?"

"'Cause he walks on that wild, dark side, like I used to before the doctors shocked me to my senses. He's not what he seems, Missy. You can't tame him, you can't hold him, you can't keep him. Not his kind."

"And what kind would that be?" How much had he witnessed, heard? Perhaps she was as guilty as most others in thinking Benjamin harmless, in believing him simple, in forgetting he had ears to hear and eyes to see. And a mouth to reveal things best kept secret.

"A wolf in sheep's clothing. Look to the scriptures. Heed the Word. Remember the warning. He has no soul. He can't be redeemed."

But Cee Cee no longer saw Max Savoie as evil and soulless. Distressed, she snapped back at the sweet, simple man. "If you were the same as he is, how is it that you have a soul, Benjamin Spratt? How is it that you've been forgiven?"

He smiled at her sadly. "I don't have one, Miss Lottie. And haven't been. I'm hellbound, and so is he. Pray for us, Miss Charlotte, but don't trust us. Don't love us. Only our Shepherd understands us. Only He can show us the way to escape the darkness without pulling in others behind us."

His gaze flickered up nervously. When he saw Mary Kate approaching he scuttled away, disappearing with his mop and bucket into the back chambers.

"What were the two of you discussing?" Mary Kate asked, catching the distress her friend was trying to hide.

"Souls or the lack thereof. And speaking of soulless, what was that all about with Legere?"

Mary Kate smiled. "Just a business call. Nothing for you to concern yourself with. Now, what did you want to talk about?"

Cee Cee took a deep breath and smiled. "Nothing important. I just wanted to spend some time with you, that's all." She reached out for Mary Kate's hand and squeezed it tightly.

She squeezed back. "Let's go eat. I'm in the mood for some *étouffé*. Benjamin," she called to the back of the church, "I'll be back in an hour or so."

"Okay, Sister. Good-bye, Miss Lottie. Don't forget to watch out for the sheep."

Forcing a smile, Charlotte waved a hand and then let it settle upon her friend's shoulder.

"What's this about sheep?"

Cee Cee tried to laugh it off. "You know Benjamin. You never know exactly what he's talking about." But she was very afraid that this time, he did.

The lunch was pleasant, a relaxed conversation discussing the better memories, the long-forgotten dreams. Cee Cee wanted to talk to her friend about Max, about the way he made her heart pound and her body hum. About her worries, her desires, her fears concerning him. But Mary Kate was no longer the one to whom she could spill those kind of secrets. She was a bride of the church. She'd pushed away all things carnal—all things terrifyingly intimate—when she'd taken her vows. Charlotte wanted to believe Mary Kate's vocation was sincere, but sometimes she wondered if her surrender to God wasn't simply a way to escape the will of Man. Of any man who might attempt to use her body in that same way they'd both been abused.

Would telling Mary Kate she was wrong in that fear be a good or a bad thing? Maybe it was best to keep that conversation for another time. When she'd had a bit longer to examine her own feelings and phobias. Maybe she should think about talking to Dr. Forstrom.

When Charlotte hugged her good-bye, her mood grew bittersweet as she saw Dolores Gautreaux, her bruises fading, smiling at Benjamin Spratt, who balanced her baby cautiously on his knee. Perhaps there was someone for everyone. Perhaps Max Savoie was that someone meant for her.

When she returned to the station and saw the custodian blocking off the ladies' room, she darted inside to dig into the waste can, pulling out Max's slightly-worse-for-wear leather jacket.

And as she shook it out to rid it of any litter, something else fell out of its folds. Cee Cee bent to pick up the small electronic device, looking it over with a frown. It was state of the art, way too expensive for their department to ever requisition, but she recognized it immediately for what it was.

It was a bug.

Ten

"MAX, COME OUT here for a minute."

Jimmy waited for the sound of his light steps. He took a deep, regretful breath for what he was about to do, and suddenly, he remembered an odd snippet of the past. He'd been sitting on the porch on an evening like this one, and nine-year-old Max had come out of the house, his expression troubled. He passed Jimmy a book he'd been reading. "Tell me," was all he'd said.

The book was *The Island of Doctor Moreau.* Jimmy had thought he was asking him to explain the concept of a novel far beyond the grasp of his young mind. But that's not what he was asking at all.

"Tell me. Am I like the beasts in this story? Is that what I am?"

"I don't know," Jimmy had replied, too surprised to think of what else to say beyond the truth. So he'd lied. "I don't know what you are, Max."

The boy's eyes had filled up with tears of upset and dread, and before Jimmy could catch him, he'd bolted. For three days he hid somewhere in the big house, not appearing at meals, not sleeping in his bed. Jimmy had no fear that he'd run away; he'd still been afraid to be outside after dark. He could hear the boy late at night, the soft whisper of those strange sounds he made, that mournful, eerie wail that was not quite sob, not quite howl.

It broke Jimmy's heart to hear him and not call to him, to not coax him out and comfort him. Jimmy knew he should have done so instead of letting him huddle alone in the dark, shaken by fear and weeping. But he didn't because that fear gave him power. And he didn't want to lose the boy he'd come to love but needed to control.

He'd been eating a sandwich in his office at dusk on the fourth day when he heard the click of toenails on the hardwood floor. He glanced up to see a low, sleek silhouette just inside the doorway. Max only assumed that simplest of his forms when he was distressed and didn't know how to express himself with words. Jimmy held out the other half of his sandwich and finally Max came to him, creeping, practically crawling to take the food from his hand, slowly, carefully, as if he wasn't close to starving. It disappeared in two quick bites. Jimmy continued to read through his paperwork in preparation for a morning meeting, ignoring Max until he came up onto the couch—keeping his distance at first, then gradually easing his head across Jimmy's knee, pushing his nose under Jimmy's free hand with a plaintive sound. He rumpled the soft fur, petting gently until the shivering creature lay down and curled close, until the sharp muzzle became a boy's smooth, damp cheek.

"Don't be afraid, Max," he'd said quietly, firmly, covering the trembling figure with his jacket. "I'll take care of you and keep you safe within these walls. What you are doesn't matter here. What matters is that you belong to me and I value all that you are. Don't ever forget that."

And he hadn't. Nor had he ever asked that question again.

Max now moved to the porch rail, head tipped back, tasting the breeze. "Storm's coming in."

"Not for a while yet. Max . . ."

"What is it, Jimmy? Just tell me. You've been hedging around it all day, all week. Whatever it is, tell me." He waited, his gaze so sincere, so unmasked and vulnerable.

"It's not something either of us is going to like."

Max stiffened slightly. "I didn't think it would be."

"Max, where's your leather coat?"

He blinked, knocked offtrack for a moment as he thought, and then thought of how best to answer. Truth won out. "I left it at Detective Caissie's. Why?"

"I'm not proud of this, and if you want to be angry, I don't blame you. It's just that this fondness you have for this woman . . . You know who her father was and what he was trying to do. He wanted me behind bars and so does she. I got worried for the both of us, and I did something I probably shouldn't have."

"Tell me."

"I had a listening device planted in your coat."

Max blinked again. Behind his flat stare, his mind raced frantically to recall all the things that he and Charlotte had said to each other, and with deeper horror, considered all the things they'd done to each other. Things not intended for an audience. He swore softly, still too shocked to be angry.

"I apologize for invading your privacy. But there's something I want you to hear."

"I was there, Jimmy."

"Not for this. She must have been wearing your coat this morning. I'm sorry, Max. This is going to hurt." He said that as if he were preparing to rip a bandage from a half-healed wound.

Braced for the worst, Max heard Charlotte's partner's voice.

"*Cee Cee, this guy is bad news. If you want to fuck him, fuck him. But don't fall for him.*"

"*I am not in love with Max Savoie!*"

"*Ceece, you don't know this guy. You don't know what he is.*"

"*I know exactly what he is. He's my way to Legere. That smug bastard killed my father, and I'm going to get him. I don't care who I have to sleep with. Savoie can get me in close. He can give me Legere.*"

"*Cee Cee, you're dreaming. He'll never give up Legere.*"

"*Yes, he will. He'll do it for me.*"

Max took a shallow breath, just to see if anything inside him still worked. He made an awkward circle to face the night, his hands lacing behind the back of his neck, standing motionlessly for long minutes. When he turned back to Jimmy, it was to say just one thing.

"It's not true."

"I know, Max."

"I would never take a step against you. Not for any reason."

"Is that the truth, Max? Then how is it that this woman, who could destroy you, destroy us, knows exactly what you are, unless you told her? Unless you showed her?"

Cornered, Max could no longer back away from the reality of what he'd done. Away from the magnitude of his betrayal. There was no excuse, so he put it plainly. "Those men were hurting them, these girls who'd done nothing wrong. I couldn't walk away from it. I wasn't thinking."

"Max, that's not true, is it? You never do anything without thinking. You knew exactly what you were doing when you killed those men. My men."

"Yes, I did," he answered softly, as guilt, and a whisper of defiance, curled through him.

"And you still say you've never taken a step against me?"

He opened his mouth, then shut it. He had no reply to that obvious truth.

"I'm not angry with you, Max." Jimmy spoke calmly, watching Max's expression to make sure his careful handling of the matter was having the desired result. Surprise, then relief flickered in the steady stare, and he knew he was taking the right approach. Defuse the situation, manipulate the emotions from rebellion and worry to relief and regret. And gratitude. As furious as he might be over what had been done and hidden from him, it was done. Now, to turn it to his advantage.

"I'm sorry, Jimmy," Max said quietly.

Not quite the apology Jimmy was hoping for, but a start.

"For what you did? Don't be. I never ordered those girls to be harmed in any way. They were just hostages, pawns for leverage. What my men did was inexcusable. I would have punished them myself if you hadn't done it for me." A pause and a heavy sigh. "It's what you *didn't* do that hurts me, Max. You didn't trust me. You didn't come to me first with what you saw. You didn't think I'd do anything about it.

"So you acted on your own, and then you hid what you'd done from me. You hid the fact that you interfered in my plans. You hid the fact that two outsiders knew your secret and used it against you to make you afraid and ashamed to come to me with that truth. Did you think I would kill them, after you'd risked so much to go to their rescue?"

He could hear Max swallow that down hard.

"Were you afraid I'd punish you? Is that why you didn't come to me? Have I ever, ever hurt you, Max? Have I ever given you a reason to be afraid?"

"No." Just a whisper.

"Then why? Tell me where I failed you. Tell me what I did to make you not trust me, to make you believe I wouldn't forgive you, to make you doubt how I feel about you."

Max's expression didn't alter as he took a shaky breath. "I don't know. I'm sorry, Jimmy. I didn't know what to do, how to make it right with you."

"You could have come to me and told me the truth at any time."

The intense stare wavered, then flashed back to meet his. "I'm sorry." Said firm and strong, with everything Jimmy needed to know behind it.

The old man held in his smile, knowing he'd staked his claim right through Max's heart. The illicit connection Max had with the two meddlers was broken; the uncomfortable wedge shoved between them was gone. He'd uncovered Max's duplicity, and he'd been magnanimous in his charity. And Max would never forget that. All the guilt and misery he'd carried for all these years was absolved.

"I should have come to you," Max said at last, very softly.

Gotcha, you bitch.

"So," Jimmy began silkily, "how are we going to keep you safe, now that they know what you are?"

Alarm showed on Max's face before he got it under control. "What do you mean?"

"You've given some very damaging information to two unreliable sources. Information that could hurt you—badly. I know you want to trust them, but do you think that's possible? Do you think it's wise?" Seeing those stoic features tense and grow still, Jimmy proceeded with caution. "I know you cared for her, Max, and I know you wanted to believe she cared for you."

Max didn't flinch. He didn't even breathe.

"I'm sorry, Max. I'm sorry that she hurt you. I know how much their acceptance meant to you, and how their betrayal must burn. But you have to understand: They never saw you as something human. To them you were just an animal to be tricked and teased and used and cast away. They could never look past what you are. You know that. You know there is no possible way that a detective with the NOPD would fall in love with someone with your past, someone who's not even a man."

Then, with condescending gentleness, "Did you really think she was going to welcome you into her world, into her life? Did you believe she was going to plan a future for the two of you together, that she'd willingly breed your offspring, whatever they might turn out to be? Did you, Max?"

His eyes blinked slowly. "No. Of course not."

"You have to put it behind you, boy. You can't let yourself dwell on how they deceived you, on how they must have laughed over your gullibility. You have value here, Max. You matter to me, and I'll do everything I can to keep you from harm's way. All I ask is that you distance yourself, quickly and completely. Then we'll see what they plan to do with what they know. Maybe nothing. Who would believe them? Who would believe in looking at you, what you really are inside? What do you think, Max? Do you think they would speak out against you, even if it meant implicating themselves with their own deeds?"

"I wouldn't have thought so before tonight." Before Charlotte tore his heart in two with her brutal words. Now he was thinking quickly, dispassionately, the way he'd been trained to, with self-preservation foremost in his mind to hold back the anguish building behind it.

"We need to protect you, Max. We need to see to that before anything else. So I need you to do something for me tonight. Something that will let them know they can't spit on you without consequence. Something that will teach them both about loyalty and love. I know you won't let me down. I know you would rather die than fail me. We'll show them how wrong they were to think they could turn us against each other."

"Anything you want, Jimmy," came the soft response threaded with steel. "Anything you want."

"SO HE SENT you," Mary Kate Malone said casually as she wrapped her tea bag around her spoon.

"For an answer," Max said quietly as he slipped from the shadows to stand on the other side of her table.

"Did he tell you the question?"

"No."

"Do you want to know it?"

"No."

Mary Kate studied his hard features for a moment until she could get her fear under control. It was time for an atonement. Time to pay for her vanity and her pride. When she spoke, her voice was soothing, serene. "I guess there's not much more to say then, is there?"

"What's your answer?"

"He knew my answer before he sent you." She took her time, stirring in milk and sugar. "I've done things in the past and even just today that are weak and cowardly, and I ask forgiveness for them. When Charlotte and I were taken, all I could think was, why me? Why were they taking *me*? I would have let them take her. If they'd opened that door for me, I would have run from there without ever looking back."

"But not Charlotte."

"No. Never Charlotte. She never runs from anything. Except maybe her feelings for you."

Max said nothing.

"I would have given you up to save myself and

to save her. I would have done it without a second thought."

"It's all right. I understand." And he did, even though he was surprised to hear her admit to it. He understood that kind of fierce love and loyalty. It's why he was here: to prove himself to a man who'd given him everything. To redeem himself even though Jimmy had said it was unnecessary. But obedience was the only way he could repay his debt to the man who'd saved his life, who'd pulled him from a nightmare with the simple offer of his hand. A hand he'd slapped away when taking a sideways step to rescue these two women. He didn't regret that action, but he'd make amends for it now.

Mary Kate's calm blue eyes lifted to his. "Do you forgive me?"

"Yes."

Distress filled her eyes. "Watch over her for me, Max. She needs someone to rein her in, to remind her to smile, to tell her it's all right to care. Love her. She has no one else."

A pained remorse jabbed through him. "I can't promise that."

She sighed. It was too much to ask of him now. She'd lost him. That tentative regard they'd held for each other no longer softened his stare. It cut through her like a laser, cold, clear, and hard. Whatever Jimmy had said or done, he'd managed to jerk him up short and bring him to heel.

"Fair enough. I won't keep you waiting, then." She picked up her teacup and carried it to the counter, then she turned to face him. Her expression, so defiant and enraged, reminded him of that tattered girl who'd dumped gasoline over the remains of her abusers. "Tell him the answer is no. Not only no, but *hell* no. Tell him that smart and brave aren't always the same thing. I'm not going to let him scare me into letting Charlotte down. For once, I'm going to be brave for *her*. I plan to fight him with everything I have."

"I'll tell him."

She held his gaze for a long, silent moment. She knew he wasn't there just to relay a message. Jimmy Legere sent Max Savoie to rid him of problems. And she'd carelessly let herself become one. She'd callously used Max to spit in the old man's eye, because he was one of them, one of Legere's vicious minions who deserved no sympathy or respect. And he'd been so easy to manipulate, torn up by guilt and grief and by whatever strange affection he held for her best friend. He let himself be subtly turned against Legere by exacting her revenge.

That was over now. Legere had him back under his control and had sent him there to kill her.

And once that was accomplished, he would own Max's soul.

She knew he had one, no matter how dark and troubled it was.

She didn't expect to feel regret, but it was a bittersweet burden to carry with her. She should have protected Max. She should have had a care for him, but she'd been too lost in her own fury, her own retribution. Max had roared to their rescue, snatching them from a hell no one should have to suffer. And he'd become her Saint Michael, her avenging sword, punishing those who preyed upon lost and frightened victims.

Why hadn't she realized until now that Max was one of those who'd needed her to save him?

And now it was too late. In taking her life at Legere's command, he would forfeit his own. The only thing that could pull him back from that black void of self-destruction was his love for Charlotte.

"Don't let him hurt her, Max. I wish I were strong enough to keep her safe. I wish I were as strong as she always has been. But you are. You can protect her for me. That's all I ask for myself." She took a jagged breath, then said softly, "Tell Charlotte my thoughts were of her."

"I will."

Was he saying yes to all or just to that last request? There was no answer in his unblinking stare.

Before she lost her courage, she turned her back to him, leaning her elbows on the edge of the sink, trying to keep her knees from shaking as she folded her hands and silently recited the rosary. She never heard him move, but the awareness of him right behind gave her a sudden start. Then her fear was gone. He would make it quick. He would do that much for her.

He leaned close, touching a light kiss to the scar on her cheek.

"Say a prayer for me."

She stood for long minutes, waiting. Then the wondering got the better of her, and she turned to face an empty room.

Her breath expelled in a shaky relief that was short-lived. Jimmy Legere wasn't about to let this go. He wasn't going to forget and forgive—not her, not Charlotte, and now, not Max. And he would strike viciously at the weakest link among the three of them to break the other two. She knew herself to be that weak spot, and what Max hadn't been able to finish would be picked up by another, crueler hand. The kind of hand she could never suffer under again. Then Charlotte would come charging in to protect her, flying into the teeth of danger. And Jimmy Legere would crush her.

Terror and fury tangled up into a panic. The need to escape Legere's retribution, to protect the one close enough to her heart to be considered family, pounded deep and desperate. What could she do to keep Legere from winning a brutal victory over both of them again? He'd stolen their innocence, their security, their ability to love and be loved.

No more. He wouldn't use her as the means to strike out at her dearest friend. She wouldn't allow herself to be the bait to lure Charlotte to her own rash destruction.

As she paced and thought and tried to pray, one solution kept returning to her fevered mind. One horrible, final conclusion that would expiate all her sins and all her debts to those she loved.

A sacrifice that offered escape from what she feared more than death, and which promised a bittersweet revenge.

Eleven

THE SOUND OF Porky and Baco madly thumping around their cage woke Charlotte. A glance at her clock told her it was just past eleven. Lightning strobed in the distance and she looked forward to a cooling rain. She closed her eyes, about to let go again, when the pigs began a frantic wheeking.

She was off the bed and grabbing up her gun in the same motion.

The living room was dark. A hot breeze came in through the open balcony doors. Odd, she thought she'd closed them. She headed across the room.

"I didn't know where else to go," Max said.

She clutched at her chest. With a fierce curse, she sought him out in the deep shadows. He was sitting on her couch, feet together, hands on his knees as if he were outside a principal's office waiting to be expelled.

"Max, you scared me out of ten years! Stop doing that."

"I'm sorry. I shouldn't be here. I know you don't want me here. I just couldn't think . . . I didn't know where else to go."

"Max, what's wrong?"

"There was something I was sent to do tonight."

She took a quick breath, her hand tightening on her revolver, as she was reminded with an icy chill of who and what he was. "Did Jimmy send you to kill me, Max?"

His eyes glittered in the darkness as he continued to speak in the same emotionless voice. "It doesn't matter. I can't talk to you about it. I can't go back. I can't go home. There's no place for me now. You're the only person I know. How sad is that? The only person I know, and you couldn't give a damn about what happens to me."

"What are you *talking* about?" She set her gun down and went to kneel in front of him, instinctively rubbing his knees in a consoling manner. "What's happened?"

Max sank back into the couch cushions, drawing his feet up, hugging to his knees so she wouldn't touch them. He stared straight ahead, not at her. "He's going to kill me. He'll have to now. He won't want to, but he won't have a choice. I didn't leave him a choice."

A shiver ran through her, but she dismissed his claim with a shake of her head. "Jimmy? That mean old bird loves only one thing more than his money and power, and that's you, Max. Don't be ridiculous."

"I can't go back. I've never been anywhere else. I don't have anything of my own. I don't have enough in my pockets for a streetcar token. I don't know what to do. What am I going to do?"

He was scaring her. She eased her hands over his. He clutched tight, then pulled away, crossing his arms over his chest, making his hands unavailable under his armpits.

"You'll stay here, Max." she said firmly. "At least for tonight. We'll worry about the rest tomorrow."

Though she didn't believe for a minute that Jimmy Legere was going to kill him for some infraction, he believed it, so she had to take it seriously. What had he done? What could be huge enough for him to seek refuge at her door? The cool cop part of her mind whispered, *And how can I use it against Legere?* Max Savoie knew Jimmy's every move, his every secret. In saving Max from Legere, she'd be within reach of her own revenge.

"You're safe here, Max. You're safe with me."

He stared at her for a long moment, and she was sure he could see right into the clever workings of her mind. But she wouldn't let guilt keep her from taking the chance to get Legere. She hadn't tried to lure Max from him; she hadn't used tricks or lies. She'd done everything she could to separate her feelings for him from the job she was doing.

But here he was, of his own accord. He'd come to her. He'd made his choice. Elation quivered through her, a thrill that had nothing to do with gaining an advantage over her enemy. He'd chosen *her.* Perhaps only out of desperation, but it was a start. And she could have him, and Legere. If she could earn the trust of this cautious creature.

"Stay," she told him softly.

He was so wary, so oddly distant. "I shouldn't. I shouldn't involve you."

"I thought we were already involved." She smiled, trying to relieve the tension pulling through him.

His smile in return was complex. "So did I."

"You're safe here." She palmed the side of his face. He leaned into her touch for a brief moment, then turned his head away. "Stay here," she repeated more strongly, rubbing his arms until he nodded.

"Okay. I'll just stay out here on the couch."

That wasn't exactly what she'd had in mind, but because of the distress and distrust she could feel churning inside him, she agreed, "If that's what you want."

She adjusted her thinking, considering him not as a man, but as a wounded wild thing who'd come to her for comfort. If she came on too strong, he'd run. And if he ran, and he was right about his break with Legere, she could be sending him into danger. How desperate and alone he must be feeling, to have everything familiar stripped away. She was all he had, and she would not let him regret coming to her. So she would be as careful with him as he'd once been with her.

"Let's get these shoes off you. This sofa is the only nice thing I have." She started unlacing his high-tops.

Armani and Converse—Max Savoie was a study in nonconformity, right down to the strangely passive-aggressive role he played with Jimmy Legere. Jimmy had to be crazy to let him go, to dismiss his love, his devotion. She would not make that same mistake. She weighed the size 12s in her hands. "The measure of a man is in his shoes."

"What did you say?"

"Just something Jimmy told me." She set the shoes aside and gently massaged his toes. "Are you going to be all right out here by yourself?"

"I'm a big boy, detective. Of all the things out there hiding in the dark, I'm probably the scariest. I just need a place to sleep. I'll be out of your hair in the morning." He was smiling slightly, but there was tremendous sadness in his tone.

"What if I want you in my hair and on my couch a while longer?" she teased, worried even more, especially when she reached out to touch his face and he winced back to avoid contact.

"You'll get used to the disappointment."

What was wrong with him? Where was the urgent lover who'd kept her up all night, the sweetly eager suitor who'd tangled about her feet with adoration? "You know where I'll be if you need anything." *If you need me.*

"Yes. I do."

He just watched her with those empty eyes until she swore softly. Cupping the back of his head so he couldn't pull away, she leaned in to brush her cheek against his. He didn't move. He didn't take a breath. Not until she touched her lips to the corner of his eye. Then he exhaled in a noisy shiver. She eased back.

"Good night, Max."

"Thank you."

On her way to her room, something started to bother her, nagging at the back of her tired brain. She frowned, then it struck her like a shotgun blast. "That son of a bitch!"

She marched back into the living room, snapping on a light. Max flinched from the brightness but finally looked up at her. His face was set in raw lines, all sharp angles and hollows.

"The bastard played you that tape, didn't he?"

Something sparked in his eyes, but then they returned to the unblinking pale jade. His voice was equally hard. "Which tape? The one with you stating I was a stepping-stone fuck on your way to Jimmy Legere? Don't look so distressed, detective; it wasn't a surprise. I'm not stupid. I never expected you to care for me. I just didn't expect to hear myself being rated as one rung on a long ladder."

She heard the anger, hurt, and humiliation rumbling just below the surface chill. "And you believe that?"

He gave a harsh laugh. "I'm not the one who said it to her partner." He took a quick breath, then another. "Are you going to tell me it's not true?" He waited, his glare both challenging and pleading.

"Of course it's true."

That sucked the wind from him for a long second, then his jaw firmed into a solid granite wall. "Care to tell me where my rung was in your grander scheme of things?"

"At the top, Max. No one's closer to Legere than you are. What did you expect? That I wouldn't look through your mail and eavesdrop on your calls? That I wouldn't take advantage of the time I spend with you to keep my eyes and ears open?" Temper stirred in her own voice.

Because Jimmy had shattered his trust. Because she'd knowingly put herself into this position to hurt him. So there was nothing to do but brazen it out with arrogant dignity. "This goes beyond me being a cop, and you know it. It doesn't get more personal than me and Jimmy. I've never kept that from you. I want his head on a plate. He's responsible for what happened to me and Mary Kate. He's behind my father's death. I'm going to make him pay for those things if it's the last thing I ever do."

"Thank you for your honesty," he said stiffly, over a boiling cauldron of emotions.

"I'm not finished. Would I tease you to keep you interested? You betcha. Would I spend time with you hoping to learn something important? Yes, I would. Would I let you put your tongue in my mouth and your hand up my skirt so I could bang another nail in his coffin? What do you think *that* answer is, Mr. I'm-not-stupid?"

She started to storm from the room, giving him time to call her back with every prideful step. He sat silently. She stopped when she reached the hall, heart pounding with fury, with insult, with shame. But she couldn't let it go. She couldn't let *him* go. She spoke without turning toward him, her back unbending, as inflexible as his posture on the couch.

"You know who I am and what I do, Max. It's more than my job. It's with me all the time. *In* me all the time. I didn't plan to hurt you with what I said. That's the last thing I meant to do. I didn't know what to tell Babineau when he asked. I don't know how to explain you and me; I don't understand it myself. You drive me crazy. I think about you all the time. I can't stay away from you. But I can't tell anyone else that."

Silence. Then a curt, "Tell me."

She revolved slowly. "How can I do my job if they see me straddling the fence between our two worlds? I don't want what we have now, to become what we do. I don't know how to keep it separate, but I'm trying, Max. I'm trying so hard, because I don't want to lose you."

There, she'd said it.

"Come here to me, Charlotte."

The tight command made her bristle up. She approached him with her chin angled high and her step defiant, because he was still all fierce and darkly intense and had triggered an "Oh, my God, you are so hot!" pulse that pounded in her ears. She yanked his feet down off the couch so she could straddle his lap and glare down at him from a position of power. He didn't move as she palmed the tough symmetry of his face, as her fingers sifted back through the black hair at his brow. His eyes never flickered as she bent incrementally until their noses brushed.

"Don't."

He spoke that single word as if it were some talisman he could fling up between them to ward her off, to hold back the exquisitely tortuous sensations that surged when she stroked her thumb over his bottom lip.

"Don't do this to me, Charlotte."

"I'll stop if you mean it."

She pulled down firmly on his stubborn chin, opening the way for her tongue to slip into his mouth, to glide over his, to taste him, to trace the hard line of his teeth and the slick softness of the insides of his cheeks.

He sat perfectly still, as if in a dental chair waiting for the drill to bite into him without Novocain.

Breath shuddering in her lungs, she looked up from her near feral crouch upon his chest. Her eyes were hot, angry. Aroused.

"Does this feel like pretend to you, Savoie?" When he refused to react, she sank back into his mouth, taunting aggressively until he made a low, tormented sound in the back of his throat, as if she were killing him, as if the hot plunge of her tongue were a dagger to his heart, carving slowly, painfully, to whittle away all resistance.

She lifted up at last, frustrated, knowing if she couldn't break him at least in this, she could never have him. And right then she knew that she wanted him more than anything else she could imagine. But he had to believe her.

"Do you honestly think I have ever done that or wanted to do that to anyone but you?"

For a long beat, he didn't move. Then, so fast it was a blur, his hand shot out to clap about the back of her neck, gripping just tight enough for her to know she couldn't break free. As he held her captive, as he stared into her eyes until his pupils swelled over hot seas of green, she was reminded again of what he was. Dangerous. A predator. Something wild and deadly and not quite domesticated. Not quite human.

Instead of struggling against those things, she relaxed within the cuff of his hand, her lips curving into a sultry smile. "There's only you, Max, and you know it."

He dragged her up until their mouths were a whisper apart. He stared into her fiery gaze, his eyes daring. "I think I need more convincing."

And he lowered her down to his lips so she could persuade him of her desire, of her need for him, with an attention to detail that had his head swimming. His hand dropped to the small of her back and pulled her against him, into the hard length of his erection.

She smiled into his kiss. "You're so easy."

"You had me at 'Drop your pants, Max.'"

"I've never said that to you."

"Say it now."

She laughed. "You're an aggravating man, Savoie." Her fingertips stroked over his brow, along the sharp ridge of his cheekbones. "A foolish man," she murmured into his kisses. "Arrogant man. Sexy, hot, dangerous man. My man."

"I'm convinced." His tongue plunged deep and his palms roamed her breasts, the curve of her hips, reckless, rough, urgent. She had on a skinny, ribbed tank top and gym shorts that provided easy access. He was wearing way too much. She started working down the front of his shirt, then impatiently gripped either side and gave a savage pull. Buttons bounced across her coffee table and carpet.

When he let her up for air, she had one demand.

"Drop your pants, Max."

"Anything you say, detective. But I wouldn't be a gentleman if I didn't say ladies first." He tugged down her shorts, then unzipped his trousers with one yank. With a quick move, he was over her. And inside her. Pinning her shoulders to the couch cushions, he took his time, teasing her with long, deep strokes even as she began to twist and beg with the arch of her body.

"Max, *hurry*."

"Wait for it."

Her head tossed. Her breath came thick and fast. Her fingers dented his arms, digging deep, making future bruises with their desperate clench. He took a savage pleasure in watching her eyes glaze. Wild for him. Hot for him. He burned with the force of his want, to take her, to claim her, to lose himself in her.

"With me, Max. Please." She was shivering at the edge, holding on for something just as fiercely as she was holding on to him. "Let *go*. Dammit, Max, I love you."

Surprise broke his rhythm. As he struggled to recapture his restraint, she gripped his hips and pounded him into her.

Sudden hot waves of urgent sensation rose and flashed through his body, the floodgates bursting open. Barreling, drowning, unforgiving, until there was no stopping the climax that ripped control from him with a stunning violence. Her name was on his lips. The only name that had ever been in his heart.

He could hear her hoarse cries through the roaring in his ears, and then silence settled.

Her unexpected laugh was soft, husky as she rubbed her palms along his damp back. "Geez, Savoie, you could have stocked a pond."

He let himself collapse upon her long, luxurious lines, crushing her beneath his dead weight. He had absolutely no desire to move. Ever.

"You tricked me," he grumbled.

"Did I?" Her fingers played with his hair. The strength of her contented sigh lifted him and let him down easy.

"Don't care. Worth it." His face nuzzled between her breasts.

"I need sleep." She kissed his wet brow. "We can crowd onto this couch and wake up all knotted and achy, or we can take a few steps down the hall and stretch out in my nice comfy bed."

"Here's fine."

"Move, Max."

He staggered to his feet, feet that were tangled in his trousers, forcing him to drop back down onto the couch to kick his way free of them. Charlotte took his hand, hauling him up, letting him topple into her. Holding him close. Panicking briefly because they fit so well together.

After herding him down the hall, she let him flop on the bed, face first. One bounce and he was out.

She smiled with wry tenderness. "Next time, remind me to enjoy a few more go-rounds with you before I say the magic words."

She busied herself washing up, locking up, too restless, too nervous to settle beside him. Because of the words she'd said out loud. Those magic words that had thrown open the floodgates of his desire and the restraint from her heart.

Finally exhaustion drew her down to the embrace of her mattress, and something deeper, stronger, drew her to Max Savoie. She curled into him, despite the sultry heat, to press a kiss to his shoulder. He muttered softly and pulled her arm up to his chest, trapping her tenderly against him. She didn't struggle.

Thinking he was asleep, she vowed quietly, "I'll keep you safe, Max."

His reply was a rumbled whisper. "You're my every dream, Charlotte."

A PHONE RINGING in the middle of the night was never good.

Alain Babineau gave her the details like a surgeon making one quick cut to minimize the trauma. She told him in a level voice that she'd be ready when he swung by in fifteen minutes. Then she hung up and sat motionlessly.

"Charlotte? What is it?"

The tremors started small in her hands. She made fists. They moved up her arms until she hugged them against her broken heart. Her shoulders began to quake, and then Max's hands were on them, turning her, scooping an arm beneath her knees to pull her up into his lap to cradle her like a child.

In the tenderness of his embrace, she wept. She sobbed her soul dry for all the times she'd denied herself tears. For the days and nights of terror when she'd had to be strong for Mary Kate. When she'd washed her father's blood out of her favorite sweater so she could wear it to his funeral. For the times she'd stood straight and tough when confronted with the brutality of her job and the loneliness of her life. And for an irreplaceable loss still too great for her to comprehend.

And while she drenched his shoulder with sorrows, Max did all the right things. He stayed silent. He held her close but not too tightly. His touch was unobtrusive on her hair, along her arm and shoulder. His mouth moved across her brow in light, gentle sweeps to express his understanding of her pain.

When her grief had worn down to soft sniffles, he asked, "What can I do?"

Her wet cheek rubbed against him. "You're doing it." Her breathing rasped like a saw across the tethers of his emotions. "It hurts so bad, Max. I don't know how I'm going to stand it."

"I'm sorry." And because that was so inadequate in expressing the panic and regret ripping through him, he desperately sought something else that might bring her some comfort. "Her thoughts were of you."

Cee Cee went still. Her breathing stopped. She hadn't told him what was wrong. Slowly, she lifted her head from the damp haven of his shoulder to look at him. She stared, expression curiously calm.

Her first blow was a surprising shock of pain, mashing his nose, momentarily blanking his mind. He instinctively held on to her, reeling while she pounded him with her fists until he no longer felt their impact. She struggled to escape him, cursing wildly, her elbows, then her heels coming into play to finally break his grip. While he floundered, hanging on to consciousness by a primal need to survive, she scrambled away.

Then the barrel of her gun cracked against his teeth. "You killed her!" she raged at him. "You came here to me after you killed her."

"No!"

"Liar." One vicious swing of the gun butt dropped him to the sheets they'd shared.

"I *didn't*. I couldn't."

She straddled him, breathing hard into the madness of pain and betrayal. She jammed the barrel against his temple, pressing his head into the mattress. "You walked away. You left her there, knowing what they were going to do. You coward—you *monster*. You let them kill her. Why didn't you tell me? I could have saved her. She didn't have to die."

"I didn't know. I couldn't tell you."

"Which is it, you lying bastard?" she roared.

At the sound of the revolver cocking, he squeezed his eyes shut. Perhaps there was an irony in dying at her hand rather than Jimmy's. He forced his head around, just far enough so the last thing he'd see was her face. "I'm sorry," he whispered. "I love you, Charlotte."

If anything, that increased her fury. He waited for her to pull the trigger. When she didn't, a deeper, darker agony filled him.

"Don't you say that to me," she snarled. "You don't know what it means. You've brought nothing but pain and death into my life, and I want you out of it. Do you hear me? Stay away from me, or I *will* kill you."

She angled off him and pushed hard, shoving him off the bed to thump onto the floor out of sight.

"I never meant to hurt you, Charlotte."

She shuddered at the wretchedness in his voice. "Really? When you walked away from us twelve years ago? Do you know what they did to us during those hours you were trying to make up your mind whether we were worth the risk of pissing off your boss? And you didn't think it would hurt me now, doing nothing to keep my best friend from dying? Get the hell out of here. Go groveling back to Jimmy Legere. I have to go claim a body."

She went into the bathroom and slammed the door, her breathing labored. Violence and grief shook her in debilitating spasms until she finally managed a fragile control.

The face in her mirror was unrecognizable. Her eyes were huge and dulled, mouth still kiss-bruised, and ice-pale skin splattered with red. The face of what she'd become. What she'd always been. Hard, cold, and empty. Alone with her vengeance.

She washed slowly, numbing her heart and mind for what she had to do. She didn't glance at her bloody sheets, pausing only to jerk on clean clothes and to strap on her holster. When she entered her living room, a rain-cooled breeze came in through the open balcony doors.

The only thing left of him were the buttons on her floor.

Twelve

THE STENCH OF smoke and wet ruin hit Cee Cee the second she opened the car door. Though the older section and part of the sanctuary had escaped with only minor damage, the only home she knew was gone—nothing but smoldering rubble.

The moment Joey Boucher spotted her, he trotted over, shaking his head in disgust. "What kind of sick animal kills inside a church?" There was no change in Cee Cee's expression. What kind of animal indeed? That's what she had to find out.

Boucher continued. "It's a miracle the rest of them got out all right. There was enough accelerant used to power a shuttle launch."

"Somebody didn't want the cause of death found," Babineau mused. "Any word on that yet?"

"Dovion just went in."

"Go see what you can find out."

When they were alone, Babineau asked what Cee Cee knew he would. What she was asking herself.

"He got an alibi for tonight?"

"From eleven to when you called me."

Her partner fidgeted. "Airtight?"

"Vacuum sealed." She took a shaky breath. "But he was here earlier."

"How do you know?"

"He told me."

Babineau blinked. "Just came right out and told you? I never figured him for that kind of careless." Seeing Cee Cee flinch, he rushed to make awkward amends. "Look, Ceece, this ain't gonna get any easier from here on out. Maybe you'd best step on out and put a little distance between you and . . . and whatever turns up."

"*Distance?* How do you calculate distance, when wondering if your lover just happened to murder your best friend before stopping by to get naked?"

That was a little too much information for Babineau. He muttered a curse beneath his breath, unable to read his partner's taut expression. "Maybe he wasn't involved."

"And maybe my butt's made of banana creme."

He wisely made no comment.

They stood hunched in the drizzle, not wanting to step on any toes of the investigating team. She couldn't force herself to step inside, nor could she leave without knowing, so Babineau stoically tucked up his shirt collar and said nothing. Because that's what partners did.

She was wearing the Armani jacket, having grabbed it out of her closet without thinking as she darted out the door. She shivered inside the elegant folds, wanting to rub her arms but afraid to touch the fine material. She couldn't let her feelings drift in that direction. She had to stay frosty. If she buckled, Babineau would boot her home and she wouldn't blame him. A murder scene wasn't a place for misty-eyed regrets. So she wouldn't think of how much she needed the strength of Max Savoie's presence while everything that meant anything to her went straight to hell. Because he was the one who'd sent it there.

Dovion himself came out with the news. He and Charlotte had spent enough long nights poking around in a cold chest cavity to share stories and swap histories. He knew how just standing on the periphery was killing her by slow degrees.

"Charlotte, darlin', I surely am sorry about all this."

"Thanks, Dev. Save it for later. What do you know?"

"They're saying arson."

"What time?"

"Maybe one thirty, two."

Her knees wobbled. Not Max. It wasn't Max. She swallowed hard. "Was she . . . harmed in any way?"

"No."

"Would you tell me if she was?"

A sad smile. "No." Then he pressed her hand. "No one touched her. But she knew they were coming."

"How do you know that?"

"She sent the mothers and their children away. She was alone, on her knees with her God. She was holding her rosary and two photographs. Couldn't tell what they were of."

Cee Cee knew. Her and Mary Kate. The Malones.

"If she knew she was in trouble, why didn't she call me?" she wondered. "If I'd known, I could have saved her. I would have been here."

"And maybe," Alain suggested softly, "she knew that's what someone was counting on."

But they hadn't counted on Mary Kate and Max both hiding the truth to keep her away. The way they'd kept secrets together for twelve years.

Because they loved her.

Just then, two officers came down the steps of St. Bart's carrying a zippered plastic bag. Both Babineau and Dovion gripped an arm, but she wasn't going to collapse. She was frozen in a strange, disconnected calm.

But the sack was too thin to contain Mary Kate Malone—there must have been some mistake. When she started forward their grips tightened. Something in her eyes convinced them to let go. That she needed to see for herself.

She never made a sound. She never blinked, never twitched, never shrank away as the plastic was peeled down for her inspection. She didn't see what they saw: the charred remains of a murder victim. She saw an exuberant smile, the tease of blue eyes, the bounce of blonde hair as Mary Kate Malone exclaimed in breathy confidence, "Terry McFee is going to love me forever."

"I will love you forever, Mary Kate," she whispered, then nodded to the officer. But as he began to rezip, she stopped him, staring blankly at a smudge of brightness on the crisped curl of fingers.

A man's ring.

It wasn't Mary Kate.

She turned to Dovion, her expression torn wide open in distress. "Who is this?"

"The janitor. Benjamin Spratt."

Then she heard the most wonderful sound in the world: an ambulance gurney working its way through destruction.

Mary Kate was *alive*.

The ambulance attendants wouldn't let her get close, wouldn't let her ride along in the ambulance. Their grim expressions told her more than any words could. Maybe being alive wasn't such a good thing.

"Don't expect miracles," Dovion told her. "She took one to the temple, then they left her there to burn."

Cee Cee couldn't go home, even after Dovion's promise to keep her updated. Babineau took her for some hot, harsh chicory coffee, and she felt sorry for him. He was so eager to offer support, to listen to her recollections or lamentations. The silence was harder to endure.

Why had Max said nothing? To protect Jimmy Legere, or to save her from rushing into danger?

Perhaps both—it didn't really matter now. Even if he hadn't been there, he'd known, and said nothing.

She couldn't go home to face his blood on her sheets and his buttons on her floor.

They drove around as the sun crawled up to color the Square's shop windows. To break the silence, Babineau was grumbling over his new bride's complaints about living with a cop. The missed dinners. The inconsistent hours. The worry. The isolation. Blah, blah, blah.

"Want me to talk to her?"

Alain glanced at Cee Cee, clearly surprised she'd been listening. "What? Talk to her about what?"

"A little girl-to-girl about putting up or shutting up."

He laughed. "Yeah. That's just what she needs. She thinks we're having an affair."

"*What?*"

"Relax. I told her you didn't like men."

She scowled at him. "You wouldn't be far from wrong. Idiot." Men in general, no. One in particular, too damned much. She sagged back against the seat. It would be hours before she'd learn anything about Mary Kate's condition. "I need more coffee. Intravenously, if possible."

He parked as close to Café du Monde as they could get. Cee Cee had climbed out and was plugging money into the meter when a call came on the radio. Babineau waved her on. "Café au lait with two beignets. Be right there."

"You just want me to pay the bill. I'm going to tell your wife you're a cheap date."

She was paying for their breakfast when his hand slid on top of hers. She glanced up and her heart took a nosedive.

"Charlotte, take a breath."

She tried, but couldn't pull anything in through the sudden constriction of her throat. She could only stare with deer-in-the-headlights terror of what was about to hit her head on.

"There's been a fatal shooting at Jimmy Legere's. The coroner's on his way out."

She dropped without a sound.

IT WAS TWENTY minutes by car. Walking, it was hours. Barely able to put one foot in front of the other, it took forever. He could have made a call and been picked up. He could have rid himself of all the hurt, all the misery on his own. But tonight, dizzy and disoriented from pain and grief, he chose to succumb to it instead. Because it was well deserved.

Max wove along the side of the road, staggering, sometimes falling to the sharp, crushed oyster-shell surface. The occasional vehicle that passed him in the rain gave him a wide berth. He could imagine how he looked—like a drunk who'd gone five rounds with a road grader. Under his leather coat, his shirt was open and stained with blood from his nose. One of his eyes had swollen shut, and his cheek pulsed with a persistent ache. He'd cracked or even broken a rib when he rolled off the balcony rail and fell hard to the ground a floor below. But those were distant, dull pains compared with the agony that dragged his steps to a slow shuffle. The road was taking him from where he wanted to be to where he was afraid to go.

He stumbled, his steps faltering, reminding him of the sick animal that had once wandered into their village. His mother had made him watch as their neighbors cornered the weak, frightened creature and beat it down to blood and bones. The sight had upset him into tears, but even worse his mother's whispered warning as she shook him once, hard enough to scatter the moisture from his cheeks.

Remember what you've seen. They will turn on you the same way if they find out you're not like them. They will hunt you and hurt you and finally kill you. Be like them, act like them, walk among them. Don't ever let them see what you are. Special. Blessed.

He tried to obey, but it was hard to realize that things that came as naturally to him as breathing were dangerous. If she caught him the punishment was fierce, because she loved him and wanted to keep him safe. So he pretended to be less than he was, to blend into the sameness, to mimic what was acceptable.

Then the shoes taught him the other lesson that would never ever leave him.

The shame of bringing her boy barefooted to church was more than she could endure. She invited a man to dinner and sent Max to bed early. In the morning, they went to buy him shoes. His feet grew fast, and soon he was staying overnight at a neighbor's while someone else stayed in his house. New shoes. They hurt his feet, pinching his toes, cramping his stride. And then he started hearing talk about what his mother did to earn them. He wasn't sure what the words meant, but he didn't like them. He didn't like the men friends who came by in the night, and he didn't like the shoes that made him look the same.

He didn't know why he was thinking about shoes now . . . something Charlotte had said. But he couldn't let himself think about her. If he did he'd drop to the side of the road, curl up like that injured animal, and wait to die.

It was raining harder. He lifted his face to it, wiping away the wetness and the blood with shaking hands. Another mile to go. Just another mile to go. But it hurt just to breathe, so it was hard to make his feet move when he knew the agony each step would bring.

Yet what was his wretched walk compared with the hours, the days, two battered, frightened girls had spent in the hands of true monsters?

He forced a step, hugging his splintered side. Another one, worse. But not as bad as the anguish that would catch up to him if he didn't keep pushing on. If he could just get home, Jimmy could make things right in his mind again. Bad things only happened when he strayed off the path. Jimmy would show him the path and he'd follow, and things would be all right again. Simple. As they'd been before. Before he'd been tempted to stray.

It had taken him by surprise that he'd paused to notice something outside the perimeters of any particular task he was on. He rarely paid any attention to his surroundings, beyond a wary caution. They simply didn't matter to him. Those blinders were the only way he could shut out the fear that would press in and overwhelm him otherwise. Only Jimmy understood his need for focus, for simplicity, for the lack of distraction so he could continue to function without the madness that came with his curse. His mother had called it his special blessing but he knew better. There was nothing special or blessed about being different. But Jimmy had taught him its power. The power to inspire fear instead of shrinking from it.

Fear was a tricky business, like balancing on a slender limb. Careful steps, with one hand holding on for safety. Looking down would jeopardize his footing. Always hold on, because there was no safety net—just a long, deadly fall. Now he'd lost his balance, and there was nothing for him to hang on to as he teetered wildly.

Help me, Jimmy. Help me. I've lost my way.

He'd sensed the two girls that day before he saw

them. He'd come down to the warehouse to deliver something for Jimmy when the intensity of their terror, their pain, struck him like a club. He meant to walk right past the partially opened door; whatever was going on behind it was none of his concern. But he slowed, and he glanced in. And then he couldn't look away.

Two girls with their hands bound behind them, clothing torn, flesh bruised. One was fair and golden, the other dark and bronze. The pale one wept and whimpered in the shadow of the other, who was on her knees in a ridiculous attempt to protect her friend. Such fire, such fury, such hatred blazed from her dark eyes as she glared up at the figure standing between her and the door. Her defiance was futile but it was unshakable, even as the looming figure ripped his leather belt from its loops.

"Why do you keep fighting?" the man had asked in irritation. "You know you can't win. You know it's only going to hurt you more."

She sent a large wad of bloody spit toward him, grinning fiercely as he jumped to avoid it. "Untie me, you bastard," she'd snarled through that ferocious smile. "I'll give you one hell of a fight."

"I don't think so." He doubled the belt, getting ready to swing, when he noticed Max at the same time the sobbing blonde girl did.

"Please, help us!"

The door slammed shut.

Max knew the rules. Do what you're told and

only what you're told. Don't ask questions and don't answer them. He started to walk away but couldn't help glancing back at that closed door, seeing that boldly combative sneer, that indomitable spirit about to be crushed because it couldn't be broken.

He'd kept walking. And there wasn't a day that went by that he didn't wish he hadn't.

He stopped to wipe the rain out of his eyes again, and was surprised to see the start of the massive wall that enclosed Jimmy's estate. He started along it, bumping it with his shoulder as his steps grew increasingly unsteady. Soon he was leaning into it, practically pulling himself toward the main gate. The cameras would be following him by now. Would they come out for him, or wait until they had him away from any prying eyes? He didn't much care either way.

The gates were closed. He wrapped his hands around the bars, sagging into them. Down the long drive he could see the house bathed in moonlight and shadows, even as the dawn began to build behind him. And he remembered the first time he'd seen it from the backseat of Jimmy Legere's sleek limousine. He'd been awed and more than a little afraid. But more than that, deeper than that, was a huge, spreading sense of safety that brought a weepy feeling of gratitude up to clog his throat.

The same way it did now.

He pulled himself up, steadying his legs enough to hold him. Then he stepped back from the bars, staring straight into the camera as if he could look right through the lens into the eyes of whomever was watching on the other end. He waited, ignoring the pounding rain, the punishing weariness, settling into a deep, still calm that would give him the strength to remain there unmoving for hours, days.

And then the gate swung open.

Welcoming him home.

Or inviting him to his death.

Thirteen

*H*IS HOPE OF slinking in unnoticed was quickly dashed.

He'd just started up the stairs when he heard Jimmy call his name. Part of him wanted to continue on up as if he hadn't. On all fours, he took a minute to gather his thoughts, to summon his waning strength before backing down the steps and reeling down the hall to Jimmy's office.

It wasn't good. Jimmy wasn't alone. Francis Petitjohn was with him, lounging on the sofa against the wall, and neither looked pleased. He stepped just inside the doorway, where the poor light might conceal him from their direct scrutiny. Or might not.

"What the hell happened to you?"

"Just a little roughhouse with my girl." He tried to smile, but the muscles of his face wouldn't work.

"And how does she look?"

His eyes welled up with the image. "She looked great." His voice softened. "She looked great."

The room did a slow somersault and he found himself on elbows and knees, his aching cheek pressed to the cool parquet floor. His heart pulsed with an equal anguish.

"Get up, Max."

"I can't." He didn't try.

"I sent you to take care of something for me."

"She said no. She said to tell you that smart and brave weren't the same thing."

"No? Stupid girl. And what did I tell you to do, Max?"

"I'm sorry. I couldn't, Jimmy. Not a nun. Not in a church." Because, for the first time, he'd seen value in the life he was ordered to take. And there was no way he could justify it as a right thing to do, regardless of the consequences. Her courage had brought him to his knees as they both struggled to protect the same thing.

And she'd thought herself a coward? Hardly.

"What does that have to do with anything?" Legere raged. "What does that have to do with you? Since when does religion apply to you?"

Max crossed his arms over the top of his head, not for protection but to hold in the sudden bittersweet memories. They flooded up to soothe the crippling pain behind his blackened eyes. Images he could barely recall except in his tormented dreams. Dreams he dreaded and cherished at the same time. "My mama took me every Sunday. I go with you every week."

"I never expected you to listen."

No, of course not, Max realized with numbing

clarity. There was only one voice he was supposed to hear and obey.

"Where have you been?"

"I went to Charlotte's."

"*Detective* Caissie's. And what did you tell her?"

"I didn't tell her anything. I've never told her anything."

"I'm to believe that's why she beat you to a pulp?"

Max tried to laugh. "A woman with an attitude and a gun is no one you want to piss off."

Jimmy wasn't amused. "And you just let her do that to you? When you could have crushed her with one hand?" He paused, then said in a low, aggrieved tone, "She should have killed you and saved me the trouble."

That settled in deep and cold where he was already shivering.

"Why did you come back here, Max? Did you think you'd be welcomed back after making such a terribly wrong choice?"

With a tremendous effort, Max lifted his head. He tried to focus on the man who had guided him through the main years of his life, but the image was vague, distant. Like the man Jimmy Legere had suddenly become.

Though he felt sick and unsteady and pain pounded through him, one thing was clear. "This is my home. I have no place else to go."

"Your home?" Legere's laugh was sharp and

cruel. Cruel in a way he'd never been before. "This isn't your home. Your home is out there, where we found you. Do you remember that, Max? Do you remember where we found you, crouched down in the muck, in the rot? A wild, dirty little beast gone crazy with fear and death?"

Max took a breath that sent panic through his heart and pain stabbing through his ribs. The way hunger had knifed through him until he'd considered . . . he'd considered . . . the unthinkable to ease it. Horror shuddered through him. The damp and the blood pooling around him on the floor became the dank, heavy stench of the swamp. The raw terror of the darkness came crowding in around him. He made a low, fevered sound between denial and petition.

Legere pressed on without pity. "Go back there, Max. Go back to that cesspool of poverty, violence, and ignorant fear. To being alone and afraid all the time. Live in that filth, in that stink, feeding on what can't outrun you: an animal, hiding and cornered. Waiting to be discovered and destroyed. Back to that hell where I found you."

"Jimmy, please." The words moaned from him, tortured, twisted by the awful things squirming through his memory.

"Please what, Max? Please save you? I did. I took you from that place, brought you to my home, allowed you to live this life of wealth, comfort, and respect. You had every luxury anyone could ever dream of handed to you. You were loved, Max, cared for, protected. And what do you do to repay that trust, that love?"

"Jimmy, please." Desperate and dizzy, he stretched out his hands. He was lost. He couldn't breathe.

"Look at you," Legere sneered. "Look at what you've let yourself become. Because of that woman. You've let her use you, hurt you, confuse you. And when she tossed you away, you crawl back here to beg for shelter.

"You've betrayed my trust, Max. You've bitten that hand that always showed you kindness and care. And now you want me to extend it to you again. Why would I do that, Max? Why?"

His eyes closed weakly, his will crumpling beneath the weight of fear and exhausting pain. "Anything you want, Jimmy." A soft, plaintive whisper. "Anything you want."

"Get up."

He didn't move.

"Stop this right now. Pull yourself together and be what I've made you. Do it now, Max."

He drew his elbows under him, looking up briefly through eyes that were hot, golden, and red-centered, then tucked his head, breathing deep and slow. A long, fierce spasm rolled through his shoulders and rippled down his spine.

And then he rose up to his feet, the movement fluid, strong, filled with powerful grace. And he regarded Jimmy Legere, his gaze cool and unblinking in a face unblemished beneath the blood.

"We'll have no more of these dramatics. Get cleaned up and come back here," Legere ordered. "Then we'll discuss what you're going to do for me."

IN A SHOWER as hot as he could stand it, Max let the blood run down the drain. All the physical discomfort was gone, but he was weak and tired. And numb. Patterned instinct took over, requiring no thought as he efficiently shaved without really seeing his face with its perfectly normal, deceptively human features. After food and sleep he'd be as good as new.

He'd be nothing again.

He stood in the bathroom doorway and glanced about his room's spacious dimensions. He'd lived in it for almost thirty years and nothing had changed. He'd brought nothing of his own into it since that first time Jimmy had showed him in. The walls were still a blank white canvas, the drapes and bedspread a simple gray-and-white stripe brushing against the polished wood floor. All the surfaces were bare; he had nothing to put on them. No wallet, no car keys, no pictures or tokens, no watch, no television, no identity.

He'd never thought there was anything odd about how he lived until he'd stepped into Charlotte Caissie's apartment. It vibrated with her strong personality, with her past, with her preferences. He'd been curious about the rodents but assumed they provided a degree of companionship. He'd asked about having an animal when he was younger. Francis Petitjohn had laughed at him and called him stupid. Didn't he realize *he* was the family's house pet? He'd never asked again.

This room was his reflection. Blank, barren, no sense of time or place. It just was.

He opened his closet and stared at the long line of tailored suits, enough to exquisitely clothe a boardroom filled with executives. The clothes Jimmy picked for him to wear. Wool and linen designer suits, shirts in fine cotton and silk, and beneath them a row of shiny shoes he'd never worn. Jimmy liked him to present a certain look, sleek, professional, and elegant. Like dressing up the house pet, to pass it off as acceptable family.

Ignoring the suits, Max pulled a dark blue track suit off its hanger. Francis had bought it for him, knowing that when he ran, he didn't wear clothes and he went on all four legs. The fleece felt good against his skin, as he zipped the jacket all the way up to his chin. He left his feet bare.

As he picked up his ruined clothes from the floor, he lifted the leather coat. Soaked with water, it was twice its normal weight. He brought it to his face, buried his unbroken nose in its wet collar, and breathed deep, hoping that a trace of Charlotte remained trapped in the lining. But there was nothing left of her.

I love you, Max.

He knew she hadn't meant it when she said it, but he'd hoped. He'd foolishly hoped that one day it would be true.

That day was never coming.

"MAX, SHUT THE door."

Jimmy was calmer, in an almost benevolent mood. And why not? He was getting what he wanted: Max brought to heel. He watched the younger man's approach with his step light, his moves easy, all strong, lethal grace. No signs remained of the broken creature weeping and groveling on his floor; he looked recovered from whatever self-abuse he'd allowed to befall him. His gaze was level, his features composed. And because he was glad to see Max looking like himself again, Jimmy forgave him the casual choice of clothing. But that's *all* he'd forgive him.

"I can't just let this go, Max. You know that."

Max said nothing, by his silence, not disagreeing.

"You know you're never going to be able to trust him, Jimmy," came T-John's soft summation. "Not until you tell him."

Max's glance flashed to the loosely coiled Petit-john as Jimmy hissed, "Shut up, Francis. Max is none of your concern."

"You're wrong there, Jimmy. You built this whole shebang on that boy's reputation. You should have told him while you could still handle him."

"Max is not going to be a problem, are you, Max?"

But Max was regarding him with something different behind his impassive mask. Suspicion. And then he looked down at his bare feet and up again. Something else was shifting in his gaze. Something not quite so pleasant.

"The measure of a man is in his shoes."

"What nonsense is that, Max?"

"Charlotte said it was something you told her. How would you know about that, Jimmy?"

"About what?"

"How would you know that's what my mama always used to tell me? How would you know that?"

"That bitch just couldn't keep her mouth shut."

"Which one? Charlotte or my mama?"

Petitjohn chuckled. "I told you he'd figure it out Jimmy. He's a lot smarter than you give him credit for."

Max's mind was turning quickly. "I doubt she told you that on the way to the cemetery, so when exactly *did* you have that conversation?"

"Max, it's been thirty years."

"Maybe to you, but it's right there beside me every time I close my eyes. What aren't you telling me, Jimmy?"

"Told you you were making a mistake, Cousin," Petitjohn drawled. "Told you that nun wasn't going to go running to her lady cop friend so you could kill them both, and keep poor Max all to yourself."

Max remained focused on the man in the wheel-chair. "Jimmy, what was the question you asked Sister Catherine to answer? Tell me."

The old man hesitated. He looked from the hard lines of Max's face to the scheming smirk of his cousin. He needed to calm Max first and regain control—then he'd deal with Francis Petitjohn, whom he'd mistakenly assumed was harmless.

"Max, everything I did was for you. They were using you—exploiting your talents, compromising your trust, taking advantage of you to get at me. I was trying to protect you."

"From what? Having some kind of a normal life?"

"Nothing about you is normal, Max. There's no place for you in a normal world. No expensive suit and smart-ass girlfriend is going to make you into a human man. The more you try to force yourself to fit in, the more obvious it is that you never will. The only place you're safe is here."

Max reared back as if slapped. Then he was carefully remote once more. "All I wanted to do was spend some time with a woman I cared for. What I am didn't seem to bother her as much as it bothers you."

Petitjohn stared at him in dismay. "Detective Caissie knows what you are?"

Realizing he'd said too much, Max offered no more.

"She'll have to be dealt with," Jimmy murmured to himself.

"Like Sister Catherine had to be dealt with? Why? What threat was she to you?"

"The fact that you don't know is what makes them so dangerous. We're going to have to keep you out of sight for a while. Keep you in here." Jimmy looked grim. "It's the only way you'll be safe. You've made a mess of things with your infatuation for her. How much does she know? She'll use that knowledge to hurt you."

"To hurt *you,* you mean."

"It's the same thing."

"No, I don't think it is." He looked at Jimmy a bit differently, as if seeing him for the first time. "I never would have betrayed you. Not to Charlotte, not to anyone. I'm not one of your belongings. I'm not a fancy suit to look good at your back, or a weapon to hold in your hand. You don't own me, Jimmy."

"Yes, I do. Everything you are is because of me. Before me, you were nothing. *Nothing,* Max. Outside these walls, do you know what you are? An abomination, something to be regarded with fear and hatred. Something to be destroyed." He saw the anxious flicker in Max's eyes and pressed on. "Without me to protect you they would be on you in a second, and your precious detective would be leading the way."

He saw his miscalculation immediately. The instant he mentioned Charlotte Caissie, Max slipped the chain he was trying to secure once more. He'd been so close.

"No," Max said softly, his tone filled with a curious revelation. "Without me to protect you, *you* are nothing."

Petitjohn laughed. "Bingo."

"When did you talk to my mother?"

"Max—"

He took a step back, brow lowering. "It was no coincidence, you finding me. You were looking for me."

"I wanted to give you something better. I wanted to keep you safe. She understood that at first—then she changed her mind and wouldn't let you go."

Horror thickened his voice. "So you had her killed?"

"I never meant any harm to come to her."

"Why? Why me?"

Jimmy had no response to the horrible pain in that demand.

"Since Jimmy doesn't want to, let me tell you a story, Max. Our fathers ran the docks," Francis began, ignoring Jimmy's sharp glare, "equal in all ways. Until Etienne made a remarkable discovery. He'd been listening to the superstitious rumblings of the loading crews, something about some mythical beast who could walk as a man. Nonsense, my father thought. But Etienne, who loved power more than he loved his brother, was intrigued and began to search for this phenomenal creature."

"There are more like me," Max whispered.

"At least one," Petitjohn told him. "And he was

ferocious. Those were different times. We owned the docks. Violence amongst ourselves was ignored by the law. Etienne and his discovery tore through the competition until the wharves ran red. And they ruled them, unchallenged, until the first Detective Caissie brought them crashing down. My father was killed; Etienne was imprisoned."

"And what of . . . What happened to . . ."

"The beast?" Francis supplied with a smile. "No one knows."

"Was he my father?" Max looked to Jimmy, his features keen with cautious excitement. When Jimmy wouldn't answer, he turned to Francis.

"I don't know, Max. There's no one left to ask. Back to my story, there were three of us to inherit: me, my brother, and Jimmy. Equal in all ways. Are you sensing a pattern here? Jimmy killed my brother in a little disagreement, and then he had to scramble to find a way to protect himself from the rest of the family. That's where you came in. You were just a kid, but by God, you could be terrifying. And with you standing at Jimmy's back, he had Vantour and his dock labor behind him and pretty much won everything else hands down."

Max let the tale digest slowly, then his eyes welled up with distress.

"Why?" He looked to Jimmy for a moment, his expression stripped down to the basic elements of hurt and sorrow. "I was just a child. Why couldn't you have waited?"

"I couldn't wait, Max. I needed to work with you when you could still be influenced."

"Controlled," he corrected bitterly.

"Yes, controlled. That's what I learned from Rollo."

Rollo. The one like him.

"He was arrogant and wild, and my father couldn't get him to suppress his more primitive . . . appetites. You were young, Max. You didn't understand the power you had. I was able to teach you restraint and respect."

"You taught me to be afraid—afraid of everything outside these walls."

"To protect you, Max."

Suddenly, insight sank in cold and clear. "To protect you from *me*."

And he watched the alarm begin to build in Jimmy's face. He saw fear collect in his posture and dread widen his eyes.

With a cry of anguish, Max spun away, crossing his arms over his head, pacing the room in an erratic path. Finally he slowed and stopped, his back to the other two. "Why did you kill her? Why did you have to kill her?"

"It wasn't supposed to happen that way. Believe me, Max."

Max made a sound halfway between a laugh and a sob.

"They were supposed to take her out into the swamps to scare her, to convince her to let you go with them. They were supposed to give her money and let her go. They must have gotten greedy, or she must have tried to run with you."

"They shot her. Right in front of me. I couldn't do anything to stop them. But I made them sorry. I made them sorry."

Jimmy watched his shoulders shake, regret swelling up in his own eyes. "Max, we didn't know where they'd taken you. That's why it took us so long to find you. You were never supposed to be harmed or frightened."

Francis leaned close to his cousin to whisper, "You've lost him, Jimmy. Let him go, or take him down. Quickly."

But Jimmy was determined to try to make amends. "Max, I wanted what was best for you."

"And I wanted my mama back." He whirled around. All traces of humanity were torn from his face as he roared, "It wasn't your choice to make for me." He surged forward two steps, then on all fours until he was in Jimmy Legere's face, lips curling back from razor-sharp teeth, eyes red and gleaming. The hands gripping the arms of his wheelchair became hair-covered claws. "You stole my childhood! You destroyed everything I loved! And I will make you sorry!"

Jimmy Legere put a frail hand to the side of those gaping jaws and said softly, wearily, "I *am* sorry, Max. I am so sorry. I tried to protect you."

In the time it took for him to take a tortured

breath, Max was once again himself. He sank unsteadily to his knees, his world spinning. And he realized the irrevocable damage that had just been done. There was no going back to what was. Everything he'd built his life upon had just been pulled out from under him. Everything, everyone he loved, was lost to him.

"What am I supposed to do now, Jimmy?" he asked tonelessly. "How can I stay, now that I know?"

"You can't, Max. You can't stay."

Slowly, Max lowered his head until it rested on Jimmy's knees. The dangerous dazzle in his eyes dimmed, becoming a dull stare of pain too deep to endure. His anger died out to a cold ash of fatigue that smothered the last spark in his soul. He had nowhere else to go.

The familiar comfort of Jimmy's hand on his hair softened the knowledge of his other hand reaching into the cushions of his chair. He was too tired to react as the slow stroke of that hand on his head had his eyes closing, his shoulders instinctively relaxing.

This was what he knew. What he'd trusted and loved. His terror of a world where he didn't belong, where he'd be so glaringly, agonizingly alone, where he'd know nothing but fear, have no one who cared, was greater than accepting the will of this man who owned his life.

You do it, Jimmy. He'd meant it then. He'd abide by it now.

"You know I've always loved you, Max. Just like a son."

"I know, Jimmy," he whispered hoarsely.

"I promised to take care of you. To do what's best for you. It's not a promise that's easily made or easily kept, but I made it to you and I'll see it through."

"I know you will."

Feeling the cold metal touch the base of his skull, he took a slow breath to calm his thoughts, and let them fill with Charlotte Caissie. With the way she'd looked in that smoky spotlight, filling up his gaze, flooding his heart: his bronze warrior woman. Where just for a moment he could pretend that she might love him.

Even prepared for it, the sound of the shot made him jump. Blood, wet and warm, was on his face, his neck, his hands. Blood that wasn't his own.

Understanding struck with the sudden brutality of the bullet fired from Francis Petitjohn's gun. With a raw cry, Max backed out from under Jimmy's crumpled form. Scuttling backward, he sat stunned into a blankness of heart and mind. His breath came fast until his senses swirled in a dizzying loss of time and place. He could smell the swamp, the rot and decay. And death; the awful, invasive stink of death. The cold ooze of it seeped along his bones, rising, sucking him under. A low wailing sound rose in his throat, but he shut it off tightly.

If they heard they would come back, and they would find him and they would take him from his mother. And he would be alone. And all the horrible things she warned of would come to pass. Without her to protect him, everyone would know. Everyone would know what he was.

Please, don't leave me! Don't leave me here alone!

"Max."

His gaze swam back into a vague focus. He didn't know where he was. The smell of blood was everywhere, thick and nauseating. He could see a hand stretched out to him, offering a connection, the means to pull him from the terrifying nothingness of the swamp.

He hesitated. Something wasn't right.

"Max, take my hand."

"Jimmy?"

"Jimmy's gone, Max. I'll take care of you now. I'll watch out for you. All you have to do is take my hand."

He stared at that avenue of escape while horror and darkness shuddered through him, pulling him back. He couldn't breathe. He couldn't move.

Please. Please, don't leave me here alone.

"Max, we're going to need each other to get through this now. I have to know I can count on you. We're family. I'll take care of you."

The voice was soft, coaxing, convincing him to look up to where Francis Petitjohn was smiling down at him.

"Max, take my hand. You can stay here. You'll be safe. I promise you."

And slowly, numbly, he lifted his hand, letting the man who'd killed the only father he'd ever known take it, drawing him back into the only world he understood.

Fourteen

Cᴇᴇ Cᴇᴇ ꜱᴀᴡ the events unfold, beginning with the stains just inside Jimmy Legere's office. Smears of blood, imprinted with Max's palms and Converse treads. She'd done that. She'd hurt him and sent him back to fall on his knees to Legere. On the far side of the room was a mess of blood, brain, and bone, bisected by wheelchair tracks and bare feet. She stared at both areas with an odd analytical distance until she felt Alain Babineau's supportive grip on her arm.

"Let go," she told him flatly. "I'm not going to fold."

That claim was reinforced when she glanced out onto the wide veranda where Junior Hammond was in his glory, taking Francis Petitjohn's preliminary statement. Petitjohn looked remarkably relaxed and compliant. Junior glanced up, saw her, then scowled.

"Would y'all mind keeping out of my crime scene, thank you very much?"

They'd passed the stretcher ferrying Legere to the coroner's wagon on the way in. Learning the sketchy details on the ride out helped her maintain a stoic front while her heart was banging a frantic rhythm.

"Where's Savoie?" Babineau yelled back, saving Cee Cee from having to make the request.

"Not on the premises. According to Petty John here, Savoie slipped the scene while he was calling 9-1-1. Don't worry, we'll pick him up. He can't have gone far on foot with Legere's thinking parts all over him."

Cee Cee closed her eyes, the image of her father at the breakfast table flashing up before her. His smile as they talked about sports. The sudden shock entering his eyes at impact. The spray on her face that she didn't notice until hours afterward.

"I need to find him, Alain." Her words were quiet but determined. "I have to find him."

She moved quickly back out into the main hall, leaving through the front door to skirt the side of the house beneath the cool overhang of the upper gallery. Francis Petitjohn was settled into one of the wicker chairs murmuring, "My lawyer should be here shortly, boys, then I'd be happy to continue."

"There are some odd prints in here," one of the investigators called from Legere's study. "Do you own some kind of animal?"

Petitjohn smiled as he looked at Cee Cee. "In a manner of speaking. Kind of a family pet."

He knew she knew.

"Where is he, Francis?" she asked quietly as she stood by the side of his chair.

"The way he looked when he showed up this morning, I don't think he's going to be anxious for you to find him, darlin'."

Her throat knotted up. "Is he all right?"

"I kept Jimmy from blowing his brain out through his eyeballs because of you, and he wasn't going to do anything to stop it." He leveled a cool stare at her. "I'd say he's about the most dangerous thing out there on your streets today. Were I you, I'd be running the other way."

She found herself wandering the big house where the staff and business employees haunted the halls like uneasy shadows, not quite certain what to do. They didn't turn to Francis Petitjohn, she noticed.

She observed Max's room with an ache. How empty and lonely it was, for all its size and sparse luxury. It was as impersonal as a hotel room. Or a posh prison.

She watched as his discarded clothing was catalogued and bagged. The officer raised a brow at the sight of the bloodied, buttonless shirt and waterlogged coat.

Cee Cee glanced about. "Any red tennis shoes?"

"No, just that parking lot of new models there in the closet. Whatever he was wearing at the time of the shooting, he's probably still got on him."

Thinking of Max alone outside the safety of these walls, covered in Jimmy Legere, spurred her into action.

She and Babineau returned to the city. Alain went

down to the docks to test the atmosphere. Vantour was still missing, probably permanently. When word of Legere's death reached the other wannabe bosses, the entire area could easily explode in violence until another leader emerged.

Where would Max go?

It was even harder than she imagined to walk up the front steps of St. Bart's, knowing there was no welcome for her inside. The sanctuary was cold and dark, stinking of smoke and ash. She moved silently up the center aisle, feeling ghosts at her back. The building was empty, waiting for arson and insurance investigations to conclude before reconstruction could begin.

She stopped. There, in the dead layer of soot, was a single print. A tennis shoe.

She looked up and around her. "Max?"

His name echoed. He was already gone.

She prowled the city all day, not knowing where to start, not knowing enough about Max independent of Legere to establish any kind of pattern for his behavior. What he would become without Legere, she had no idea.

A check-in with Babineau provided no relief. The situation simmered. Everyone was restless, nervous, uncertain. No one wanted to make the first move to claim Legere's territory. The city wouldn't sleep that night, and neither would she.

Tired, distressed, and drained, she unlocked the door to her apartment, noting a car parked down the block. Someone else was looking for Max, whether it be on her side or his. She waved a hand to let them know they'd been made, and locked her door behind her.

The pigs usually greeted her with greedy whistles for food. Now they were silent, watching her through anxious eyes as she stuffed in a handful of alfalfa. Instead of leaping on it with their usual enthusiasm, they stayed huddled and alert.

Then she noticed red high-tops just outside her bathroom door. She snapped on the light, finding clothes strewn in a bloody trail leading to her shower. The curtain was still dotted with water.

"Max?"

She unsnapped her holster and returned to the hall, cautiously nudging the door to her bedroom wide. The protective grill from her window lay twisted and broken on her bed. The wooden sill was splintered. At first she thought the room was empty. Then she heard the soft snag of his breathing. She circled the foot of the bed to find him huddled, naked, wet, and shivering, with his back to her wall, hugging updrawn knees.

And her heart was gone.

She crouched down, sliding her palm along his shaking shoulders. His head lifted at her touch; an agony of loss filled his unfocused stare. She didn't say a word, simply joined him in that tiny wedge of space. With a soft sound somewhere between a whimper and howl, a sound that stirred the hair on her neck because it couldn't have come from anything human, he tipped forward, crawling into her lap like an injured animal, curling around her knees, balling up tight in misery. While she surrounded him with her embrace, with her warmth and care, he began to rock as those eerie wails continued.

She couldn't see through her tears, lost on the tide of her own remembered anguish, the unforgettable and almost unsurvivable pain of watching a father die. For that's what Jimmy Legere had been to him.

It was hard to find a place for her hands, with all of him so sleek and bare. She threaded the fingers of one hand through his damp hair, and the other between his own. He clutched tight as her damp cheek pressed to his shoulder.

I'm sorry, I'm sorry, I'm sorry, her heart wept. Sorry she hadn't trusted him, that she'd hurt him. Sorry she'd driven out to the violent event on River Road. Sorry she hadn't been there for him while he wandered lost and in pain, not knowing what to do or where to go.

But he came to her. He'd come back to her.

She kissed his warming skin as a huge knot of possessiveness swelled in her throat.

Slowly he quieted, and simply let her hold him.

No huge sense of closure came in knowing Jimmy Legere was dead. She'd hated him, respected him, and even half liked him at times. He'd been an irascible adversary who'd filled her with purpose, but now that he was gone, the only things that mattered were those he'd left behind: his vast criminal empire, and this man who meant more to her than glorying in her revenge. She would tear one down and build the other up as a final flip-off to Legere.

"Everything's going to be all right, Max." She wouldn't tell him she was sorry about Jimmy; that wasn't true. He'd started shivering from the chill and shock, so she pulled the comforter from the foot of her bed and bundled it about him, tucking in the bulky ticking, rubbing briskly through the batting. In consoling him, she found herself comforted. The taut, raw feelings inside her began to ease into a manageable ache of loss.

"You're safe, Max. I'll protect you. I'll take care of you. You're safe with me. Can you trust me?"

A slight nod, but more telling was the way his body relaxed against her.

"You'll be all right, Max," she said softly. "We'll both be all right."

SHE AWOKE, STARTLED, not from the clutches of her nightmare but because of its absence. It was early, not even five o'clock. Curiously content, she burrowed back into the cocooning warmth with a sigh. An answering murmur had her eyes snapping open wide.

The sense of security came from the wrap of Max Savoie around her.

Sometime during the night, he must have moved

them from the cramped huddle on the floor up to her bed. Under the comforter she was still dressed, right down to her holster and shoes. He wasn't. They were curled together, limbs tangled, bodies overlapping in an intimate sprawl.

A purely irrational longing overtook her: the desire to have him here in her bed, sharing heat, sharing closeness and comfort, every night. To wake up each morning lost in the strange beauty of his eyes.

Her lack of resistance to the idea should have scared her to death, the same way all the unsavory and supernatural elements of Max's life should have scared her. But she found herself oddly unafraid.

Aroused by his proximity and lack of attire, she enjoyed the luxury of not having to act on it. As Max had said, there was no hurry. He wasn't going anywhere and for a few more hours, neither was she. She dozed happily, putting the sorrow, the panic, the uncertainty aside to simply absorb the fulfilling sense of sharing this space with this man. She thought of him as a man, even though that's not what he was. It was less complicated that way. The heavy drape of his arm across her middle, the soft brush of his breath against her ear, the warm, comforting hollow created by arm, shoulder, and bare chest. Perfect.

When the room lightened with morning, she reluctantly slipped away to make the necessary calls, then returned, unable to help herself, to sit on the edge of the bed and watch him sleep.

There was no sign of the punishment she'd

dealt out on his features. Again, she marveled at his strange regenerative abilities and was glad for them. She couldn't bear to be confronted with how badly she'd hurt him in her madness and rage. Now those emotions seemed far away, and the only thing that was important was protecting Max from those who would misuse him as Legere had. He had risked everything to rescue her from uncertainty and pain; now she would return that favor.

She checked the time, which was passing much too quickly. Leaning forward, she brushed the back of her hand down his cheek.

"Max, time to wake up."

His eyes opened to a sharp awareness of everything. She watched the events of the past hours fast-forward through his gaze; flickers of hurt, shock, devastation, and loss. Then his stare was carefully guarded.

"Good morning," she told him with a gentle smile. "I wish I could have let you sleep longer, but it's going to be a busy day."

He nodded. "I'm sure you've got lots of work to do."

She expected an edge of irony in his words, but there was none—just a heavy weariness. Her determination to protect him from the events soon to unfold firmed. "And I have to make sure you're taken care of, first."

"Taken care of?" He frowned slightly. "What does that mean?"

"My partner's on his way." She put her hand on his shoulder to still his recoil. "He's bringing some clean clothes for you."

His tension eased a bit. "Okay."

"Then I want you to go with him. He'll take you down to the station to make your statement. He's going to stay right with you through the whole thing."

"What whole thing?" He sat up, the covers falling to his lap.

Her breath caught. It was extremely difficult not to explore that newly bared terrain with her gaze, with her touch.

"What we talked about last night: keeping you safe and protected." She put her hand over his, pressing tightly. The instant her grip loosened, he eased his away.

"And where will you be?"

"All hell's going to break loose, and I'm going to be in the thick of it."

He smiled faintly. "Where else? You'll be careful?"

"Of course." Her hand rubbed along his arm, along the top of his thigh. She wanted to make that touch more personal in the worst way, but didn't dare with Babineau en route. And she wasn't sure she should, with Max regarding her so warily.

"And I'll see you here later?"

"Here? No. I'll come visit as soon as they okay it. It may be a while, but that's because I've asked them to go the extra mile with you. I don't want anything to happen."

"I thought . . ." He glanced around in confusion, then his expression grew impassive once more. "Where will I be? Are you arresting me?"

She laughed, combing her fingers through his hair. "No, of course not. But you've got a lot of awfully valuable information that they're going to need, especially now. They're going to want to keep you tucked away from any harm."

"Who's they?" he asked quietly.

"The district attorney's office. When I talked to them, they were ready to make you any kind of deal you wanted to throw their way. Make them give you plenty, Max. You deserve it. You'll be giving them the city on a silver platter."

"Why would I do that, Charlotte?"

She paused, really looking at him for the first time. Seeing his genuine confusion and objection. "Because you came here for help. And I promised to keep you safe."

"I came here because of you—not so you could extend me a professional courtesy."

A terrible suspicion began to unfurl. "Max, what exactly did you think I was offering you?" He didn't answer, but she read it in his eyes for an unguarded instant.

Sanctuary. Here. With her. And how much more? Then it was gone behind his impenetrable stare.

She touched his unresponsive hand. "I'm sorry. I didn't know that's what you were asking."

He laughed it off with a careless gesture. "Always the cop first. I was being stupid. It was too much too expect. Don't apologize. I've got to go."

She was losing him.

She reached for him, catching the covers as he slipped out from under them. "Max, listen to me. Let me help you."

"Your official help wasn't what I came here for, detective. I'm sorry for the misunderstanding and all the trouble you went through on my account. I can take care of myself." He was pulling away quickly, defensively, erecting an insurmountable wall of distance.

"Max, *please* don't run. Don't go back. You don't owe them anything. There's nothing for you there."

"And apparently nothing for me here, either, detective."

A knock at the door distracted her, and by the time she turned back he was standing naked at the window. The sight of him literally stole her breath.

She gulped, then scowled. "Don't be ridiculous. You can't run around town like that."

"Good-bye, Charlotte."

He turned and jumped. By the time he'd cleared her broken window frame, he'd gone completely from man to four-legged beast.

"Max!"

She raced to the window. Looking out, she saw a big lean wolf loping across her street, disappearing between the parked cars into the shadows of the city.

"I'LL BE DAMNED. Will you look at that?"

The comment dragged Cee Cee's attention from the mound of paperwork she was shuffling through while waiting for news on Mary Kate. She followed the direction of everyone's attention and the shock hit her like a blow.

In the company of Legere's high-powered attorney, Max Savoie strode through the station like a visiting celebrity. In a black, beautifully tailored Giorgio Armani suit with stark-white shirt and silk tie that probably cost a cop's monthly salary, his black hair slick, his skin taut over aggressive bone structure, and his eyes hard as chips of glass, he was no longer the boy who'd snagged her heart at first sight. But he controlled the room with that same purposeful indifference.

"Mr. Savoie has come in to give his statement," Antoine D'Marco drawled out in his $1,500-an-hour voice. "He wants to cooperate fully in order to bring this matter to a quick resolution."

"Mr. Savoie, this way." Junior Hammond was all cold civility.

The moment they were out of sight, Cee Cee rushed to get a front-row seat at the monitor to watch the taping of the only other witness to Jimmy

Legere's death. Max sat calmly and composed at his attorney's side, while Junior gloated over the turn his case had taken.

"Not hiding behind Detective Caissie's skirts this time, Savoie?"

"I went a bit higher up the legal food chain." His gaze shifted to the camera for an instant. He knew she was there, watching. "I'm here voluntarily, Hammond, so play nice or I'm gone."

Taking him seriously, Hammond launched into his line of official questions. Each was answered completely in a low monotone that broke only slightly when he described the concluding events.

"Let me get this straight, Savoie. You were going to let the old guy take you out without a fight?"

"It was his life to take, detective. I don't expect you to understand."

Hammond looked dumbfounded, then shook his head. "You got that right. In his statement, Mr. Petitjohn said that he stepped in to keep Legere from shooting you in cold blood. That when he intervened, Legere turned on him with gun in hand. Fearing for his life and for yours, he had no recourse but to fire. Self-defense, or the gunning down of a helpless old guy in a wheelchair? What's your take on that, Savoie?"

"It happened very quickly. I heard the shot but I didn't see what occurred. It could have been that way. Jimmy was armed and determined, and he wouldn't have taken kindly to being interfered with.

There was nothing helpless about him. If Francis went cross-grained of him, he had every right to fear for his life. He would have been foolish not to."

"History repeating itself, and all. So this was a sort of falling out amongst thieves?"

"If you say so, detective."

"According to Petitjohn, you showed up yesterday morning after having been in a fight. The shirt you were wearing was covered in blood. Whose?"

"Mine."

"You don't look any worse for wear."

"I heal fast." A slight smile. "And she hits like a girl."

"She being Detective Charlotte Caissie?"

"That's right."

"And you were visiting Detective Caissie in her apartment on on the night of the twenty-third on official business?"

Another faint smile. "No. It was personal."

Hammond put his hand over the microphone, leaning forward man to man. "How was she?"

Max leaned in close. "You'll never know."

Hammond sat back, annoyed. "So you were in Detective Caissie's apartment for personal reasons when her partner, Detective Alain Babineau, called to inform her of the events at St. Bartholomew's?"

"Yes."

"And how did Detective Caissie react to that information?"

"She was very upset with me."

"Why was that, Mr. Savoie?"

"She thought I might have been involved."

"With the murder and the fire?"

"Yes."

"And why would she assume that?"

"I have no idea, detective."

"Really?"

"I was very fond of Sister Catherine. I had no reason to harm her."

"Did Jimmy Legere have a reason?"

"I don't know."

"Were you that reason, Mr. Savoie? You and your relationship with Detective Caissie?"

"I don't know."

"Wasn't that one of the things you argued about with Mr. Legere? He didn't like the fact that you were in a relationship with a policewoman?"

"He didn't like the idea of me keeping bad company."

"Why would he think that?"

"He thought Detective Caissie was only after information that might incriminate him."

"Was he right, Mr. Savoie?"

He never blinked. "Yes."

"So he assumed Detective Caissie was banging you to put him away?"

Nothing changed about Max's attitude or tone but suddenly he seemed to bristle. "You speak of Detective Caissie disrespectfully again and we're done here."

"I apologize."

"Don't apologize to me. Apologize to her."

"I will when I see her."

"Do it now."

Hammond hesitated, then swiveled toward the camera. "That was out of line. I apologize."

"Yes," Max continued in the same neutral tone. "That's what Jimmy assumed."

"And that upset him?"

"Very much so."

"So why not just whack her, if you'll pardon the expression? Why would he want *you* dead?"

"A trust issue."

Hammond chuckled. "I understand Mr. Legere was one who reacted with extreme prejudice if he thought trust had been compromised?"

"I don't know about that, detective."

"Right. You don't know that he killed his own cousin, Mr. Petitjohn's brother?"

"That was before I came to live with him."

"Mr. Petitjohn didn't elaborate on what other trust issues Mr. Legere might have had with you. Could you shed more light on that for me?"

"No, I'm afraid not. I don't know what he was thinking. He'd told me just before his death that he wasn't well, that he didn't think he had much longer to live."

"Do you think he might have been trying to hurry that along by having this confrontation with you? By attacking Mr. Petitjohn? A sort of assisted suicide?"

The dampness that welled up in his eyes was dispersed with a blink. He didn't wipe it off his immobile face. His voice was without inflection. "I don't know."

"Do you know of anyone else who might have a grudge against Sister Catherine or Benjamin Spratt?"

"Who?"

"The janitor who was murdered."

"I'd forgotten his name." Max's brow furrowed. "Both of them were killed?"

"Just Spratt."

"And Sister Catherine?" he whispered.

"She's critical in ICU, with burns and a bullet in her brain."

"She's alive." He looked disconcerted; then, with a blink, his expression blanked once more. "That's good. That's good to hear."

If Hammond were an astute investigator, he would have jumped all over Savoie's quiet surprise. Charlotte never would have let him back away without demanding an explanation. Why did he expect to hear different? What did he know about the attack on the church and its true target? Why had he been there earlier that evening talking with Mary Kate? On Legere's business, or his own?

But Hammond veered off onto another road altogether. "Mr. Savoie, do you know who Jimmy Legere passed his business interests to?"

Max looked him straight in the eye and said

flatly, "According to my attorney, he gave them to me."

Hammond stared, mouth unhinged.

Cee Cee had the same reaction.

Antoine D'Marco stood up. "I think Mr. Savoie has answered all your questions. If there's anything else, you can reach him through my office."

As the two made their way through the column of police who regarded them in a stunned silence, Cee Cee tried to approach, but D'Marco put himself between her and Max. His smile was cold and condescending. "Mr. Savoie has other matters to attend, detective. I'm sure you understand."

Matters involving the largest criminal empire along the Gulf Coast?

Why had he come to her if he knew he'd be stepping into Jimmy's shoes, where he'd quickly be over his head in everything she despised?

"Max?"

There was a slight hesitation in his stride. But he didn't stop and he didn't turn around.

And that's when she noticed his shoes. Black, glossy, and a perfect match to the suit.

Fifteen

THEY CONDUCTED BUSINESS informally in one of the double parlors. Max refused to go into Jimmy's office. He sat still and silent while Francis Petitjohn paced in agitation.

"Tony, this is ridiculous. He has no identity, no papers, nothing. And you're going to put him at the top of a multimillion-dollar business?"

"I'm not," Antoine D'Marco drawled softly. "Jimmy did. We discussed it quite frequently over the last few months. I have all the paperwork prepared: birth certificate, Social Security, voter's registration, etcetera. By tomorrow, Mr. Savoie will be a registered, tax-paying citizen in the state of Louisiana, on his way to becoming one of its richest men."

Petitjohn snorted. "A few pieces of paper won't change what he is and what he isn't. What he *isn't* is capable of handling things."

"I don't know, T-John. He handled himself with the police and with the press. And he has a better education than you or Jimmy."

"But he's not family. He's a nobody. He's a—"

"Thug in a silk tie," Max supplied.

"Exactly. No one is going to take orders from him. Vantour's people think he killed their boss."

"But we know differently, don't we, Francis?" Max interjected softly.

Petitjohn stared long and suspiciously at Max, but couldn't read anything on his stoic face. "Jimmy was fond of Max, that's true. But he wouldn't have given him control of our family business. Not if he was in his right mind. Tony, you *know* I'm right. It should go to me. That's the way it was supposed to be. Blood is blood, and Max is just hired muscle. Jimmy was about to put a bullet in his head."

"But you were faster, weren't you, Francis?" Max murmured. "In self-defense."

A slight flicker passed through Max's eyes, glowing hot and red, and Francis Petitjohn knew a sudden, sharp terror. He hurried on.

"I'll take care of Max. That's what Jimmy would have wanted. He'll always have a place here—but not in charge. He doesn't want that kind of responsibility. He has no experience in negotiating or diplomacy. No one's going to listen to anything he has to say."

"Jimmy thought they would," Antoine remarked as he shut his briefcase. "He had the utmost faith in Mr. Savoie."

"But he doesn't want it. Right, Max?"

Max was seeing Frankenstein's monster in that flaming windmill. "I haven't decided yet. Thank you for coming out, Mr. D'Marco, and for getting me through today."

"My pleasure, Mr. Savoie. You did very well. I've always thought Jimmy was right about you."

It took Max a moment to master speech. "I'll let Francis see you out. I'm going to go upstairs to change. My feet hurt."

He started from the room, the pinch of the new shoes not nearly as painful as the one about his heart. He'd reached the hall when Jasmine, the girl from the kitchen, approached him hesitantly.

"Mr. Savoie, there's a call for you."

"No calls, Jasmine."

"It's Charlotte."

He took a shaky breath. "No calls."

"Yes, sir." She paused and then lightly touched the back of his hand. Her voice was shy but sincere. "I'm very sorry for your loss, sir."

Swallowing with difficulty, he managed, "Thank you."

When she hurried off, he stood in the hall, head hanging, shoulders slumped, drowning in all the emotions he'd been struggling to suppress all day.

"Mr. Savoie?"

He looked up to see the two burly men he'd faced down over their game of cards with the threat of eating their eyeballs for breakfast. They looked uneasy, but not afraid.

"Me and Teddy," one of them began gruffly, "we wanted you to know how bad we feel about Mr.

Legere. If there's anything we can do for you, you just let us know."

"Thank you."

Their driver came in to let D'Marco know the car was ready. He paused on his way out, hat in hand. "Mr. Savoie, it was my pleasure taking care of Mr. Legere. I'd feel privileged to do the same for you."

"Thank you, Pete."

One by one, as D'Marco and Petitjohn watched from the parlor, Jimmy Legere's people approached Max Savoie. He responded to their condolences with a quiet thank you. None extended the same courtesy to Jimmy's cousin. After the last of them paid their respects, a weary and mystified Max went upstairs.

"I guess that answers that," D'Marco said, his smile small and satisfied.

Francis Petitjohn scowled after the retreating figure. Time to rethink his strategy.

His room was dark and cool and so very empty. Max levered out of the tight leather shoes and flexed his toes. He'd taken three steps when he jerked up sharply to sniff the air.

Voodoo Love.

Charlotte had been in his room.

Of course—she'd come with the police investigating Jimmy's death. But the knowledge that she'd stood where he was standing acted strangely upon him, making him restless, anxious, angry. And alone.

"Mr. Savoie, Detective Caissie is here."

"Yes," he said without thinking. She was. Then he turned in surprise to face one of the older house-keepers. "You said she's here?"

"Downstairs. Shall I show her into the parlor?"

Anticipation jumped before he grabbed onto it. "No. Extend my regrets to the detective. Tell her that on the advice of my attorney, I won't be entertaining any private interviews with the police." He could hear her voice: *You're a coward, Savoie.* Yes—in this, he was.

He paced his ample room, half expecting her to burst in with irritation to demand that he speak with her. His brush-off would make her furious and he smiled a bit, imagining how that flare of temper would flash in her eyes.

But she didn't come up. And after a minute or two, he heard the gears grind in her little sports car as she tore down the drive. He didn't go to the balcony to watch her pull away.

"Mr. Savoie?"

"Yes, Helen?"

"Detective Caissie left this for you. She said the rest had to be entered into evidence. She said you'd understand."

He took the plastic grocery bag from her. "Thank you, Helen."

He waited until he was alone to open the sack, which contained one thing.

His red shoes.

———

HE WOULDN'T TAKE her calls and he wouldn't see her. But she saw him everywhere. On the television, in the newspapers, one of which proclaimed, *Mob boss killed in quarrel over employee's affair with policewoman.* She was called in and questioned and gave a terse version of her involvement with Max Savoie. She laid it out as cold and concise as the look in Max's eyes when last she saw him. They'd had an intimate relationship while she was investigating Jimmy Legere. She'd asked questions. He'd given her no answers. They no longer saw each other now that Legere was dead. Case closed. At least on paper.

JIMMY LEGERE WAS buried with full media attention and overflowing attendance. It was tabloid fodder. Francis Petitjohn took center stage as his grieving, murderous cousin, with a silent and emotionless Max Savoie standing sentinel. Cee Cee watched from a distance, wishing there was some way to extend her support. But it was too late for that. Too late.

At the cemetery, a long line of criminal dignitaries filed by to shake Petitjohn's hand and give Savoie the once-over, wondering who they'd be dealing with once the obligatory mourning was done and the crypt was sealed.

She heard Max inhale sharply when his gaze turned from the person ahead of her to fix on hers. He didn't take her hand or show any reaction to her whisper of his name. He held himself rigid as she leaned into him, one hand cupping one side of his face as she touched her lips to the other. Longing hit her so hard and fast, she couldn't tear herself away until he finally spoke in a low, flat-toned voice.

"Step back, detective. There's no need for dramatics."

She put distance between them, not expecting the fierceness beneath his blank mask. "Max, I need to talk to you."

"Why, detective? You used me to get to him, and now he's dead. Job well done. Move on." He turned to the next person in line, forcing her on to stand in front of Francis Petitjohn.

She told him, "If you harm him in any way, it'll be your funeral next."

Petitjohn smirked at her. "Always a pleasure, Detective Caissie."

FOUR HOURS LATER, she stood at Benjamin Spratt's graveside, this time without the fanfare or the crowds. She listened to Father Furness speak of the loss of a simple servant loved by God with her head bowed, her tears falling unashamedly. Warm fingers slipped between her cold ones. Thinking it was Babineau she opened her eyes, then stared at the pair of red shoes next to hers.

She couldn't look up at him. She didn't dare. Instead she angled slightly, her arm curving about his waist beneath his open coat. He drew her in close, letting her wet his shirt front with her grief, saying nothing since words weren't what she needed.

When the service was over, she wanted nothing more than to linger against his solid strength. When she felt him press a good-bye kiss to her temple, she resisted the urge to hang onto him with tight desperation. She rubbed her cheek against him to dry it, then eased away, never looking up.

"Thank you."

His fingertips brushed beneath her jaw, and he was gone.

As she squared her shoulders and stood straight, she looked across the plain casket to see Dolores Gautreaux with her baby in her arms.

Later, with the squad room empty of all but the watch commander, she sat at her desk and emptied the pouch containing Benjamin's effects. Not much had survived the fire. The remains of a cheap watch, the keys to the church. And the ring she remembered seeing on his hand.

She picked it up, surprised by its weight. A little coaxing from a tissue restored the fiery brilliance of the stone. A ruby; she'd bet her next paycheck on it. Where would Spratt, who was practically homeless, come up with such an impressive piece of flash?

She set the ring down to study Dovion's report. A professional hit; two taps to the back of the head. As if Ben had been the target, not Mary Kate. As if she'd been struck down after surprising the assassin. Benjamin Spratt's body was found kneeling before the remains of the altar. Mary Kate was in her quarters with the door shut. A single shot to the temple had rendered her unconscious as flames devoured the church.

"What's wrong with this picture?" she whispered.

She read through the report again, identifying what was bothering her: the insinuation that Mary Kate was an afterthought. The casual investigator would, and did, agree with everything the way it was laid out in the report.

But that investigator hadn't grown up in St. Bart's. That investigator wouldn't know that with the sanctuary doors and Mary Kate's door closed, the way they were every evening when Benjamin was cleaning, she couldn't have heard anything going on. She would have been in her quarters, exactly where they found her, not wandering about, surprising a killer in his work. If the shooter was going after Spratt alone, he would have had no reason to seek her out and shoot her down. The timing was wrong.

Then she looked at it another way. Mary Kate first, then Benjamin Spratt. But why Ben? To throw off suspicion? But then, why not make it look like an accident? Mary Kate falling while overcome by smoke, hitting her head, perishing in the fire?

Someone went to a lot of trouble to set up this elaborate front to cover up what should have been simple.

Mary Kate knew they were coming for her. She'd

taken the time to clear the shelter area, sending the women and children to the Gospel Mission under the pretext of a suspected gas leak. But there was no problem with the gas, according to preliminary reports.

Benjamin had taken the women and children to the mission. Then he'd returned, perhaps against her instructions. She'd wanted to be alone with her God and her memories when Legere's man came to finish what Max had started.

But why kill Benjamin?

She, Mary Kate, and Max. One, both, or all three. Who had Legere meant to dispose of?

Or was someone *else* pulling the strings?

Cee Cee leaned back in her chair, rubbing her eyes. Max didn't know. She believed what he'd said in his statement, or at least what he'd put on record. But he *had* gone to St. Bart's. To threaten Mary Kate, to kill her, or warn her? Mary Kate might never be able to tell her tale. Cee Cee took a deep breath to stave off the sorrow.

Dammit, what was she missing?

Max, Mary Kate, and Legere. Were they the only main players, or were more people involved? Maybe she was making it too simple. Maybe that's what someone was counting on.

Sighing, she looked back at her files, expanding her focus to encompass factors outside the microcosm on River Road. The deaths of Gautreaux and Surette: Those were no mystery to her anymore. The disappearance of Victor Vantour: There was an avenue to explore. The docks were always a site of friction. Control the docks: control the city. That's what her father had said. She remembered Max's muddy boots the morning she'd paid a visit to Legere. Had Max been planting evidence in the ever-popular bayou graveyard? Legere had to know he'd be the prime suspect. Would he have been so bold as to openly start a war?

She came across a magazine photo of Legere and Vantour posing on the site of a riverfront reclamation project. Their staunch opposition had been news for months, as they fended off those who would leach civic progress into their tightly held territories. Legere in his wheelchair, Vantour behind him, hands resting easy on Jimmy's thin shoulders . . . wearing what looked like a huge ruby ring.

"Sonuvabitch."

THE BURN UNIT was chilly and emotionlessly antiseptic. With the risk of infection so great, she wasn't allowed in Mary Kate's room. She watched her nearly mummified friend through glistening eyes as she listened to the doctor.

"We've done all we can for her here. Arrangements are being made to fly her to a center in California. They specialize in the kind of intensive care she needs for both the head trauma and the burns."

"She doesn't have any insurance. Who's going to pay for it?" Cee Cee knew St. Bart's didn't have the resources, and doubted that the state would be that generous.

"It's all been taken care of, detective."

Her attention sharpened. "By whom?"

"By a party who asked to remain anonymous."

She knew immediately: Max. Somehow he'd arranged to get around probate to use Legere's fortune. What irony—Jimmy most likely wanting her dead, and Max using his money to keep her alive.

She looked back into that stark, colorless room where tubes and machines worked busily. "Is she in pain?" Her voice hitched slightly.

"We try to keep her as comfortable as possible."

Which meant yes. She clenched her hands to keep them from trembling. "How long a recovery will she have?"

A pause.

"It's a very long, very arduous process, Ms. Caissie. Debridement of damaged tissue, grafting, physical therapy. She's been drifting in and out of a comatose state. At this point, we have no way of gauging her cognitive function. Nothing's going to happen quickly unless she takes a turn for the worse."

"Years," she summed up quietly. "When can I see her? Talk to her?"

"Someone from the Center will contact you when she reaches that point."

If she reached that point. "I would appreciate that."

She turned and found herself face-to-face with Dolores Gautreaux.

"I came to pay my respects," the slender woman murmured. "I owe the sister everything."

Cee Cee gave her an assessing sweep. She was a strawberry blonde with deep blue eyes. That surprised Cee Cee, for the woman she remembered seemed so colorless. With the bruising gone and a little makeup, Dolores Gautreaux was pleasantly attractive. It would seem the death of her husband not only saved her life but also breathed it back into her body.

"Dolores, can I buy you a cup of coffee?"

ACROSS A SMALL square table, over harsh coffee in the crowded hospital cafeteria, Cee Cee laid her cards out.

"Dolores, I'm about to lose the two people who mean the most to me in this world, and it all started with you. I'm not here as a cop. I'm speaking to you as the best friend of that woman suffering for imagined sins, and on behalf of the man who lost everything to set you free. I think you owe me and them an explanation."

Very quietly, Dolores asked, "What do you want to know?"

"Whose idea was it to kill your husband and his pal?"

"Mine." Softer still.

"And you went to Sister Catherine with that

request. Why would you do that? Why would you think a nun could arrange a hit for you?"

Hands twisted about the foam coffee cup. "The sister and I talked about it last time I was there. I told her I wished he were dead, and she told me to be very, very sure I meant that."

"And?"

Haunted eyes lifted. "I wasn't sure. He was so good to me when I came home, buying gifts for me and the baby, fixing things around the house. But I knew it wouldn't last. So I told him if things got bad again, I would take my case before my people."

"Your people?"

Her gaze grew evasive. "My clan. Those I left when I married."

"Your family?" Cee Cee asked carefully.

Her stare drilled into Cee Cee's, and her answer answered everything. "No. My kind."

"MAX, A WORD with you before you go meet with D'Marco."

Francis Petitjohn was sitting behind Jimmy's desk, sorting through papers. The sight tightened around Max's belly like razor wire. He stepped just inside the room and waited to hear what Petitjohn had to say.

"We need to come to a decision between the two of us. Better now than later."

"All right."

"You and I haven't always gotten along well, have we?"

Max didn't answer. There was no need to.

"It's time to put all that aside. If we're going to hold everything together, we're going to need to work together starting right now."

"How?"

"We both bring different things to the table, Max. Important things. I have my family's name and the respect it carries. I'm a familiar face. The others know me. They'll work with me.

"But I don't kid myself. I've never had the kind of power and authority Jimmy had. The kind of strength to control the rest of them. I'm smart enough, but I've never managed to earn their trust or their fear.

"But you have, Max. You've always been the power behind Jimmy's words. If he said them, no one doubted you would carry them out. That could work for us, too."

"How?"

"We'd be partners. I do the talking, you do the enforcing. It's what they're used to, and it won't spook them. They're scared of you and the way you do things, so they'd be more likely to take you out than learn how to work with you. They know you're different, and they fear different.

"I can be a buffer between you and them, the same way Jimmy was. Your secret would be safe, and I'd be strong. What do you think, Max? Deal?"

Max studied the man behind the desk, seeing shades of Jimmy Legere in his features and gestures. Hearing him in his voice. Comforted by the similar scent that blended with Jimmy's here in this room where he'd been raised and loved. That familiarity triggered a stirring of anguished loneliness.

Stronger still was the restlessness—the yearning for someone to follow, somewhere to belong. Surrendering control to Francis Petitjohn would be easy. It was what he knew, what he understood. He could serve and be safe. Purpose and direction would soothe the aching emptiness and panic shadowing his every step. All he had to do was place himself in Petitjohn's hands.

He saw again that hand reaching down to him to offer rescue; he felt the massive relief that came with taking it. It was what he'd been trained to do, to passively accept the commands of one voice. He'd never chafed within that yoke before. Why did he find it so difficult now?

In his thirtysome years, he'd instinctively trusted two humans—Jimmy Legere, upon taking his hand, and Charlotte Caissie, upon tasting her lips—and both had twisted that trust to their own advantage. Maybe it was time to set instinct aside in favor of intellect. The words *equal in all ways* returned to mind.

"So," he drawled slowly, "the next time someone decides to shoot me down on the steps of a church, you'll be there to protect me, is that it?"

To his vast surprise, Petitjohn didn't jump to deny it. "That was Vantour. He wanted you out of the way. He was getting disenchanted with Jimmy."

"And you know this how?"

"Vic and I were in unofficial negotiations." He put up his hand to stop Max's aggressive step forward. "Jimmy asked me to do a little test of his loyalty. He failed."

"So you killed him."

Petitjohn never so much as blinked. "I thought you did."

Uneasiness rippled through Max. "Did you tell Vantour how to bring me down?"

"No. I only found out about it after the fact. When you didn't mention it to Jimmy, I just assumed you took care of things yourself."

Petitjohn held his stare without a flinch. He could have been telling the truth, or it could be yet another lie.

"Max, we need to stand together on this. Agreed?"

A long silence, then, "I'll talk to D'Marco."

A slow smile. "All right, Max. You do that." Then his gaze chilled. "There are some other matters that need to be dealt with."

"Such as?"

"You have a weakness, Max, a secret that could destroy you. That could destroy us."

Max went very still.

"The good news is only a couple of us know it. The bad news is one of them is a police detective."

Max's expression grew as smooth as ice. "She's not going to say anything."

"I'm so happy to hear you have that kind of faith in her. But I don't. And none of the rest of those who depend on you will either. Jimmy let it go for far too long. He knew what had to be done, but he was too soft on you to take care of it.

"I'm not going to do anything about it yet, Max. I'm going to leave that up to you. You want to help run things, you have to be able to make those choices. You take care of her now, or someone else is going to later. And if someone else does it they're not going to be gentle about it, the way they were with her and her friend the last time I ordered it."

Max went cold.

"She's not going to just walk away with a broken arm and a concussion," Francis continued. "Do you understand, Max?"

"Oh, yes." He was beginning to understand a lot.

MAX MET ANTOINE D'MARCO at a small sidewalk café where the immaculate attorney was sipping white wine and slurping oysters off the shell.

"Ah, Mr. Savoie, join me for some lunch."

"No, thank you. I don't drink and I'm not partial to seafood." His nose crinkled up at the odor as he took a seat.

"Something more to your taste, then? Perhaps some steak tartar."

Raw meat. Max regarded him unblinkingly. "What did Jimmy tell you?"

"Everything. There were no secrets between us.

And yours is safe with me." He extended an oyster. "Are you sure? It's quite delicate."

Max reared back, the odor of shellfish stirring unpleasant associations. "No. Thank you."

A dainty slurp and a sigh. "Suit yourself. Now then, Max, I need to know what you plan to do with what Jimmy's left you."

He eyed the prissy lawyer cautiously but found nothing to alarm him. His flamboyant marigold-colored suit, fluffy handkerchief, and perfect hair suggested an effeminate softness, but Max had seen his eyes go cold and dark like a swamp gator's when he latched on to an opponent and executed a purposeful death roll. Jimmy had always surrounded himself with the best his money could buy, then made sure they understood that failure was not an option. Not ever. Jimmy's faith was good enough for Max, and he laid out the discussion with Petitjohn with quick precision.

"And are you inclined to accept this offer of partnership?" The attorney didn't reveal any of his own opinions.

"No. I'm not so inclined. He killed Jimmy, after the situation he forced us into didn't push me into doing it for him. I'd be a fool to trust him and I'm not a fool."

"I didn't think you were, but I wasn't positive until now. You want to take it all, then? Jimmy wanted you to. He trusted you to. Let's finalize the paperwork."

Max sat back, his expression contemplative. "Not just yet. I need to think something out first. I can't take it until I'm sure Francis doesn't have any control over me. Jimmy's final mistake was thinking Francis harmless. It won't be mine."

"I like you, Max. I'm going to like doing business for you."

Max hoped the lawyer's confidence wasn't misplaced as he trudged down the street, hoping some idea would surface. What came up instead, screeching almost onto the sidewalk, was a little sports car.

"Get in."

Charlotte Caissie was behind the wheel, wearing oversized sunglasses and a colorful scarf over her hair. When Max hesitated, she set her service revolver down on the shifter column.

"Get in the car, Savoie. Now."

Without a word, Max hopped over the door to drop into the passenger seat. He grabbed on when her double clutching practically threw him into the dash.

Cee Cee drove fast, weaving around traffic with a desperate recklessness that had her passenger whiteknuckling the edge of his seat. She kept her eyes on the road, but the rest of her was humming with awareness of him. He was wearing the gray suit and blue striped shirt he'd worn on their first disastrous date. An omen? And he had on those polished shoes she abhorred. She snuck a glance and her pulse shuddered like the little car's transmission.

He was staring straight ahead, jaw set, eyes narrowed slightly against the cut of the breeze. Finally he glanced at her, annoyance betraying itself in his tone.

"Are you abducting me, detective?"

"There was a time when it would have excited you to no end to think so."

He didn't smile. "I have places to be. People will be looking for me."

"Yes. You are so very important these days, aren't you? Since you always seem to be so busy, I thought I'd remove you from distraction so we can have that conversation."

"I don't believe we have anything to say to each other, detective."

"I believe you are wrong, Savoie."

She hadn't known it was possible to ache for someone the way she ached for Max. Not the coolly elegant heir to Jimmy Legere's legacy, who wore shiny shoes and took meetings in private rooms. But the aggravating, overly attentive, and ever smoldering Max with his leather coat and red sneakers, who could suck up her common sense with his kisses and conquer her night terrors.

She never slept now. The dreams were back, crouched in the shadows waiting for her eyes to close. Horrible, dark visions from which she awoke screaming.

They spun out of the city, away from the crowds and the noise and the witnesses, and out onto quiet, shaded lanes. She abruptly pulled off down a narrow two track and stopped the car, then threw her sunglasses onto the dash to glare at him in worry-fueled fury.

"What are you doing, Max?"

"About what, detective?"

"What game are you playing with your shiny shoes and snotty attitude? Why are you trotting behind that little weasel Petitjohn? Jimmy Legere at least had class."

"Don't talk to me about Jimmy."

"Why? Afraid you won't like what you hear? That he was a bully and a thief and a murderer and a liar? That he used you and would have thrown you away like an old pair of shoes because you stood up and said no to something you knew wasn't right?"

He grabbed her forearms, the movement so quick, so violent, she cried out as he jerked her up to him. "Don't tell me what Jimmy Legere was. Don't you dare. Not unless you want to talk about how *you* used me. How you got me all hot and bothered just to provoke Jimmy, to become a wedge between us and make him mistrust me. He was going to put a bullet in my head, detective. He was going to kill me because I couldn't convince him that I hadn't betrayed him to you. Does that excite you? You have stripped me naked, literally and figuratively, for your own amusement. You've ripped the heart from my world, the safety from my soul. Why? Because I was foolish enough to want to protect you? Because I stopped, when I could have just kept walking?"

She yanked away from him, falling against the door. Breath tore from him in harsh rips of sound over a low, rumbling growl. His eyes gleamed a fierce hot gold, then swam blood red.

Suddenly she feared she'd made a huge, possibly fatal miscalculation.

She grabbed for her gun but he caught her forearm with a hand that wasn't a hand any longer. When she pulled back, his elongated nails sliced through her flesh nearly to the bone. Pain and terror grabbed her by the throat, and she fought for her life.

Punching, slapping, struggling, she finally got the door open, falling out onto the loose gravel on hands and knees. She caught a blur of motion as he went up and over the car.

She propelled herself forward, running hard until he grabbed the back of her shirt. The fabric ripped at the shoulders. She planted her feet and came around swinging with a roar of pent-up rage and fear, but he caught her wrists. Trying to pull free, she sent them both tumbling to the ground. He fell across her, his weight driving the breath from her lungs and the courage from her heart. Her shriek was caught by his sudden hard kiss.

The taste of her, the scent of her, the furious beat of her heart against him had his adrenalin spiking in a wild, intoxicating rush. Excitement was pumped by the chase, by the challenge of her strength, and the need to have her, to claim her, to love her in the dirt, on the side of the road controlled him.

She was wearing a short leather skirt. His hand shook as he stroked the firm curve of her thigh. Her underwear was a little scrap of nothing, no barrier as it came away with a quick tug. It was damp. He tore open his trousers, kneeing between her long legs. Her balled hands were braced against his shoulders, the gesture denying. Her face turned away from the hot, heavy scorch of his breath.

"Tell me you want me," he demanded, his voice raw with the effort of holding back, even for the second it took for her to look up at him through eyes filled with angry distress and desire. For her hands to unfist, then clutch with need.

For her to whisper, as if in agony, "I want you."

He drove inside her, over and over, lost to the hard fist of lust that finally softened into something else after he'd emptied into her. Then, when he was wonderfully weak and tenderness pooled, he turned to her to share those gentler emotions. But there were tears on her face, and fire in her eyes.

"Get off me." When he was slow to respond, the sharp snap of her voice deepened into a more panicked rumble. "Get off!"

He backed up, crouching on the balls of his feet as she struggled to drag some dignity into the wanton sprawl of her position. Her blouse was torn, her knuckles and knees scraped, her arm bleeding. But it was the caution behind her fierce stare that put a scare into him. And he was suddenly filled with frustrated anger that she could so easily reduce him to the beast within him.

"I didn't mean to frighten you." His apology was as stiff as his expression.

She started to deny it, but the shaking of her hands as she tried to close her tattered shirt betrayed her. She sat up slowly, scooching farther away from him. They stared at each other for a tense minute, breathing hard.

"For a minute, I thought Petitjohn had convinced you to kill me," she confessed.

She expected him to laugh off that fear, but his reply was brutally candid.

"He did."

Sixteen

SHE STIFFENED IN fear when he moved beside her, but it was only to examine the tears in her arm. His expression was distant as he used her scarf to crudely bind the wounds. Because she was shivering, he pulled off his jacket and draped it about her shoulders. The heat and scent of him lingered in its folds, oddly calming her despite his words.

While she watched from her defensive huddle, he made a brief phone call in a voice too low for her to hear. She gauged the distance to her car while his back was to her, the muscles in her legs bunching.

"Don't."

She froze at his soft warning.

"As much as I'd enjoy chasing you, I don't think you have the strength to make it a real race."

"Sorry to disappoint you," she snapped. "I'm afraid I'm not much of a challenge."

"Oh, I wouldn't say that, detective."

He kept his distance, just watching her.

"Are you going to do it here?" She made her tone hard, provoking.

He smiled. "We just finished doing it here."

"I didn't mean that."

"I know you didn't." Layer upon layer of complexity wrapped about that short statement. "Did you think I was going to step over there and tear out your heart? The way you did mine? The suspense must be killing you."

He was angry and hurt, but that's all she could tell from his odd, distracted mood. He might have infinite patience, but she hated to wait.

"Just do what you have to do."

He regarded her unblinkingly. "I am."

"What are you waiting for? My permission?"

She said it to goad him, to spark some sort of response off his flinty surface so she could prepare. So he wouldn't know how afraid she was of him and of what he was capable.

But he knew her bravery was a pretense and withdrew to an even chillier plane.

"Don't be an idiot, detective. I'm not going to harm you. I just need you out of the way for a while."

Her huge relief couldn't quite overcome her suspicion. "Why?

"So I can take care of things."

"What things? What are you up to, Max?"

"Nothing I feel compelled to share with the police."

He couldn't have stated it more clearly: She no longer held a position of confidence. She was one of the opposition. And while he might still want to take from her physically, there was nothing he was willing to give on any other level. She fought back uncharacteristic tears.

She was worried about him. Jimmy Legere had at least cared for Max and kept him out of harm's way as much as possible. She remembered what Max had said about being on a chain and the comfort of knowing those limitations. He was off the leash now, paralyzed by his freedom and not sure which way to run. If he wouldn't come to her, where would he go? And with him, the power Legere left behind?

He hadn't called her by her name since leaving her apartment.

There was no trust in his stare anymore, no naivete when it came to his affections. He believed she'd only been using him. He wasn't totally wrong. But he wasn't totally right, either.

Legere's big town car pulled up on the side of the road and sat there idling. Before she could get up, Max bent to scoop her into his arms. His hold was tight enough to convince her not to squirm. As he walked to the car, she looked back at what they were leaving behind. Her car with the driver's door open, her blood splashed on the interior. Her purse, her gun. Evidence of a struggle there and on the grass. Her DNA on the torn panties. And no sign of her footsteps leaving.

She had just become a missing and presumed dead statistic.

If the driver was surprised to see his new boss

carrying a battered policewoman in his arms, he didn't express it. He held the rear door open as Max said, "Home. Ring up Dr. Curry, Pete, and have him meet us there. Discreetly."

"Yes, sir, Mr. Savoie."

The interior of the car was almost too cool after the steamy late-day heat. Max slid into the center of the wide seat with her in his lap, holding her firmly but carefully, almost impersonally. One hand held her head to his chest, the other curved behind her knees, keeping her close but doing nothing to comfort or alarm her.

As the big car moved smoothly onto the road, the full weight of her exhaustion settled in. The sleepless nights, the sorrow, the nightmares, the worry, all gnawing away at her ability to rest until she was one knotted nerve. She rode the slow rock of his breathing, feeling the strong, mesmerizing beat of his heart, letting the warmth of his embrace seep into her like a soothing balm. She took a breath and released it slowly, letting go of the tension along with it. This was where she'd longed to be: wrapped in his powerful arms, floating on his tantalizing scent, safe in the care of the most dangerous being alive. Pulling his coat more closely about her, she nestled her cheek into his shirt and, on a sigh, was asleep.

EYEBROWS ROSE AMONG the house staff when Max strode up the front steps carrying an unconscious woman. Most of them knew who she was. Every time she'd left before, Jimmy would curse her name for hours. Some of them were aware that she'd been a point of contention between Jimmy and Max. But none of them had ever seen the aggressive side of Max as he snapped out concise orders.

"Send the doctor up to my room when he gets here. Giles, collect every one of the camera tapes. I want nothing of our arrival on record."

"Yes, sir, Mr. Savoie," the bulky Giles murmured, remembering the threat about his eyeballs being devoured on toast.

"As far as anyone here knows, I've just returned from visiting with my attorney in the city and I am alone."

"Yes, sir. I didn't see anything."

"If Petitjohn shows up, put him in the parlor and come get me at once."

"Yes, sir. Happy to do it for you."

Max paused, giving the man a closer look. "Don't let the eyeball remark concern you. I rarely eat breakfast."

A weak smile. "Yes, sir. Never gave it a second thought."

Max carried Cee Cee upstairs. The moment he laid her down on his bed, the cavernous space in which he'd spent nearly thirty indifferent years became a warm, intimate surrounding. Because she was in it.

She made a small sound and nestled into his covers in a way that tightened everything inside him.

He reached out to touch her hair, but held back. She seemed so fragile, with the dark bruising of weariness beneath her eyes. So he sat on the floor, his back against the bed, content just listening to her breathe.

She was safe. For the moment, she was safe. But he didn't kid himself. As much as he disliked Francis Petitjohn, he couldn't argue with his logic in this instance. Charlotte Caissie would be seen as a liability and as leverage. If he went forward in Jimmy's place, anyone close to him would be in danger. He'd be compromising her safety; she'd be jeopardizing her job. And those were things neither of them were willing to negotiate on.

So where did that leave them?

With no future.

That's what Jimmy had been trying to tell him. What he did, what he was, wasn't compatible with this woman.

He'd been so careful all his life to stay protected, to keep himself from being vulnerable to anything and anyone. And here he was, his emotions on display, before the one person who could truly hurt him. He had no defenses. He couldn't harm her, he couldn't help her, he couldn't stay away. The only common ground they had was sex, and while that was marvelous for them both it wasn't enough. Because he liked her—he always looked forward to her conversation, to the clever turnings of her mind, to the way she looked at him as if he were . . . normal.

Her hand touched the back of his head, startling

him from his thoughts. For an instant he froze like her little furry pets, the heartbeats hurrying in his chest.

Her unexpected touch was like everything about her. So simple, so straightforward, yet stirring up a chaos of reactions he didn't know how to deal with. Just from the brush of her fingertips through the hair at his nape.

He leaned his head back into her palm, his eyes closing. And he found himself talking, because he hadn't had anyone to talk to. He'd actually never had anyone to talk to but her, and there were things inside him that needed to be said, whether she wanted to hear them or not.

"I don't know what to do, *sha*. They're looking to me to tell them, and I can't abandon them. I can't leave them to T-John. I'm a coward—I'm not a leader. I don't know what they expect from me."

He turned his head to look at her and couldn't look away. She was lying on her side, scuffed and bruised and worn, and so beautiful.

"Step up, Savoie," she told him with more scold than sympathy. "They expect you to take care of them. To do the right thing by them. To be worthy of their trust."

His sigh wavered. "I never thought I'd be responsible for anyone, and now I've got all this. I'm going to lose it if I can't think of a way to hang on tight. Vic Vantour is dead."

"I kinda figured as much."

"I didn't kill him, but someone went through a lot of trouble to make it seem like I did." He paused, his brow puckering. "Someone who knew about the thumbs."

"What?"

"Mr. Savoie?" Giles stood awkwardly at the door. "Dr. Curry is here."

"Show him up." He gave an easy hop to his feet, seeing Giles step back as if something dangerous had reared up in front of him. Max crossed to the door and, with a flush of embarrassment heating his face, said quietly, "Giles, see if you can come up with a pair of ladies underwear for my guest."

Giles blinked, then cleared his throat in what sounded suspiciously like a laugh. "Yes, sir. I've been looking for an excuse to charm Jasmine out of her panties. And don't worry, sir. I'll be discreet."

Max glared at the big man, pitching his voice low and menacing. "You find something amusing?"

"No, sir. I wouldn't dare." But a small, contrary smile twitched about his lips until Max muttered, "Thank you, Giles."

Stuart Curry had lost his medical license due to operating while under the influence. After that, he developed a lucrative practice with clients who couldn't afford to go through regular channels for treatment. He was a round, gaudily dressed man with a bad combover and more gold hanging off him than the average rap star. He charged a small fortune and never asked questions.

"Max, sorry to hear about Jimmy."

"Thank you."

Cee Cee perched on the edge of the bed as the doctor's close-set eyes skimmed over her. As he set his case on the side table, he asked quietly, "Are you all right, my dear?"

She glanced at Max, who remained by the door, wearing his inscrutable face. "Yes. We had an accident with my car and I've cut my arm."

"If you say so. Let me see."

Four groves ran from her elbow over the swell of her forearm. There was no mistaking them for anything other than claw marks.

"I'll have to do some needlework or you'll have a good deal of scarring."

"Go ahead."

She sat unflinching while he ran neat seams. It wasn't the first time she'd been stitched up, and it probably wouldn't be the last. She was aware of Max's scrutiny but didn't look up at him. When she made an involuntary sound as the needle took a bit too much meat, he went to stand out on the balcony.

Bandaged and dosed with antibiotics, Cee Cee left the bottle of pain pills on the nightstand and went to join Max after Curry departed.

"He left his bill. Extortion, if you ask me. Do you want me to turn it in to my insurance?"

"I'll take care of it."

She leaned against the frame of the French doors. Her arm ached dully and her palms and knees stung.

But the worst pain came from his refusal to look at her.

"I'm sorry," he said at last. "I never meant to frighten you or hurt you. I had no right to . . . touch you."

"I overreacted."

"This isn't your fault," he bit out fiercely. "None of this has been your fault. I walked away. I just left you and your friend, knowing what they were going to do. Now I'm no different than they were, taking what wasn't offered to me."

"Would you have stopped if I asked you to?"

"Yes."

"Then don't *ever* say anything that stupid again."

When Max finally spoke, his voice was deep and raw. "I keep thinking about those hours, and everything that I could have kept from happening. I go over and over it in my mind. I tried to make it not my problem, to not matter. But I couldn't."

"The worst had already happened, Max. I doesn't matter."

"Of course it matters!" He shoved his fingers through his hair, clenching it tight. "Every *second* mattered. Every second that I did nothing. I can never be forgiven for that."

"Is that what you asked Mary Kate to pray for? For God to forgive you?"

"No." He turned. His eyes glittered in the failing light. "I asked for you to forgive me." A pause.

"Don't tell me that you do, because I know that's not true."

"Why did you bring me here, Max? To keep me safe if your world goes to war?"

He didn't answer, looking away.

"Max, my job is dangerous. It's what I do. I'm not going to hide from it here. You'd lose all respect for me if I did."

"I'll take that risk," he said grimly.

"No, you won't. I won't let you. Tell me what's going on—off the record. Talk to me, Max."

His relief at finally releasing the tension was so great, the words spilled out in a rush. "Petitjohn wants a partnership. He doesn't think Vantour's people will trust me alone." As he filled her in on the rest that he could tell her, she listened and processed the information in her clever cop brain.

"And you trust Petitjohn?" she asked.

He shot her a frown. "Of course not. He killed Jimmy. And I'm pretty sure he killed Vantour to frame me, after the arrangement for someone to shoot me at the church failed. And he wants you dead."

"Well, I'm not about to oblige him."

"He wants me to do it, or else he'll have someone else take care of you. So let's let him think I took care of it. For a while, at least."

"And then what? Max, he's a dangerous man."

"So am I." His eyes glowed.

She stayed silent, seeing him transform into

something more deadly than a beast, something more beyond her control: a thug in a silk tie.

"You don't have to become Jimmy in order to honor what he wanted for you," she said quietly.

He looked startled, then turned away again. "I don't know what you mean."

She studied his bold, angular profile. Of course he knew; he just didn't want to deal with it. Well, too bad for him. He'd brought her here as his quasi-prisoner, so he could damn well listen to her. "If you pick up where he left off, you and I will have to go toe-to-toe. Maybe not right away, but someday. You know that. Then I'll have to do something about you, before you do something about me."

"It doesn't have to be that way, detective."

"Yes, it does. You know it does."

"I would never let anything happen to you."

Her silence mocked the forcefulness of his vow.

"I'm not Jimmy Legere. I'm nothing like him," he swore.

She didn't respond.

"He had my mother killed." Horror quivered in his voice. "He killed her so he could take me and use me to control the docks, the same way his father did by using one of my kind. My *kind*. I don't even know what that means."

"I think I do."

Max's gaze was glittery, anxious, and vulnerable. "Tell me."

"That's one of the reasons I came looking for you. I spoke to Dolores Gautreaux."

He shook his head slightly; the name meaning nothing.

"I was wearing her brutish husband on my new boots."

"Ah."

"She didn't know who you were, either. But she knew *what* you were. She told me you were one of her kind. That's why she felt justified in calling on you to take care of her situation.

"I want you to go someplace with me, Max. No questions; just trust me. Can you do that? Will you do that?"

He stared into her eyes for a long moment. "Yes."

"We're going to a club in the French Quarter. You're overdressed, and I'm underdressed. I'm going to clean up and then we'll go."

"Like a date?"

She smiled. "If you want to call it that."

He watched her walk across his bedroom, admiring her no-nonsense stride.

Trust me. How easily she said that. How quickly he'd agreed. Jimmy would have called him a fool, and perhaps he'd be right. But if he had to place himself in someone's hands, he'd rather it be hers than Francis Petitjohn's.

She went into his bathroom and closed the door, then he heard the shower turn on. He stood for a long moment, thinking of her hands on her wet body, of her standing naked under the spray. A tap at his door tore him from the direction of his thoughts, making him testy when he glowered at Giles in the hallway.

"Here you go. Jasmine probably would have preferred you to ask her for them yourself."

Max took the small bundle of nylon, then grinned. "Yeah? Well, my girl wouldn't have liked that. That's an extra problem I don't need. Thank you, Giles."

"No problem, boss man."

Max stood in the doorway, bemused. Boss man. Apparently they had an easier time accepting him in the role than he had in taking it. *Step up, Savoie.* Still perplexed, he pulled a white silk shirt from his closet and carefully opened the bathroom door. Steam billowed out, along with the scent of Charlotte Caissie.

What are you waiting for? My permission?

Yes, he was. Because no one else had.

He hung the two garments on the inside of the knob and backed away.

CEE CEE PAUSED under the spray. Had she heard the door open? Gathering the curtain in her hand, she peered out, ready to call his name in invitation.

The room was empty.

She awkwardly finished rinsing with one hand, trying to wash away the fear that she was losing Max. He'd treated her differently since she'd failed him that morning in her room. Ever since she'd been too afraid to say what really motivated her concern. She wanted to keep him safe not to testify, not to earn kudos on the job. But because she just plain wanted him.

But the moment to tell him was gone. Now he'd never believe her. She'd pushed him in the direction he was going, not Jimmy. And if anything happened to him, it was her fault.

After drying off, she put on the luscious silk shirt, growly ill temper stirring at the sight of the red scrap of nylon and lace hanging behind it. She put the panties on, then stalked into Max's bedroom, as steamed as the bathroom mirror.

Max had changed into slouchy jeans, a plain white tee shirt, and his red shoes.

"Thanks for the change of clothes," she snapped as she tugged up her skirt.

Understanding, he grinned at her. "They aren't mine."

"Obviously. Did your little playmate lose them in your game of chance?"

He blinked, not immediately catching the reference to his alibi from Gautreaux and Surette's murders. Then he grinned wider. "I just made her up to make you jealous. Did it work?"

"Don't flatter yourself, Savoie."

"Then why do I feel flattered?"

"Because you're an arrogant beast, that's why."

"And you love that about me."

She sighed. "Yes, I do."

"And you love me."

She started to reply but his fingertips pressed to her mouth, halting the words he feared were going to be no, and she feared would be yes.

"Let's just leave it at that," he suggested softly, then turned for his raincoat. He settled it on her shoulders, then shrugged into his leather jacket. "You drive. I don't know how."

In Jimmy's big garage, Cee Cee ignored the Porsche, the BMW, and the Mercedes, rushing over to a bright green Nova with a black roof and white striping.

"Is this a '69 Yenko? There were only forty of them made."

"Thirty-seven," the chauffeur corrected.

"She's *beautiful*." She looked to Max and explained that the hot muscle car was the brain-child of a Chevy dealer in Pennsylvania who'd gotten the factory cars through GM, then swapped out the Nova's lightweight engine for an asphalt-ripping RPO L72 big block V-8, and tossed in a tachometer along with his "Yenko Super Cars" striping and badging, to create a mouth-watering classic. To Max it was just an ugly little car with all the sex appeal of a shoe box.

"Zero to sixty in under four seconds." The husky sound of Cee Cee's voice made him forget about the car as she nearly begged, "Can we take this?"

Max watched her hands caress the square hood

and his throat tightened. "Give her the keys," he told Pete.

She slid her long legs under the wheel. When the engine roared to life, Max buckled up apprehensively. She pumped the accelerator and the vehicle shuddered with power.

"Oh baby," she purred, her hand stroking the gear shift in a way that made him go all hot and cold. "I like things that are fast, dangerous, and wickedly sexy," she crooned, then grinned at Max. "That's why I like you."

She popped the clutch and sent them hurtling out of the garage.

AT A QUARTER to midnight, New Orleans was just waking up. Pedestrians crowded the narrow sidewalks, wandering in and out of the open doorways where blues and zydeco and laughter floated on the smoky air. Cee Cee parked on a side street, locked up the car, then started looking for the address Dolores had given her.

She paused, frowning. "This can't be right." The building was shuttered tight and dark. It looked more like an abandoned warehouse than a nightclub.

Max walked around her and headed down an alleyway barely wide enough for his shoulders. In back, they could hear the faint pulse of music and conversation seeping through a heavily barred door.

Cee Cee tapped twice, paused, then tapped

again, feeling vaguely foolish using the code Dolores gave her.

The door opened and Max took a quick step back, his posture tense, his senses quivering. "What is this place?"

"Let's go see."

They went down a long, narrow hall with warped floors and worn rugs. It was almost too dark to see anything; the promise of light ahead kept them moving forward.

"Good evening. Welcome to *Cheveux du Chien*." *Hair of the Dog*. A stunning woman greeted Max with a smile, but her face stiffened when she observed Cee Cee. "I think you're in the wrong place, honey." It wasn't a friendly suggestion.

Max put his arm about Cee Cee's shoulders. "She's with me."

The woman pouted. "No accounting for taste. This way."

Max gave Cee Cee a hard squeeze and a chiding, "Behave."

The club beat like a wild heart with sound and light. Café tables circled a dance floor, with two tiers of seating rising behind them. Exposed pipes and conduit were painted flat black. Chains and pulleys hung from the high ceiling, stirring in the breeze of the fans. The tables were full, the bar crowded with customers drinking and shouting over the hard techno music.

Max pulled up to scent the air. His expression

grew strange—sharp with tension, yet dreamy at the same time. Cee Cee put her palm on his chest. His pulse lunged beneath it.

"Max, what is it?

"I don't know," he whispered, advancing into the room with a stiff-legged gait. She could feel him shaking, and suddenly she feared she'd made a terrible mistake bringing him into this unknown.

As they followed the waitress between the tables, heads turned, eyes fixed and followed, and postures became guarded. In the dark, smeary light, she thought she saw eyes flashing gold and red.

"Stay close to me," Max rumbled, so low it was nearly a growl. She didn't need to be convinced to take his arm. Tense and agitated, he sank into a booth, pulling her into his side. His body vibrated with tension, and she rubbed his hand as it spasmed around hers.

Scanning the crowd, Max found all focus on him. In hoarse amazement, he told her, "Charlotte, they're all like me. I'm not alone!"

Seventeen

CEE CEE'S HAND tightened on his. Feeling very much like Porky and Baco, she tried to adopt a toughly confident manner, but something about the patrons of *Cheveux du Chien* was so alien, her skin prickled. She could see in them that difference that set Max apart. The quickness, the power, the strange attentiveness, the sudden feral gleam in the eyes. Eyes that gauged Max as a threat and her as . . . dinner.

Two men approached. One was huge, with a bald head and massive hands, and the other was all sleek muscle topped with a mane of bright red hair. The big one leaned on their table, showing his teeth. It wasn't a smile.

"This is a private club."

Max met his glare levelly. "So invite me to stay."

"You have a lot of guts coming here. Or very little brain. Which is it?"

"You decide."

"Do you know who we are? What we are?"

"Not by name, but yes, I know you. From the docks. From Vantour. What you are is like me."

"Jacques LaRoche. This is Philo Tibideaux. And your friend?"

"She's mine and not a part of this." His hand tightened to quell Cee Cee's objection.

LaRoche took Cee Cee's other hand and tugged firmly. "Philo will entertain your friend while we talk." He waited for Max to slowly, reluctantly, let her go.

"Keep her where I can see her."

The redhead grinned. "Just a dance. Right over there." He took the hand LaRoche passed to him, bending over it, running the tip of his tongue across her knuckles.

"Be careful with her," Max warned mildly. "Her bite is much worse than her bark." His gaze locked on Cee Cee's for a moment before turning to LaRoche, who'd assumed her seat.

"So," LaRoche began conversationally, "Legere passed his business to you. Amazing. Vantour wanted us at his back, but he would never allow us any power. He had no interest in our kind, only in what we could do for him. Legere was the same. What about you? What would you do for your kind, Savoie?"

"Tell me why I should care about people I don't know, and who never reached out to me until I held something they wanted."

"We were afraid of you. You walk on the outside of us. You stand in the shadows of those who would use us and hurt us. Why would we trust you?"

"Because I can protect you if you work with me."

LaRoche's eyes narrowed as he watched Savoie's attention drift to the human woman he'd brought in with him. A weakness. "You don't have that kind of power."

"But I could, if I can control the docks. I didn't kill Vantour."

Huge shoulders shrugged. "We don't care if you did or not. He enslaved us. We would follow someone who would set us free to walk as men do. Would that be you, Savoie? I'm not sure. You bring one of them in here with you, and ask for our trust. Leave her with us and you have it."

Max's stare fixed on his, chill and unblinking. "She brought me and she leaves with me. And if anyone gets in the way of that, I will crush you all and scatter your bones in the river."

LaRoche chuckled. "You have a big reputation, Savoie, but we've never seen for ourselves the truth of what you can do. Take her if you can." He sat back and waved a hand toward the dance floor.

Max slid out of the booth, the movement gradual and sleek. "We'll talk again soon."

"Perhaps we will."

Max strode out onto the dance floor to pull Cee Cee out of Tibideaux's loose embrace. "Time to go."

Clued in by the quiet tension in his voice, Cee Cee was instantly alert to danger. And to the fact that they weren't getting out of the club without a fight. There was subtle movement in the shadows all around them, figures circling, closing in until they stood in the center of the dance floor under the strobing lights. Like wolves surrounding sheep. And she thought suddenly of Benjamin Spratt.

Only, Max Savoie was no sheep, and she hadn't been a little lamb for a long, long time.

Max said, "I'll distract them. You get the hell out of here."

Her gaze flashed up at him. "Run and leave you? I don't think so. I'm not much for running."

He cursed softly as he stripped off his jacket, tossing it away. He assumed a slightly crouched position, looking lethal as he said quietly, "Don't worry. I'll protect you."

"I was about to tell you the same thing."

He caught her quick grin before Tibideaux grabbed her arm, too swiftly for her to react in her own defense. He flung her into the group of tables, where ranks quickly closed her off from Max. Sprawled on the floor, she heard a hair-raising sound ripple through the room, a rumble starting low and building in intensity into dangerous snarls. She stood to see Max smiling ferociously, his hands beckoning.

"Step up," he called with mocking amusement. "Who wants to see what I can do?"

He made fists and when his hand opened again, each finger was tipped with a razorlike claw.

He didn't wait for them to make a move. He

grabbed the back of Tibideaux's head and drove his face down into the floor, then threw him up into the second tier of tables. And then they were on him.

Cee Cee pushed her way through the fringe of onlookers. She'd been in her share of hand-to-hand situations, but she'd never heard sounds as horrible as these—the snarls, the yips, the roars, the groans, the awful thuds of body contact and rips through fabric and flesh.

Max became hidden by the tangle of combatants scrambling up and tumbling down, then he rolled free and up to his feet. He hadn't changed form, though most of the others had become variations on the creature she'd seen in her bedroom—blazing eyes, perverted canine features, and deadly fangs and claws.

Max was breathing hard, streaked with blood: some of it his, most of it theirs. He dodged a paw aimed at his throat, nearly buckling as deep groves tore through his shoulder. He grabbed his attacker's arm and pivoted, using his body to bowl over a half dozen assailants. Then, in a quick evasive move, he vaulted onto one of the pool tables.

"Max!"

He turned to catch the two pool cues she tossed up to him. Grabbing the handles of a couple of beer pitchers, she rolled up onto the table beside him, smashing the heavy glass on the side rails before standing with bristling shards rimming the knuckles of either hand. His gaze took her in from head to toe as she braced beside him for battle.

"You are the most beautiful thing I've ever seen in my life," he vowed, tone rough with passion. "I want to take you down and have you right here."

"Pick a better time and place, Savoie, and I'm all yours." A quick slash from her left hand sent one of the mutated creatures falling back with a howl. The others became more wary.

Max swung the pool cues in a dangerous arc to keep those on the other side of the table at bay. "Then let's make short work of them so we can get on to better things."

"Max?"

"Charlotte?"

"I've loved you since the first time I saw you."

He inhaled sharply, but didn't dare look at her. He struck out with swift, stunning blows to knock several aggressors to the floor. "You pick now to tell me? When I can't do anything about it?" His voice was gruff with emotion.

"Get us out of here alive, Savoie, and you can do anything you like."

"Consider me very highly motivated."

And he jumped right into the thick of them with a roaring cry.

What they had on him in numbers was overcome by the constant shifts of his physical form. They simply couldn't get a grip on him before he'd alter in size, in shape, from man to towering monster to sleek wolfish creature, each transition smooth and seamless to the confining limits of his clothing. They were nowhere near his match with their bulky, furred bodies and brutish power. And while he was careful not to kill, he was fierce beyond comprehension, shattering bones, tearing with fangs and claws through an increasingly smaller force as the injured crawled away to lick their wounds. Hardly unscathed but completely unstoppable, he whirled fearlessly to take on whomever was next.

Watching him, a huge swell of emotion overtook Charlotte. For a moment there was nothing but him, glistening with sweat and blood, savage, wild, yet tightly controlled. My God, he was magnificent! And he was hers. Nothing in the known universe could be as stunningly amazing, as humbling, as searingly hot, as knowing he was fighting for her. He was also doing it to impress the hell out of his kind with his wicked display of alpha dog superiority, but that was exciting, too. A hard fist of lust and longing and pride made her go hot and cold and shivery. When they left this place, he was going to take her the way he had on the side of the road, with hard, claiming purpose, and she was going to do everything she could think of to encourage him.

Then a larage hand clamped about her neck from behind and Tibideaux shouted, "Back down, Savoie, or I'll tear out her pretty throat."

Tibideaux dragged Cee Cee from the pool table, his thumbnail poised to rip through her jugular.

Max paused for a terrified heartbeat before saying firmly, "Take him, Charlotte." He was moving even before she drove back with her head and bit down on the sensitive membrane between Tibideaux's thumb and forefinger, making him howl.

LaRoche looked shocked as Max lunged through his minions to take him to the floor. The fallen man's windpipe clamped by his hand, Max leaned in until he was inches from LaRoche's face, letting his own shift into its vicious alter ego.

"Enough of the foreplay. Do we stop this, or do you die?"

LaRoche put out his hands, fingers spread wide, and stared up at Max in amazement. "You're everything they said you were. I've never seen a pureblood before."

"Do you yield, or do I have to pee on you to mark my territory?"

LaRoche laughed at his audacity. "Let's talk, Savoie."

Max pulled him to his feet. Shifting into his human form in a shredded tee shirt, licking the blood from around his mouth, he then turned to seek out Charlotte. Tibideaux still held her by the back of her shirt. A seismic rumble came from Max's throat. "Let her go before I eat your face."

Tibideaux let go.

She didn't run to him, or cast herself into his arms. She approached him with a long, steady stride, caught either side of his jaw between her hands, and kissed him hard and deep. When she pulled back, his eyes were molten.

"Wait for me at the house, Charlotte. I need to do some business here."

"Play nice, baby." She took his lips again, softly this time, then picked her way over the fallen without looking down.

"Quite a woman," LaRoche allowed.

"And this was just our second date."

HIS ROOM WAS dark when he stepped inside. When he saw the empty bed and the evidence that she hadn't returned to it, his heart plummeted.

"Max?"

She stepped in from the balcony, where she'd been watching for him. She was wearing just his shirt. This time she ran, hurtling into his arms, clinging as tightly about him as shrink-wrap.

"It's all right. I'm all right."

"I just need to hold on to you for a minute. Okay?"

"Okay."

He pulled her close, letting the shivers shake through her until she finally relaxed on a fragile sigh.

"I was so worried about you."

"About me?" He was too surprised to respond.

She leaned back to take his face in her palms. "I don't know what I'd do if anything happened to you."

His smile was wry. "It's all right for you to poison me and torture me and break my face, but God forbid someone else should do it?"

"You're mine, Max. No one hurts what's mine."

"I feel so much better."

"*I* feel better," she murmured. "And you feel wonderful."

Her kiss quickly sidetracked him from her misuse of him. "Is there anything else you'd like to get off your chest? Like my shirt?"

She chuckled. Then her expression grew so serious, his throat seized up tight. *Don't tell me good-bye. Don't say good-bye.*

"I love you, Max."

His eyes closed. His breath caught. "Tell me again."

"I'm in love with you."

"Show me."

And so she did as she undressed him, as she rolled with him across the bed, holding him, touching him, kissing him, welcoming him inside her with the soft cry of his name. Taking him, strong, greedy, and demanding with her mouth, with her hands, with the hot clench of her inner walls. Not content to let him bring her paradise, but pursuing it at the same urgent pace. Wildly aroused by their shared combat, by the strength of the dark and hotly dangerous lover she held captive with her kisses and the wrap of her long legs, the pleasure was fierce and sweet and satisfying. She came screaming. Then she cradled him, exhausted, in her arms.

Sometime later, Cee Cee stirred with a ridiculous sense of contentment. Her hand moved across the sheet beside her. Finding it cool and empty she flipped over in alarm and was immediately comforted. Max was sitting on the floor next to the bed, eating something that sounded . . . fresh.

"Late-night snack? Anyone I know?"

"The wrapper identified the deceased as Top Sirloin." He sucked at his fingers, and she realized he was eating it raw. "I can finish this downstairs."

"No, I don't mind." She nestled her head on his shoulder. "I'm not squeamish, for a girl."

He nudged her with his head. "My girl . . . right?"

There was just enough hesitation for her to smile. She looped her arm about his neck. "Right."

He made a pleased sound and continued to tear into his meal.

"How did your meeting go?"

"I guess I'll find out soon enough." A pause. "Before you start interrogating me, that's all I can tell you for now. Things are in motion. I'm cautiously optimistic."

She paused, then blurted, "That's all I get? After putting it on the line for you, that's *it*?"

"Darlin', you're a police detective and I'm a thug. That's going to make for a bit of guarded conversation from time to time."

She pouted for a moment, but his endearment went a long way toward soothing her temper. "Fair enough. Point taken." She made herself more comfortable on his shoulder, her hand rubbing lightly across his chest. He'd showered; the dark, springy hair was still damp, and his skin smelled wonderful. She sampled it with small kisses, then sighed, unable to shut off the ever-turning wheels in her brain. "LaRoche called you a pureblood. What does that mean? Or is that privileged information, too?"

"That's personal, not business, so you can poke around there all you like."

"So?"

"What?"

"Are you going to answer me? Then no more questions, and I'll let you 'poke around' all *you* like, too."

Silence, then a slightly shaky laugh. "I'd take you up on that right now if I didn't have Mr. Sirloin all over my hands."

"Go wash them. Or," her voice lowered, "you can wash me later."

His breathing shuddered, then he pushed to his feet. "I'll be right back."

She sat up to follow him with a lustful appreciation. Moonlight from the open balcony doors caressed the cap of his shoulder, the curve of his flank, the out-turned toes of his bare feet. Watching him move was erotic verse in motion, a strong, aggressive tempo refined by an almost delicate grace.

"You make me hot, Savoie," she whispered under her breath.

He looked back at her over his shoulder, his grin wide and white.

She'd forgotten about his acute hearing.

He returned moments later, then sank to his knees at her feet and rested his head in her lap. Startled by the incredible trust and humility of the gesture, she sat unmoving, then began to run her fingers through his hair.

"Do you know how odd it feels to have a stranger tell you things about yourself that you don't know?" he began.

His shoulders were tense beneath the stroke of her other hand. Gently, firmly, she began working the knots from them.

"All this time, I had no idea there were others like me. I thought it was just me—a freak of nature, an abomination. Alone and different. Jimmy never told me."

To control him—the bastard. She bent to kiss his temple.

"These . . . beings who are like me aren't men, aren't beasts, but sort of a blend of both. They've banded together to hide what they are and protect their secrets. LaRoche's group works the docks and does the dirty work of the mob bosses. Since they have no papers, they're powerless to act on their own behalf. Where would they go? Who would believe them? So they take nasty jobs, huddling together in cheap homes, living in poverty with their human mates. And the more they mix and dilute their powers, the weaker their natural abilities become, until there are no purebloods. Purebloods like my father. My mother. Me. And the one Etienne Legere found to help him claim his fortune. The others, they all have some degree of power, the males much more so than the females."

"But none like you?"

"No. None like me."

He closed his eyes, letting his physical self be soothed and calmed by her touch while his spirit prowled restlessly.

"They have no one to lead them, to organize them, to take care of their interests." He felt a strange unhappiness, even guilt. Because he'd come from where they were, but he'd had advantages they were denied. They'd been virtually slaves to Vantour and others like him. No one cared about these proud, angry, helpless, and frightened people who lived outside the laws of man.

"Do you trust them, Max?"

"I don't know them. Part of them is as strange to me as it is to you."

"And the other part?"

"It's like finding a huge family you never knew you had."

"Then I'm happy for you, Max. But be careful."

His chuckle was cynical. "Even in families, there's no such thing as equal in all ways."

Family. He still trembled at that notion, but he couldn't deny his huge relief when he'd dropped his defenses and let them touch him with tentative mental overtures.

He'd immediately wanted to pull back, to close down, to throw up barriers they couldn't penetrate. But he didn't. And it was harder just to sit there and let them learn him by scent and psychic signature, than to half-kill them in battle. One was an impersonal show of strength, the other a terrifying display of trust. He had no experience in that and was quickly overloaded with sensations. It was like having all their hands on him at once, touching, pushing, stroking, gripping. Like suddenly having sight and hearing for the first time, and being bombarded by input he'd hungered for but couldn't control. Greedy for it, dizzy from it, until finally LaRoche put up his hand to motion them back and he was able to breathe. And then the sudden, awful ache of being separate from them, after knowing the embrace of unity.

He didn't share this with Charlotte, afraid she wouldn't understand and yet afraid she would all too well. He needed to adjust, to accept first, before he could tell her about it. And he needed to decide on how to respond to their claim that they'd consider it a betrayal for him to pollute his heritage with one who was not their kind.

His kind. A strange and beautiful notion. He had so many questions.

He closed his eyes, letting Charlotte lure him back to her with her siren's caress. Her fingers buffed lightly across the back of his hand, the short, blunt-cut nails rasping in sexy little shivers of sensation that nearly blanked his mind to her soft question.

"Does it hurt?"

"What?" For a moment, he was confused. She could be raking through his flesh with talons like Freddy Krueger and he wouldn't have equated it with pain at this moment.

Her hand curled about his, her touch maddeningly gentle, stroking his palm, gliding up his fingers to their tips, then pushing to spread them so that her fingers could mesh in between. Fascinated by the journey and the incredibly intimate result, he fought to keep his focus on what she was saying.

"When you change form. Is it painful? Does it hurt you?" Her gaze lifted to his, her dark eyes liquid with concern.

He smiled, keeping it light because something strange and powerful was happening within his chest, a tightening that squeezed about his heart like a vise. "Only when I forget I'm no longer on four legs, and try to scratch behind my ear with my back foot."

She scowled. "Go ahead and make a joke. Laugh at me."

He pulled her hand up to his lips, pressing a heated kiss on her knuckles in apology. "No, *sha*. It's no different than changing an expression." His voice lowered to a husky rumble. "Would it distress you if it did?"

She tried to maintain her annoyance, grumbling with reluctance, "Yes, it would." Then her tone quieted, smoothing out like warm silk. "It would very much."

He fit her palm to the side of his face, liking the notion of her being upset on his behalf.

"Does anything else change when you're in a different form?"

"Change how?"

"The way you think, the way you feel?"

He smiled slightly. "You mean do I become a slathering beast without a conscience and a taste for human organ donors?" He nibbled lightly on her fingers.

Yes, that was exactly what she needed to know. When he changed, did he become any less the man she loved?

"I'm the same inside; the same memories, the same emotions. My senses are sharper, different. It's hard to explain. I'm more aware of my instincts. I have tremendous strength and speed. But I'm always in control of what I am and always remember what I do."

"And you can change whenever you want?"

"No full moon necessary. I control my form: how much it changes, a little or a lot. Whatever I need." He fisted his fingers, then extended them, now hair covered and claw tipped. Then his hand was back to normal. "From man to beast to the animal on all fours, and anything in between. They're all elements of what I am that I can change within certain limits, just by visualizing it."

"Limits?"

He chuckled. "I can't become twenty feet tall or fit through a keyhole, which might be nice on occasion. But you have to plan ahead. There's nothing more embarrassing than ripping out of your clothing, only to find yourself in the middle of company with no trousers on later."

"I don't know," she mused. "I rather like catching you without trousers."

He grinned and relaxed. Her questions conveyed an acceptance that quite frankly astonished him. She was curious, not uncomfortable or recoiling. But then, what else should he have expected from someone who enjoyed poking about in a Y incision with Devlin Dovion?

"When you're in your full dog suit . . ."—she paused when he chuckled, not offended by her analogy—"you can hear me?"

"Oh, yes. My hearing is excellent, but I can't speak the way I can in beast form. The change alters my vocal chords. It's amazing what people say and do in front of the family pet. I've had some naughty erotic fantasies there." His tongue stroked over her knee in a long, wet tease. "If you'd like to wear a red cape, I could be your Big Bad Wolf. Picnic basket optional."

"Why, Grandma, you're packing a mighty big picnic basket yourself."

"I could make you howl at the moon, Charlotte."

"And you'd never be tempted to gobble me up?" She smiled, but there was a slight edge of worry behind it.

"Only in ways you would enjoy, *sha*. Only the shape changes—not my feelings for you."

"A shape shifter. Is that what you are?"

Again, the caution, as if by putting a folkloric name upon it, he would become alien and separate from her. He wasn't about to let that happen.

"I don't know yet what we're called, or if we *have* a name. I know so little and need to learn so much. I'm many things, detective, and all of them love you."

His hand settled on her bare calf, kneading in slow circles. "I love your skin," he murmured. "Its warm color, its softness, its strength, its smell, its taste." His tongue slid down the length of her thigh until he nipped sharply at her knee. Her hand fisted in his hair. "You have no idea how much you mean to me."

She angled, parting her legs so he was trapped between her knees.

"Show me."

His gaze met hers, all smoldery and warmed by desire. Never breaking his intense stare, he strung delicate kisses up the inside of her thigh. By the time he got to where he was going, she was trembling. His eyes drifted shut and he breathed her in.

"I could find you anywhere." His soft whisper

started a quiver in her belly. "Across a room, in the dark, in the middle of a crowd. The scent of you, so hot and warm and . . . mine."

The slow stroke of his tongue started her body humming, and she waited for a torturous eternity for the touch of his mouth. Soft and teasing, kissing, tugging at the tender folds to reach the slick sweetness of her center. Feasting there with a fearsome concentration that had her falling back helplessly to the mattress. She groaned at the feel of him caressing inside her, wondering wildly just how long a tongue her Big Bad Wolf had, as he seemed to reach all the way to her tonsils. Her hands fisted in the sheets; her bare toes curled atop his thighs as sensation sizzled through her.

The sudden, surprisingly sharp nip of his teeth punched the breath from her lungs and sent her into a hard, rolling orgasm. He came up over her, taking her body with a hard thrust, her breath with a devouring kiss, her senses up into a fierce, tightening spiral until that surging pleasure spiked all over again, punctuated by her hoarse cries.

WAKING TO THE sight of Charlotte Caissie in his bed, her tawny body bare to the covers at her waist, filled Max with bittersweet longing and alarm. All the fierce, heated adrenaline had calmed; that possessive urgency to have her, to hold her, to love her. Now there was just a new day, and with it, a harsh reality. She wasn't safe with him and he wasn't safe with her. They could hurt each other emotionally now, as well as physically and professionally. With so much in the balance demanding his attention, he couldn't afford the distraction she brought into his life.

But what would that life be without her?

I love you, Max.

His heart still shuddered with it, and his mind still couldn't wrap around the enormity of it. He wanted to shake her awake just to hear it from her again. And again. And again. If only he could hold her here forever, where the outside world couldn't touch or spoil what they'd shared, where he wouldn't have to consider the danger swirling about the both of them, where he could enjoy this one thing he'd longed for for nearly half his life: the cherished love of this woman. But that was a foolish wish, and he couldn't afford to be weak. He couldn't keep her here, and she wouldn't agree to be kept. He didn't think he meant more to her than her work, and to keep her safe, he couldn't allow himself to consider feelings above practicalities.

He quickly tugged on jeans and a tee shirt, then trotted downstairs barefoot in search of coffee. After she consumed that first pot, maybe they could continue their conversation without the desperate need to undress each other. But then again, maybe not. He wasn't quite sure what to do with her, now that she was in his bed, under Jimmy's roof, or where she would fit into the unsettled chaos of his world. After today, he would have a better idea. Or else he would be dead and it would be a moot point.

As he rounded the newel post at the bottom of the steps, a gun barrel notched up under his chin and a cold voice said, "Max Savoie, I'm taking you in on suspicion of murdering Detective Charlotte Caissie. Unless I blow your fucking head off first."

Eighteen

MAX ASKED CALMLY, "Would you like some coffee, Detective Babineau, or have you already reached your limit?"

"I'm way past my limit, Savoie." He looked very fierce and very dangerous. "I've been up all night trying to track down my partner. Seems some kids used her car to do some joyriding, and got in a bit of mischief at a convenience store that ended up in a high-speed chase. Totaled the car, sent one of the kids to the hospital and the other to jail. Funny thing was, the blood in the car wasn't from either of the kids. I think the lab will confirm it's Cee Cee's.

"One boy said they found the vehicle abandoned on some back road with the door open and the keys in it. When I took a team out to check, we found evidence of an assault. Cee Cee's a smart girl. She wouldn't take a spin with just anybody in her passenger seat. To get the drop on her, it would have to be someone she knew, someone she trusted. Are you following my logic, Savoie?"

"So far, so good."

"Mind telling me where you were yesterday?"

"I met with my attorney in the city. I can give you his name–"

"I know his name. What I don't know is what you did to her, you son of a bitch."

"Nothing I didn't want him to do, Alain. Don't blow his head off yet. We've just started dating."

While her partner stared, dumbstruck, Cee Cee came down the stairs wearing one of Max's tee shirts over her rumpled skirt.

"We have company, *cher*. Did you want coffee, too?" Max asked.

"A little sugar first, then the coffee." She looped her arms around Max's neck and kissed him soundly. "Why didn't you wake me?" she scolded against his lips.

"You looked too beautiful to disturb. I'll bring a tray out to the side porch." He smiled slightly. "Detective Babineau, make yourself at home."

Babineau gave Cee Cee a hard once-over as they started down the side hall. "It looks like *you* already have."

"Don't be pissy, Babs."

"Pissy? I was about to order a dredge of the river!"

"That's sweet. I didn't know you cared."

"Well, it's damned inconvenient having to teach someone new what radio stations you like, and how much hot sauce to put on your po'boy. *Savoie*? For the love of Christ, Ceece, what a time to get all hormonal over the guy, just when the whole district's about to explode."

"That's part of why I'm here."

"You're working? Undercover or under the covers?"

"You are very irritable in the mornings, Alain. I don't know how your wife puts up with you."

He dropped heavily into one of the wicker porch chairs and stared out at the overgrown gardens. "Seeing the blood in that car scared me to death, Cee Cee."

She pressed her hand over his. "I'm sorry. It had to look like I was out of the picture."

"What happened to your arm?"

"An accident. That's how the blood got in the car."

He turned to her with a low demand. "What's going on with you, detective? You are so far out on the limb, how are you going to know if he's cutting the branch off behind you?"

"Because I trust him."

"Is that the cop or the starry-eyed girlfriend talking? He's a criminal, a killer."

"But that doesn't make me a bad person," Max said.

He set the tray with cups and carafe on the tabletop, then poured a cup for Cee Cee, strong and black. "You'll have to fix your own, detective. I don't know how you take it. And I'm afraid I don't know your music preferences, either. I guess I'll be learning all sorts of new things this morning. You didn't answer him, Charlotte." He still stood studying her unblinkingly.

"The girlfriend is a believer. The cop is cautiously optimistic."

"The criminal is grateful. The boyfriend is slightly disappointed." His tone chilled. "I have a meeting this morning, if you'll excuse me, I have to get dressed. Detective Babineau, if I don't see you before you leave, keep her safe for me."

He brushed his knuckles along the side of Cee Cee's face, then went back into the house.

"Oh, for fuck's sake," Cee Cee grumbled, looking after him with annoyance and distress. "What the hell is his problem? I *so* suck at this stuff. Now he's all torqued off and I don't even know what I said."

"No one said relationships were for sissies. Go after him if you've gotta. I'll just sit and enjoy my coffee."

HE'D ALREADY PULLED on dark blue slacks and was buttoning the cuffs of his crisp white shirt when Cee Cee's hands slid up beneath the loose tails to rest against his bare middle. Her thinking was simple and direct: toss him back on the sheets and smooth out the misunderstandings on a horizontal plane. Passion fired her blood in full support of that logic. A quick, hard tumble would cure any insult she might have inadvertently delivered.

A fine plan, until he neatly circumvented it. He caught her hands, lifting them to his lips, then held them tightly to his chest. His voice wasn't any friendlier.

"Charlotte, I'm afraid I don't have the time to work out the particulars of our relationship at this moment."

"Who are you meeting this morning, Max?"

"Petitjohn and . . . some others."

"LaRoche?"

"Perhaps."

"What for?"

"It's business."

"Dangerous business?"

"All of my business is dangerous business. As is yours, detective. We can't separate that out, can we?"

She pressed against him, rubbing her cheek along his hard, muscled back. He tensed but didn't turn. "I want to beg you not to go. You know that, don't you?"

"I do now."

"I want to beg you just to walk away from it."

"And do what? Sell shoes? I have obligations to the people here, Charlotte. To Jimmy. If you wanted me to walk away from them, you should have convinced me of that last night."

"And to me? Any obligations there?"

He lifted her hands, kissing her palms, nipping her fingers, licking along her knuckles, then holding them clasped beneath his chin. He didn't answer.

"I want to beg you, but I won't ask you."

"Charlotte, what am I going to do with you?"

She felt the breath shiver from him. Then he spoke softly, his words filled with a quiet emotion she couldn't identify. But both the tone and the sentiment scared her.

"Stay out of sight for a few more hours. After that, it shouldn't matter."

"Why?"

"I love you, Charlotte."

"Max—"

"Go downstairs and finish your coffee so I can finish up here. Go. Please." Then much softer, "Please."

She drew her hands out of his and left.

Seeing her expression when she rejoined him at the table, Babineau wisely made no comment. Her cup rattled on the saucer when she lifted it, so she put the coffee down and simply sat, trying to control her panic. She wasn't thinking like a cop, with her head and controlled instincts. She was lost to the confused emotions of a woman so in love, she couldn't see beyond the anguish of letting him walk out into his brutal world.

She heard him come down the stairs, his light, quick step unmistakable, but she stayed at the table, gripping the arms of her chair. He didn't come out to the porch. When she heard the front door open and shut, her stomach lurched. Wasn't he going to say good-bye?

Then she heard voices in the hall, low and serious. Business. Legere's business, now Max's business. She wasn't sure how she felt about that yet. Only how she felt about him.

"Charlotte, come see me out."

She moved carefully, lest she hurry and betray how fragile her emotional state was. Max was speaking to several of his household people while two burly body men and the chauffeur stood waiting. In the dark blue suit and sober tie, he could have been a banker or stockbroker—if not for the red shoes and the subtle hint of violence that clung to him like a mysterious cologne.

He stopped talking when he saw her and waited for her to join him. He took her hand, drawing her close to his side while he told the others, "This is Detective Charlotte Caissie, my girlfriend. She's to have full access to anything of mine, anytime she requests it."

"Mr. Savoie," began one of the bulky duo uneasily.

"Giles, anything, anytime. I have no secrets from her. I trust her with everything I have and everything I am. Is that understood?"

Uncomfortable assenting murmurs replied. The women grew a bit misty-eyed, thinking what a romantic he was, and the men exchanged knowing glances, enviously figuring she must be great in bed.

Embarrassed, Cee Cee muttered, "This is hardly necessary, Max."

"It might be, Charlotte. It might be very necessary."

If he didn't come back. Her gaze flew up to his, wide with shock and disbelief. If anything happened to him, he'd just handed everything concerning Jimmy's empire to her—and, if she chose, to the New Orleans Police Department.

"Max, no."

Waving his people away, he looked down into her liquid gaze. "It's already done, Charlotte. Antoine D'Marco, my lawyer, will come see you. I want you taken care of. I want you to have the knowledge to keep yourself safe."

If I don't come back.

She pushed at him, but he was holding on tight. "I don't want your lawyer or your secrets."

"Charlotte, don't do this now," he petitioned awkwardly. He knew how to handle her anger, her contempt, her sarcasm, but this unexpected vulnerability had him rather desperate. "Hush, now. What do you want?"

"I want dinner and dancing. I b-bought these great shoes and—"

He silenced her with the fierce crush of his mouth,which gentled so quickly with the first taste of her tears, she had to cling to him in a free fall of emotion. When her knees went weak, his arm scooped about her waist to haul her up against him while he kissed her damp cheeks, her closed eyes, and her mouth.

"I want to see the shoes. When and where?"

"Tonight. Seven. PaPa Legba's."

"I'll be there. But you have to let me go now."

"Max . . . don't be late."

"I won't be. Let me go, detective."

"I don't think I can." She gulped.

"Nonsense. You're the strongest, bravest woman I've ever known." Gently, firmly he worked her fingers free from his coat, holding them in the curl of his own. "How could I not come back to you?"

With a quick squeeze of her hands, he stepped back and walked briskly away. She could see his posture straighten, his stride grow more aggressive and controlled as he drew out his sunglasses and slipped them on, transforming into the man Legere had made of him.

"I want you, Savoie," she sighed softly.

He looked back over his shoulder, his sly grin flashing. Then he was gone.

Cee Cee stood in the hall, waiting for her heart rate to return to normal. For the first time in her life, she was paralyzed by helplessness. She couldn't fight her way out of it, she couldn't think her way through it, and she simply could not accept that Max Savoie might be walking out of her life just when she'd finally realized how much he meant to her.

"Is there something you need, Detective Caissie?"

She glanced at the pretty young woman who

looked about the right size for those red nylon and lace panties, and a swift surge of possessiveness shocked her from her stupor.

"Thank you . . ."

"Jasmine."

"Thank you, Jasmine, but I have absolutely everything I need or want." And she was going to hold on to it.

She went back to the porch. "Babineau, if you're finished lapping up the benefit of those ill-gotten gains, we have work to do."

He tossed back the last of his coffee and scrambled to join her. She was back to the hard-thinking, tough-edged partner he'd follow into hell as she bit out crisp orders.

"I need to know the whereabouts and scheduled meetings for every major crime player in the city this morning. Something's going on and I need to know when and where."

As they strode to the door, the pretty housemaid intercepted her again.

"Excuse me, detective. Mr. Savoie wanted you to have these."

A set of keys. Familiar car keys.

She grinned wide. "Savoie, you're going to find me *so* freaking grateful."

"The key to his heart?" Babineau drawled.

"No, to mine. Let me borrow some money. I need to get some clothes and I can't go back to my apartment yet. I'm supposed to be dead."

"I'm married. You know I'm not allowed to carry money."

"Plastic, then."

"Oh, yeah, and I get to explain a purchase for the woman I'm not having an affair with to my wife?"

"I'll let you drive." She gestured out to the cherry ride parked out front.

Babineau gave a wolf whistle. "Your shacking up with Savoie might have its good points. Any others I should know about?"

She arched a brow. "None I'm willing to share."

She dropped him off at his car an hour and forty-five minutes later, feeling capable and focused in new jeans, a snug lime-green tee shirt, and some scandalously inappropriate underwear.

"In about an hour, make a report that you found me sleeping it off here at Savoie's. Tell them the kids boosted my car while we were rolling around in the grass, and that Max had his chauffeur pick us up when we discovered the car was gone. Elaborate. Tell them I was too drunk to remember I owned a car." She put up her hand to stop his protest. "I don't care—it's not going to sound pretty no matter how you put it."

"And everyone's going to know Savoie is putting it to *you*."

Leave it to her partner to serve it up unwincingly plain.

"At the moment, that's the least of my worries."

FRANCIS PETITJOHN RAN his various enterprises out of a dockside warehouse refurbished into an office park. While Jimmy had preferred the isolation of his country home and to have business come to him, T-John enjoyed keeping his finger on the pulse of the workers, and his foot on the back of their necks.

He looked up from behind his paperwork to smile thinly at his visitor. "Good morning, Max. Are you ready for our big day?"

"As ready as I'll ever be." He stood halfway in the room, not yet committing.

"Come in and sit down. I'm almost finished here." This was the first time he'd ever offered a seat or any courtesy.

Max remained where he was, his gaze roving the room as if he hadn't been there hundreds, probably thousands, of times before. He'd always found the decor retro trash, with its bright splashes of color and chrome and a shag rug out of the '60s. It wasn't the type of place conducive to business, Jimmy had always grumbled after sitting on the oddly formed artsy chairs. Max silently agreed.

"I heard something interesting this morning from one of my contacts in the police department." Francis glanced up to gauge Max's interest, finding no flicker of it in his features. "It seems Detective Caissie is MIA"

Max said nothing.

"So you decided to take care of things yourself,

did you?" Surprise, possibly grudging respect, edged that comment.

"Jimmy taught me it was never wise to do business from a position of weakness. And as you pointed out, Detective Caissie was my weakness."

Petitjohn gave an uneasy laugh. "You're a heartless creature, Max."

"I am what you and Jimmy made me."

Petitjohn smiled slightly. "Indeed you are. Max, sit."

He came in cautiously to take the proffered seat. Then he simply stared with a flat, unreadable gaze until T-John was twisting nervously beneath it.

"The meeting's in an hour. Are we in accord, Max? We can't afford to show any uncertainties, not in front of these people. Let me do the talking. We'll give them a minute or two to express their condolences, then we'll stake a firm claim for what's ours."

"Ours," Max echoed quietly. "Whatever you want, Francis."

Petitjohn studied him for a long moment, a cunning smile on his face. Then he sighed as if he'd come to some decision.

"We'll toast to it." Petitjohn reached for a pitcher of orange juice, splashing the drink into two glasses and pushing one toward Max. "To Jimmy Legere."

Max lifted the glass. "To Jimmy." He drank it down, almost immediately realizing his mistake.

"I'm sorry, Max," Petitjohn said as he watched

Max try to catch his breath. "You should have let it go. You should have stayed at my back where you belonged, instead of getting in my face.

"But you didn't. You took out Caissie. How could I trust the kind of monster who kills someone he loves? Jimmy let you get too smart and too damned dangerous. I'm not sharing my fortune with an animal. Nothing personal," he finished as Max dropped from the chair onto the carpet. "Like I told Jimmy, you're just too hard to control."

CEE CEE TAPPED on the dark-tinted glass, and Pete rolled down the window.

"Where's Max?"

"Up with Mr. Petitjohn. He told us to wait."

Cee Cee glanced at the elevator door, an uneasy feeling creeping in. She faded back into the shadow of one of the support pillars as the bell rang for the basement garage. The doors opened and Francis Petitjohn strode out, flanked by two of his men. No sign of Max. She swore, low and fierce, and began sprinting across the lot to where Petitjohn was climbing into his big Cadillac. His surprise at seeing her was monumental.

"Where's Savoie?"

He was quick to recover. "You tell me. We have a meeting in less than an hour. We were supposed to go there together but he never showed. If you'll excuse me, detective, I have an appointment. If you see Max, tell him I'll be expecting him." He closed the door before she could ask any further questions.

She waited until the car drove off, then raced for the elevator. By that time Giles and the equally muscle-bound Teddy were out of the car, concerned and looking to her for directions.

"He must still be upstairs." She didn't have to tell them that wasn't a good sign as she jabbed at the button. They joined her in the elevator without a word. As the car rose up, she took out the back-up gun borrowed from Babineau, cool instinct blanketing the awful terror that she'd be too late.

She strode into Petitjohn's outer office, flashing her gun at the alarmed secretary, then ordered, "Don't," as the woman's hand darted for the intercom. "We'll announce ourselves."

Three armed men leapt up as she pushed through the double doors.

"Detective Caissie, NOPD. Stand easy or go down hard."

Max was balled up on the floor, his back to her.

"Get them out of here," she snapped to Giles. "Keep them in the other room. No calls to anyone."

The second the door shut behind them, she was on her knees.

"Max?"

Her hands shaking, she rolled him toward her and cursed. His body was rigid, his knees tucked tight as he started to convulse. His eyes were rolled back.

"Max. Max, it's Charlotte. What did he do to you? What did the bastard do to you?"

She noticed the glass on the floor and what looked like chemical burns around his mouth and guessed the worst. He'd ingested liquid silver served up by the treacherous Petitjohn, and it was eating him from the inside out like a corrosive. She frantically tried to think of what to do. Remove the silver so he could heal himself was the only answer she could come up with.

She dragged him up to his knees and forced two fingers down his throat. Max fought the gag reflex and, more weakly, her. "Come on. Give it up for me." She rammed her fingers again and this time, his choking produced the desired result. She didn't look at the bloody mess he retched up onto Petitjohn's plush carpet. "Good. That's good," she soothed, stroking the sweat off his fevered brow. "We're not done yet. Throw it off, Max. Come on—you can do it. That little weasel isn't going to beat us."

But the sound of Max's breathing was harsh and awful. If the silver was in his system, she didn't know how to stop its spread, how to keep him alive.

She pushed him back onto his heels where he sagged against her palms, sucking for air in that horrible clogged-hose fashion. His eyes had glazed and began to roll back.

"No! Stay with me, Max. Fight it! Come on." His head lolled when she shook him, and snapped back when she slapped him. Once; again; then harder. "Max, it's Charlotte. Look at me. See me. Come on—don't be a coward. Don't you *dare* give up. Don't you run away from me now. I'm right here. Look at me!"

He blinked.

Encouraged, she got even tougher. "Come on, baby. Fight for me. Fight for *them*. You've never done a single thing for yourself your whole life. You've never taken a single stand. Make it count this time. Are you just going to roll over and play dead because that's what Petitjohn wants you to do?"

"For you," he whispered.

"What?" She stroked her hands over his gaunt face. "What did you say?"

"For you. I took a stand for you. Twelve years ago."

His eyes took on that eerie brilliance, then he tucked his head, a hard shiver passing through him. When he looked up, that gaze was warm and clear. And hard. "I've never regretted that choice for a second. I'm not sorry, but T-John will be when I catch up to him."

She smiled in relief. "Can I give you a lift?

Nineteen

SIX DOUBLE PATTIES, hold everything but the meat, and I'd like that just thawed, not cooked. And coffee, large, black."

Silence.

Cee Cee could imagine the teenager on the other end of the order box and smiled, adding, "For religious purposes."

She pulled through to the pick-up window and paid the nervous kid who passed her the order as if it contained toxic waste. After taking the coffee, she tossed the bag into Max's lap where he was dozing in the passenger seat.

"Breakfast. You can consider this our third date."

Opening the sack, he inhaled deeply and sighed. "Do you think we could go out sometime when it doesn't involve a near-death experience on my part?"

"So far you've been picking the places. Eat."

While they sat in a far corner of the parking lot, he made quick work of the raw burger. By the time he was licking the wrapper, his energy level was back.

"How are you feeling?"

"Besides stupid?" He smiled wryly. "I'm fine. Thanks to you." His brow puckered slightly. "What were you doing there, anyway?"

She started the car. "I meant it when I said I had your back."

"Ah." He sat back, pleased with her answer. His hands latched instinctively onto the dash as she wheeled out into traffic.

"What are you going to do about Petitjohn, Max?"

"Well, I can't exactly file a police report, can I?" He looked away. "I'll see to him. Eventually. But I want some answers from him first."

"I probably shouldn't be listening to this," she remarked casually. "But I can't think of anyone who would miss him if he turned up on the bottom of my shoes. Not my *new* shoes. If you're going to disembowel him, please don't do it tonight."

"I have other plans for this evening. You have this wonderful all-new smell to you that I need to investigate."

"New all the way to the skin. And I think you'll enjoy what you discover."

"Really?" Interest piqued, he craned his neck, trying to see down the scooped neck of her shirt. "What?"

"Later." She slapped his hand away. "You have to earn it."

"Detective, are you trying to bribe me with sex?"

He gave her a shocked look, amusement playing about his lips. "To do what? Stay alive?"

"We certainly won't be having sex otherwise. Do you have a problem with that, Savoie?"

"Not in the least."

They pulled into the upscale restaurant's parking lot, edging up between the long lines of sleek, non-descript town cars and glossy SUVs, all with tinted windows.

"This must be the place." Cee Cee cut the motor and turned to Max. "By the way, thanks for the use of the car."

"My pleasure. But it's your car."

Her eyes widened.

"I owe you one. And I really like watching you handle the gear shift."

"Do you think anyone would mind if I slid onto your lap and we started making out like crazy?"

"I know I wouldn't mind." He sighed heavily, glancing toward the front door. "But duty calls. Come on, detective. Escort me in."

THE INTERIOR OF Michael's was all crystal and silver elegance. The bulky patrons in the bar area, wearing suits cut to conceal their firearms, looked as conspicuous as Cee Cee felt. A pompous staffer stopped them outside the banquet room, raising an eyebrow at Max's shoes.

"I'm sorry, sir, madame. Private party."

"It's my party," Max announced coolly.

"I beg your pardon, Mr. Savoie." He pulled back the sliding doors to reveal a horseshoe of the who's who of Crescent City crime.

"Oh my God," Cee Cee whispered. "And here I am without any handcuffs."

"Behave, detective. You're here as my guest." He smirked. "Besides, they're probably thinking the same thing. I do every time I see you. Shall we?"

He strode into the room with her on his heels, aware of all the attention turned his way. But only one reaction interested him.

Francis Petitjohn paled dramatically.

"Sorry to keep you waiting, gentlemen. Couldn't find a place to park. You know my girlfriend, Detective Caissie."

Nothing like laying it all out there, Savoie. Charlotte smiled tightly across the sea of bristling hostility. "We've met."

Max approached the head of the table with a stalking intensity while Petitjohn sat, pinned prey. "You didn't save me a seat, T-John. Charlotte told me you'd be expecting me." His stare brightened, all cold fire, and his voice lowered to a murderous rumble. "Take my hand, Francis, and maybe I'll save you."

He gripped the sweaty palm in his own, nearly crunching bone. To his credit, Petitjohn didn't flinch.

"Gentlemen." Max turned to the elite company. "I'm not one for long speeches, so let me get this out of the way. Thank you for the cards and flowers. Now it's time to pony up with something a little more tangible. Jimmy Legere trusted me with all of his interests, and I'm taking them. Anyone have a problem with that?"

Rafert Thoms, who controlled the city's transportation, spoke up for the rest of the group. "Max, nothing personal, but how do you plan to hold them?"

"The same way Jimmy did, the way he taught me. By being smart, by knowing who my friends are—and aren't. By crushing anyone who gets in my way without mercy or regret." He glanced to Cee Cee with a chill smile. "Pretend you didn't hear that, darlin'."

"Big words, Savoie," another challenged. "How are you going to back them?"

"With big, sharp teeth. I'm the top dog now and nobody steps in my yard. Anyone tries to take a bite out of something that's mine, I'll tear out his throat." For a long moment, no one in the room exhaled. Max smiled with a slow show of gleaming white. "Figuratively speaking, of course. You'll be dealing mainly with Jimmy's cousin, T-John. You know him. He's one of you, but make no mistake: He answers to me and only me. Right, Francis?"

"Whatever you say, Max," came the faint reply.

Thoms leaned back in his chair, amused and interested, but unintimidated. He was an expert at it; they all were. "I had a great deal of respect for Jimmy, but I don't know you, Savoie, except by reputation. It takes more than scary stories to make me a believer. Don't you agree?"

"Absolutely. I wouldn't step up if I had any intention of stepping down any time soon. You want references." His face went still, his eyes cool and remote. "If anyone has any further doubts or questions about how seriously I take my business, I can arrange for him to take them up with Vic Vantour. I settled him into some property over by Lake Pontchartrain. He found himself ready to retire, and figured what was good enough for Jimmy was good for him. What was his is now mine, too."

There was a sudden commotion at the entry doors, then Jacques LaRoche filled the opening with his bulk and brashness, his gaze on Max. When one of the restaurant staff gripped his beefy forearm, he was flicked off like an annoying tick. LaRoche came forward, in his steel-toed boots, tight jeans, and tighter tee shirt, smelling of labor and the docks.

Max stepped back from the table, waiting for the big man to reach him, while Cee Cee swept the room with her hard gaze, alert for trouble.

LaRoche had one quiet question for Max. "Who do you stand for, Savoie?"

"Stand with me."

LaRoche hesitated, caution narrowing his eyes. "You'll be our voice?"

"To my last breath."

LaRoche studied his face, the unblinking intensity of his gaze, and finally allowed a slight smile. "We're yours."

He leaned in to butt the top of his head against Max's shoulder. Max's hand came up to clasp the back of his neck, holding him there for a brief instant before releasing him, letting him step back to motion to Tibideaux, who stood at the door.

The redhead opened it, and a line of solemn workers, men recognized by the guests at the glitzy table as those who ran their various interests on the grassroots level, approached Max Savoie to pay homage in the same subservient fashion.

Standing at his side, LaRoche shot Cee Cee a quick, grudging smile. "I see you're still determined to protect his back."

"To my last breath," was the steely reply, earning her a wide grin.

When the silent laborers flanked him, Max regarded the elite company once more. His tone was smooth, even smug. "Control the docks, control the city, the saying goes. Gentlemen, the docks belong to me, and if you want to do business in the city, you go through me. We can agree on that here and now like civilized men, or would you rather I come into each of your yards and piss on everything before I take it away from you?"

No one moved or spoke, stunned by his arrogance.

Rafert Thoms broke the quiet with a booming laugh. He stood and approached the head of the table to take Max's hand in a firm clasp.

"Mr. Savoie, I look forward to doing business with you. No need to turn up your nose when, together, we can turn a profit."

One by one, the highest echelon of the New Orleans underbelly came up to do the same. Cee Cee faded back without complaint, feeling unnecessary now that LaRoche and his kind were there to guard their alpha. Especially since half the men in the room had spent time behind bars at her invitation.

Francis Petitjohn looked up at the press of her hands on his shoulders. She smiled, but there was no mistaking her words for anything other than a threat.

"I told you not to hurt him. If he doesn't settle things with you, I will. And you'll find out you were wrong to think he's the most dangerous thing out there on the streets."

She pushed her way through the crowded room. The air was a tad too polluted with the stink of illegal activities for her comfort.

At the door, she looked back and saw Max glance behind him on either side. His head came up as he sought her scent in the crowded room, then his gaze snapped right to where she was standing. She held up seven fingers and pulled the neckline of her shirt over to reveal her thin, black, rhinestoned bra strap. He stopped in mid-sentence, his grin wide and wicked before his attention was called away.

She watched Max work the group. He was direct and assessable, gripping hands, holding eye contact, his posture confident and effortlessly lethal. Powerful and in control.

She smiled reluctantly. Jimmy Legere should have been there to see him. He would have been so proud.

"Are you another part of his scheme, Detective Caissie?"

She glanced over at the balding importer who moonlighted as a midlevel arms dealer. "What do you mean, Artie?"

"Control the docks and control the NOPD? Our boy Max found himself a pretty beneficial bedfellow. And he's pulled your teeth, too." He chuckled. "Who's going to believe you're not in his pocket, as well as his pants?"

"Oh, damn. I left that warrant for your arrest in my other purse."

Artie scowled. "You're a laugh riot, Caissie."

She looked up at Max, surrounded by the cadre of hoodlums. How many of them were thinking exactly the same thing? How long before they started pressuring Max to cull favors for them? Until the things she couldn't share with him became greater than those she could?

She left the room, troubled by an uneasiness that wouldn't go away, and almost ran into the group of photographers who leaned in to snap pictures through the momentarily open door. She dodged back, head lowered, stiffening when one of them grabbed her arm.

"Can you tell me what's going on in there?"

"I don't know anything. Sorry," she muttered, trying to escape the reporter.

"Hey, I know you. Aren't you—"

She jerked free and moved as fast as she could without running toward the front door, not slowing until she reached the car. Huddled behind the wheel, her heart hammered, her breath chugged in unfocused panic. Her hand shook as she inserted the key, and the numbing anxiety just kept getting bigger.

SHE HADN'T GOTTEN three feet inside the locker room when Babineau caught up to her.

"Captain's looking for you. And he ain't happy. It was your gun those kids used in the stickup. He's talking about a suspension."

"Fine. I deserve it."

He pulled up short, his mouth hanging open. "Ceece, everything all right? Where have you been? I've tried to cover for you."

"I've been witness to the swearing in of criminal royalty. I need a shower."

"Wouldn't that new royalty be the one you're showering *with*?"

"Yeah." Her laugh wobbled. "My God, Alain. What am I going to do? I'm a cop, and I'm the girlfriend of the head of organized crime in New Orleans. He took me into a meeting with every Most Wanted in the city. I don't want to think he did it to hamstring me in my job, but how can I be sure? That's what Jimmy would have done. There were photographers there. Do you think the captain will just be talking a suspension if my picture turns up on the front page tomorrow? How would I ever do my job? Why would anyone take me seriously ever again?"

"Sit down. Come on. Sit down."

"It was one thing when he was just in Legere's shadow, and nobody knew or cared if we had a little fling. But now he's high profile, and it's going to be my job to put that profile on a police blotter with a number over his shoulder." She dropped onto the bench and lowered her head between her knees to combat the sudden waves of vertigo. Thinking of the pieces and parts of four victims in Dovion's lockers, of crimes she was supposed to be solving, committed by the man who controlled her heart. "I'm in love with him," she moaned.

Her partner's soft curse summed it up nicely. "Fuck me."

"Fuck me sideways," she agreed on a sob.

SEVEN O'CLOCK CAME and went.

She sat outside the restaurant in the car for almost an hour. He didn't come out, and she couldn't go in. She couldn't make that committing move to open the door. If anyone had looked through the rainy car windows they would have thought her a crazy woman, weeping uncontrollably over what was waiting for her. Over something she wanted with nearly mindless desperation. Over what she could never claim. A dream that was never meant to be.

She loved her job. She loved her role in defending justice, in standing for the weak, the vulnerable, the deserving. It was everything that defined her, everything that gave her purpose, meaning, and validation. It was the link to her past, the need to make her father proud, to continue to honor his memory in the only way she could. It was her only tie to family, those men and women sworn to uphold the laws and rights of the citizens of their city.

She didn't know how to do anything else. She didn't want to be anyone else. If she didn't have her badge, her integrity, her focus, what would she have? If she was no longer that person, who would she be?

She would be an empty possession in Max's yard, unable to go beyond the limits of her chain. And she would grow to hate him for holding her back. She'd spent her whole life fighting on her own behalf and to protect those she loved. If he took away that freedom, there would be nothing left of her.

But how could she give him less than everything?

Max had her heart, her body, her soul. She would give her life for him without a second's thought. But to *have* him, to keep him, would require a sacrifice of her spirit. And that was a compromise she couldn't make. Not even for him.

And he would never forgive himself for demanding it of her.

She finally started the growly 427, and after wiping her eyes on her sleeve, she tore away from the curb. Zero to sixty in under four seconds—even dragging her heart behind her.

SHE NEVER HEARD his step until he was beside her. He smiled slightly.

"Heya. I thought you might be here."

She scooched down the smooth wooden pew to give him space to join her.

He kept an incremental distance, waiting for her to speak. When she didn't, he asked, "Why didn't you come in?"

"Because I'm a coward."

Afraid of what that might mean, he stayed silent.

"They moved Mary Kate to that center in California this afternoon. I haven't thanked you for that." She took a big, shaky breath. "I miss her so much. I wish she were here to talk to."

"You can talk to me." When she didn't respond, his smile tightened. "Oh. I see. I'm the problem."

"I'm sorry, Max."

He'd known something was wrong. He'd been stuck in business dealings all afternoon, handling matters that demanded his presence and attention. But even as he was seeing to Jimmy Legere's interests, marveling over the sudden realization that they were now his interests, part of him refused to heel. The part of him held by Charlotte Caissie. While he talked and negotiated and smiled, he was watching the clock, anticipation simmering beneath his cool surface. Because he could not wait to be with her again.

I love you, Max.

The newness of it had him excited and trembling. His only regret was his inability to share all the spectacular events of his day with her, because he wanted to impress her. He wanted her input and advice and mourned the fact that he could never ask for it. Because they toed different sides of the narrow line of the law.

As he sat in the club waiting for her, chafing with eagerness, flushed with a foreign sense of personal accomplishment, with a happiness he still couldn't quite comprehend, worry had begun to build.

She was late. He'd given no thought to how his schemes might affect her career. He'd only been thinking of her safety—and his future. She was so capable, so confident, it never occurred to him to try to protect the other aspects of her life, aspects that would be damaged by her association with him. And then he could think of nothing else. When he sensed her right outside, every minute that passed twisted his panic tighter.

And then she drove away without him. Without even talking to him.

"Tell me what I did wrong and how I can make it right again."

She scrubbed her hands over her face, her answer

steeped in misery. "You can't make it right. You can't change who you are. Who I am."

"Oh." He swallowed hard. "I could sell shoes," he offered quietly. He tried to take her hand, but she pulled it back with an anguish sound.

"It's too late for that. We can't go back. We can't pretend everything hasn't changed."

"What's changed?"

Cornered, she attacked. "You're so smart, so damned smart—taking me with you, marching me up in front of all those mobsters like I was on your leash, letting them think you'd pulled my teeth, that I was with you."

"You *are* with me," he growled softly.

"Not like that," she snapped. "You used me. You made it business, making them think I was part of yours, that you had that extra leverage. Dammit, Max, how could you do that to me?"

She gave him time to deny it, to convince her that she was wrong, that it was never his intention to take advantage of what they had together. If he did, then maybe, just maybe, there was chance . . .

He stared at her unblinkingly. She watched the angles of his face harden and she saw the truth there.

"I love you, Charlotte. I want to keep you safe. I wanted them to know you were under my protection."

"By letting them think I'm under your thumb?"

"I'm sorry," he told her flatly. She could tell by

his lack of expression that he wasn't sorry for what he'd done, only that it upset her. "I haven't changed. What we have hasn't changed."

"You're not my Max anymore. You're their Mr. Savoie."

"I'm still just Max when I'm with you. Don't do this, Charlotte. Please."

"It's my fault," she went on in a dull voice, anger ebbing into helplessness. "I just didn't see how impossible it was going to be. I was so caught up in looking at you, I forgot to look around. I didn't want to see it until today, when it hit me so hard I couldn't breathe. I can't be with you, Max."

"Don't make any decisions yet. Just think about it for a while. I won't push you. I'll give you all the space you need." He snatched her hand, gripping it hard, bringing it up so he could press kisses on her palm, on her fingertips, so he could hold it to his cheek as his eyes searched hers, hoping to find something other than sadness and finality there.

"Time and space won't make any difference. It won't change who we are."

"Who do you want me to be? Tell me."

"Oh, Max, I don't want to change anything about you. I wouldn't love you so much if you were any different." She leaned into him, resting her head on his shoulder.

"I don't understand. If you love me for who I am . . ." He broke off abruptly as an unwelcome revelation slashed through the heart of him. He pushed her back to stare into her eyes, his own astonished. "You're ashamed of me."

She opened her mouth to deny it, but no words formed.

He drew a quick breath, and just as quickly drew back behind a tightly shuttered blankness. His voice was deathly quiet. "I see. I guess that's it, then."

He backed out of the pew, stumbling slightly as Charlotte reached out for him.

"Max—" He evaded her. "Max, I am so sorry."

He stood staring down at her, panting slightly. Then his expression softened and somehow strengthened at the same time. He framed her tear-stained face with his hands and, as hers covered them in a frantic grip, he said, "I'm not sorry, Charlotte. I will always love you."

He bent down to press a whisper of a kiss on her brow. By the time her eyes opened, he was gone.

Twenty

*F*OR THREE WEEKS, Charlotte tried to pretend she wasn't in hell. She didn't suffer from fiery torments or self-recriminations; that would require feeling. And emotionally, she was dead inside. It was the hell Mary Kate had warned her of, one of her own making. Isolation.

She'd left the church with a calm sense of closure, knowing she'd made the right decision. But as the minutes, hours, and days went by, that calm iced over into a cold, deep numbness not even brutal sixteen-hour shifts on a new high-priority case could crack.

Tourists in an airboat had found pieces of Vic Vantour out in the swamp, which had surfaced after a storm. The tentative truce on the waterfront threatened to buckle.

Max's bold words as he claimed his criminal mantle haunted her, and she knew that every hour she put in on the case was most likely taking years of freedom from his future. The distance she'd put between them didn't help, it just made it impossible for her to tell him . . . tell him what? That she wasn't going to do her job? That because she'd let him walk away twice, she'd forever turn her back?

She'd known what he was when she fell in love with him. And she couldn't protect him when he chose to break the law. He knew that. He knew what she did, what she'd have to do with the pieces he'd left for her to find: put them together into a case that would convict him.

Heartbroken, her spirit wounded, she went to St. Bart's, where the battered but proud building was struggling to be reborn. Seeing workers yank down the burnt rafters into a pile of rubble was like watching dirt thrown on the graves of those she loved. In her heart, she knew Mary Kate would never return. So when Father Furness offered his broad, familiar shoulder, she poured out her soul in cautious generalities, putting no name to her misery.

"How can I find such decency in a man who's done evil?" she asked woefully. "How can I love what I've sworn to destroy?"

"There's nothing that walks on this earth that is all decent or all evil, child," Father Furness soothed with the quiet confidence that had helped center the world of an angry young girl some twenty years ago. "Good *and* bad is done in the name of both things. Love knows the difference. Look to your heart."

"But what possible good can come of what happened to Mary Kate and Benjamin? What good comes from punishing someone who stands up for the innocent? How can you judge a wrong that's done for a right reason?"

"It's not up to us to judge, Lottie. We can only accept." He chuckled softly at her scowling expression. "That's the best answer I have, and you never seem to think it's enough." He kissed her brow and bestowed the knowing smile that always aggravated her by its certainty. "You've lost too much not to appreciate what you have."

Because she knew he was right, had always *known* he was right, her tone was sour. "You should write fortune cookies."

He smiled. "Something to fall back on in my retirement."

But Charlotte had nothing to fall back on except her job, and doing it as best she knew how. Worrying about how Max fit into the equation was screwing up the math.

She started up the little Nova, palming the knob of the shifter wistfully before shoving it into gear.

Legere, Vantour, and Benjamin Spratt. What was the link? How had the mild and meek Benjamin come by the mobster's ring?

I didn't kill him, in case you're wondering.

Max had never lied to her. Omitted the truth, perhaps, but he never spoke words that were completely untrue.

With circumstantial evidence stacking up on her desk, she needed to be sure before she plowed in and ended up plowing him under.

She went to his new office on the waterfront. She'd been there several times before to question Francis Petitjohn, but not since Max had assumed power. She noticed the difference immediately. Everything tacky was gone, replaced with dark teak, black and taupe, with occasional glints of crimson. Rich, aggressive, sexy. Like the man behind the double doors of L.E. International. Max Savoie was coming into his own.

"Can I help you?"

Cee Cee laid her badge down on the reception center. "I'm here to see Mr. Savoie."

The elegant black woman wearing a jacket and skirt in the same sumptuous red tones regarded her identification without a change in expression. "I'm afraid Mr. Savoie is unavailable this morning. If you'd like to leave your name."

The doors to the left pulled open. "That's all right, Marissa. I have a few minutes for Detective Caissie."

"I won't need that long." Her voice was cool to counter the sudden heat flashing through her at the sight of him. Dark, sleek, and elegant in a suit that couldn't quite tame the harsher elements growling behind that exquisite cut. "Just one question."

He stepped aside, waving her in. "Ask it."

Just walking past him made her break a sweat. He closed the door behind them, and suddenly she couldn't remember how she'd ever found the strength to let him go.

"Your question, detective?"

He looked so relaxed, so indifferent to all the things tearing through her like a Category 5 hurricane. She moistened her lips and could taste him there.

"Did you kill Victor Vantour?"

"No." Just that, flat and final.

She took a breath, hoping he couldn't hear it shuddering in relief. "Did you dispose of him in the swamps for Jimmy Legere?"

A slow smile. "I don't believe that was the question, detective."

But she had her answer. "I'll let you get back to work. That's all I wanted."

"Is it?"

He stood between her and the door. To get by him, she'd have to move him aside. Which would mean touching him, putting her hands on that long, hard frame, feeling his warmth, his strength. God, she was a mess.

"Yes," she replied, her tone daring him to tell her differently. "What else would there be?"

He held her bulletlike stare for a heartbeat, then stepped out of her way. The minute her hand closed over the knob, his pressed above it to keep the door shut.

"Come back."

"If I have any more questions—"

"Come back to me, Charlotte."

Then there was nothing cool or remote about him.

He leaned in.

She let him.

The way he sniffed up her scent tickled along her throat. He eased behind her, settling like a hot iron on crumpled silk, pressing close, steaming his impression upon her. Long, firm legs, lean hips. Fierce erection pulsing against her spine in an erotic massage. Hard chest, broad shoulders. And the sudden sweet assault of his mouth beneath her ear, tasting, seducing. A low sound rumbled from him, part growl, part groan. Her hand went to the back of his head, black hair sliding through her clutching fingers.

"Max, don't," she whispered as if words alone could keep her will from collapsing. The instant his tongue slipped into her ear, she surrendered a wild moan.

She turned, gripping him hard as their mouths met in a shock of desperate longing. A hot, greedy kiss that awakened each other's need like a blow torch. The need to hold tight, to reclaim, to frantically mate as their tongues were doing.

Blood roared in her head, so loud she wasn't sure her feet had actually left the floor until her butt met the edge of his desk. She had a fistful of his hair in one hand while the other snaked under his exquisite coat to roam up and down his back, hungry for his heat through the fine silk shirt. She wanted him naked. She just plain *wanted* him. Now.

Driven by the same mindless urgency, Max plumbed the sweet heat of her mouth while he palmed her breasts through her polo. It wasn't nearly enough to satisfy the chain reaction she'd started the second she got off the elevator and her perfume reached out to him. Her body arched against him, rubbing, offering everything and anything he desired. She was his all, his everything. Her hands groped fretfully as he stepped back to pull off the sexy little panties she was wearing and undo his slacks. Then he thrusted inside her so hard and deep, his blotter and all the papers on it went skidding off the desk. Almost instantly, she bowed in a taut spear of orgasm. But that wasn't enough.

He wanted to hear her sigh and moan his name. He wanted to believe things would be all right between them again. For her to admit that she'd missed him with the same soul-crushing panic that he missed her. To hear her say she still loved him. He needed to hear it. Was dying to hear it.

But there was only the harsh rush of their breathing and the frenzied slap of flesh on flesh. He tried to hold out for it, sure she'd let the foolish barriers fall while lost to the magic between them. But she was sucking on his lower lip, licking his cheek, biting his earlobe until the sharp little jab of pain ignited all the compressed fuel of his emotions. Even as he felt her tense and shudder, he emptied in a glorious, mind-blanking rush.

He leaned into her, his knees weak, nuzzling her

neck. *Tell me you love me, Charlotte. Right my world.*

Instead, he heard his own whisper. "Stay with me. Please, stay with me."

"Mr. Savoie." Marissa's efficient voice was a shock back to reality. "Your eleven o'clock from the Port Authority is here."

Before he could assemble his thoughts, Charlotte ducked under his arm and was gone, leaving him with empty arms braced upon his desk.

As he slowly straightened his clothing he saw her silky underwear, a scrap of bright pink against his carpet. He picked it up, tucking it into his inside jacket pocket where her scent could reach him like pure, revitalizing oxygen.

He rearranged his desktop, his actions smooth and steady, letting the hammering of his heart slow and his hopes cool. Finally he was able to press the intercom and say with professional calm, "Send Mr. Voissom in, Marissa."

ALAIN BABINEAU'S GAZE rose when Cee Cee slipped into her desk chair, then held for a quick once-over. Her hair was damp from showering and, instead of the skirt and polo shirt she'd worn that morning, she was wearing jeans and baggy tee shirt. And no makeup. That alone was enough to alarm him.

She pretended not to notice him, plunging into a file so she wouldn't have to meet his curious look.

"Fresh seafood for lunch?"

She glanced up, frowning and wary. "No. Why?"

"Looks like an octopus got a hold of the side of your neck."

Her hand flew up to cover the love bites that were blossoming into bruises.

"Can I hope you found someone to replace Savoie?"

No one could ever do that. Tears glittered in her eyes as she growled, "End of conversation."

Her partner sighed. "If that's what you want."

"It is."

But none of it was what she wanted. Father Furness's words came back, bitter and strong: *We can only accept.* So she'd accept it, and life would go on without the one thing that made it worth living.

She stared for a long moment at the fat manila envelope sitting on the corner of her desk. It hadn't come in with the mail. She studied the unmarked envelope, then gave it a nudge with her pen. Nothing suspicious rattled or ticked.

Using a tissue to hold one corner, she slid the blade of her knife under the flap and tipped the contents onto her blotter. Medical records. More specifically, psych records and two photos. One of a young Benjamin Spratt. And underneath . . .

"Holy shit!"

Babineau's head shot up. "What?"

"Did you see who dropped this on my desk?"

Alerted by her breathless voice, he said, "No,

sorry. I was taking a statement on the phone while you were gone. Why? Whatchu got there?"

"The answer to prayer." She let out a shuddery breath, then was all business. "Get the print guys up here. I need this dusted. I want to know where it came from. Check with the desk. See if anyone saw who brought this in here; if anyone asked for me or where my desk was. Now, Babs."

As he made the call, then scrambled out, she pushed the gruesome, graphic photo clear: A slice of horror preserved for twenty or more years. A horror she recognized all too personally. Mutilated throat. Empty chest cavity.

She began to read the reports. Then dialed.

"Savoie."

For once, the sound of his low, rumbling voice didn't send her heart stuttering. It was already pounding at a fierce, tribal pace.

"When you last . . . saw Vantour, was he wearing that big, vulgar ruby ring?"

"Why hello, detective. This is a pleasant surprise. Did you call to apologize for leaving without saying good-bye to me?"

"Just answer."

His voice grew as cool as her own. "I don't fancy jewelry myself, but yes, he was wearing it."

"Are you sure?"

"Yes."

She hung up. And started to put together the pieces to a picture as surprising as it was unexpected.

THE RECORDS SHE subpoenaed from the source listed Barnaby Pratt, thirty-two, as dangerously psychotic, and suffering from lifelong paranoia and delusions that he was some sort of half man/half animal. After he was found in the backyard on all fours, attempting to devour the family's pet, he went through the rest of his childhood drugged and shocked into a stupor. Weaned from the medication in his late teens with the help of extensive psychotherapy and a zealous plunge into religion, he had some productive years in his twenties working the docks, until experiencing another serious break with reality.

He'd gone on a rampage that covered the front pages for months with his wild-eyed, bearded face. After disemboweling his girlfriend and her mother, he stalked and slaughtered Marco Vantour, the man he believed had seduced and impregnated the girl he'd planned to marry. He'd also savagely murdered a meter reader ticketing cars on his block and the police officer who'd come to the door to question him. They finally brought him down with big-game tranquillizers at the zoo, where he was found sleeping naked in the wolf exhibit.

Tests done at autopsy proved that Marco Vantour wasn't the father of the dead girl's unborn child, although the close markers indicated it would have been a relative. Pratt's attorney claimed the insanity plea, and during pretrial psychiatric testing, Pratt ripped the head off his doctor, leaving a young nurse so traumatized that she swore the killer had transformed into some monster. Barnaby Pratt disappeared.

A year or so later Benjamin Spratt, with his soft, pudgy face and gentle gaze, came to live at St. Bart's. There he'd lovingly tended the church and its parishioners with a blissful smile on his face, and ill will toward none in his faded blue eyes.

Cee Cee threw herself into building the case, which would lead away from Max, whether that was her conscious focus or not. Through photos and interviews, she discovered that both Vantour brothers were given matching rings by their father when they turned twenty-one. Since the rings were identical, there was no way to tell which one was found on Benjamin's hand.

Tests done on the remains recovered from the swamps concluded that Victor, not Marco was responsible for luring the innocent girl into a predicament that ultimately led to her death. Barnaby Pratt had killed the wrong brother.

Had he waited twenty years to rectify that mistake?

The evidence said yes. Pratt, or Spratt, had been seen on the docks asking about Vic Vantour's routine. Cee Cee documented the testimony, but a bad feeling began to twist her intuition. A very bad feeling that had nothing to do with how much she'd liked Benjamin, or how much she wanted to protect Max.

She knew, deep inside her very sensitive gut, that Legere's people, not Vantour's, were responsible for what had happened to Mary Kate—and that she, not the janitor, had been the true target that night. And she knew that even though Benjamin Spratt had trailed behind Dolores Gautreaux and her child like a puppy dog, he wasn't the one who had eliminated Gautreaux and Surette.

Though she was sure of these things, she couldn't prove them. And no one wanted her to. The district attorney and her department heads were satisfied to believe what might have been the truth because it closed an open wound when a cop killer went down.

They wanted to believe that criminally disturbed Barnaby Pratt had resurfaced to protect Dolores Gautreaux. That he'd probably butchered the two men in the alley for reasons unknown. That with his psychosis in full swing, he'd tracked down Vic Vantour and killed him for ruining the woman he'd loved. That in retaliation, Vantour's lieutenants had slain Pratt, and Sister Catherine was a regrettable sidebar.

It could have happened that way—but Cee Cee didn't think so. It was too neat. Too convenient. The envelope on her desk, the ring on Benjamin's finger—pieces left for her to fit together. But by whom and for what purpose?

Her department and the fickle press showered her with praise for the diligence that broke the investigation wide open. The man who'd slain one of their own was no longer at large. The superstitious fear that had shivered through the night was stilled by a logical explanation. Even though it wasn't the correct one.

Cee Cee knew Barnaby or Benjamin hadn't been insane, at least at first. He'd been a shape shifter. But no one wanted to hear that truth so she accepted the attention, the commendations, the drinks, the pats on the back with a smile. And she went on to the next day with no enthusiasm. Because there was nothing to look forward to. Nothing waiting except the next empty day.

As she was catching up on paperwork one day, a big, flat box was delivered to her. When she opened the note, those nearby heard her soft, strangled cry and turned to watch as she ripped into the package with shaking hands.

Well done, detective. Pretend it's me.

MAX HEARD THE car. It was impossible to mistake the sound of that big block engine, revving with impatient power. Then her scent, equally unique.

He stayed at his back table in *Cheveux du Chien* and waited for her to come to him.

She appeared at the other side of the dance floor, tall, sleek, and every inch an Amazonian warrior in the long, dark coat. She swept the room with her stare, finally fixing on him. When she started forward, two unwise fellows intercepted her. She cut them down with a fierce growl. "I'm a detective with the NOPD. And I'm Max Savoie's girlfriend. Get the hell out of my way." They moved.

Max angled his chair to watch her approach, loving the determination in her stride, the purpose in her beautiful face.

"Heya, detective. What a pleasant surprise."

"I thought you might like to see how well it fit." She revolved slowly, the expensive raincoat belling out around her calves. She was wearing a short skirt and platform sandals. Her toenails were painted bright red, the same color as his shoes. She came to a stop, her stare direct. "And I got to thinking about other things that were a nice fit."

"Step up, detective." He tapped his mouth with two fingers. "Thank me."

She straddled the chair, settling on his lap, settling on his lips with warm familiarity. Tasting him sweetly, deeply, devouring him.

He eased her back after a long minute. "So tell me, detective," he began coolly. "Are you here only because your recent newsworthy deductions have erased the stigma of shame and blame from me? Is my character clean enough not to embarrass you now?"

The insidious suspicion had prickled the back of Cee Cee's thoughts. *Had* Max manufactured the evidence to close her case, freeing him from its stain and her to return?

Not the Max she'd fallen for. But what about the man who sat behind Legere's desk? Oh, yes, he was capable. But he was also clever enough to make sure she never found out about it. Would he do such a thing? Play such a vile trick with her emotions?

And then the unexpected gift. *Well done, detective.* Congratulations or smug insult? Was he mocking her even now?

Father Furness's voice replayed in her mind. *It's not up to us to judge. We can only accept.*

Max's gift was a test. Could she accept what she knew in her heart, or should she back away, heeding the whispers of doubt?

At that moment, she knew. And she accepted. What could have, should have, would have been the truth didn't matter as much as what she knew for a fact: She couldn't go another day without him.

Now, to convince him.

"Is that what you think, Max?"

"I don't know. That's why I'm asking. You're going to have to spell it out for me, Charlotte."

She took a breath, then let it out. "This last month has been hell without you."

"For me, too." No break in his cautious armor.

"I want to be with you, Max—to sleep with you and wake up to you in the morning. I need to hear your voice. To know you're there to come home to."

"I haven't gone anywhere, detective. Why did you run from me?"

That soft question finally broke her. Her chest hitched painfully; her eyes welled up with weeks of misery. She crumpled against him, her head on his shoulders, her arms clutching tight. "I got scared for a minute," she whispered against his neck.

He stroked her hair and buried his face in it. "You're not scared anymore?"

"I've never been scared of anything when you're holding me."

"Remind me never to let you go."

"Oh, Max—I've missed you."

The feel of his embrace tightening was a Welcome Home.

"Max?"

"Charlotte?"

"It's going to be . . . complicated."

"What is?"

"Us. Being together. You being you and me being me."

"I wouldn't want it any other way." He nuzzled her throat, nipping down that soft column to her collarbone.

"We should set up boundaries, guidelines about how it's going to work. That would be the smart thing to do, don't you think?"

"I'm having a little trouble thinking about anything right now, except how much better that coat and these clothes would look on the bedroom floor."

She laughed softly, confidence and relief returning in a warm wave. "We don't have to talk tonight. I took a week off of work. I'm the hero of the hour and they can deny me nothing."

Neither could he.

"Going somewhere in particular?"

"Wherever you're going."

"Your place or my place?"

"Either or both. But something tells me we're not going to get much farther than the front seat of the car."

His eyes grew heavy-lidded, his voice a low caress. "Are you going to make all my gear-shift fantasies come true, detective?"

"Yes, I am."

"I'm ready to leave now." He put his hands on her waist and lifted her off him, then stood, red toes to red shoes. "Let's go fog up your windows."

IN A FAR corner of the bar, deep in the shadows where he could see the entire room without being seen, as he had for the past week, a stranger's eyes flared hot and gold. He gripped a passing waiter, startling him with the bite of claws. His urgent growl and fierce expression silenced any protest, as did the twenty-dollar bill. "Who's the kid with the upright female? Kinda reminds me of someone."

The waiter looked at him as if he were from another planet. "That's Max Savoie. He took over Jimmy Legere's action. He's one of us."

"That right?" The stranger leaned back with a chuckle that sounded darkly dangerous. "Max Savoie. Whaddaya know? Life has a funny way of bringing things full circle." His teeth flashed white and sharp. "Time for us to get acquainted." *Before your time runs out.*

"Bring you another?"

"Sure."

He tipped his glass to the figure below. Life had just gotten interesting again.

Game on.

AS THEY CROSSED the dance floor, Max felt an odd tug on his senses. It wasn't exactly danger. It was something else—something unfamiliar. He slowed, his gaze scanning the room as the hairs on the back of his neck prickled. But he saw nothing to alarm him in this place he now thought of as his sanctuary. Still . . .

Charlotte pressed against his side. "Max? Is something wrong?"

There were so many unknowns in his new life, he didn't know where to begin. He no longer knew who he was, let alone *what* he was as he stood at the crossroad of two very different paths. He now uneasily wore Jimmy Legere's criminal crown, and it was Charlotte's job to make sure it was one of thorns. In this place, with these strange beings, he'd found a heritage he didn't understand, and something he had yearned for all his life: a place to belong. Then there was Charlotte and the promise of a future he wasn't sure he could hold on to, once he started down either of the two roads.

He smiled. "Nothing's wrong."

His arm tightened about her in a protective curl as he realized one unshakable truth. No matter what journey he chose, his first priority was to see that Charlotte came to no harm because of it.

This strong, brave, passionate woman had trusted him with her heart. And he would not fail her.

She smiled up at him, and he saw his whole world in her eyes.

"Hey, they're playing our song," she said.

He listened, then grinned when he recognized Warren Zevon's "Werewolves of London." With a laugh, he slipped his arms beneath her coat and twirled her around the floor, tugging her in tight. Her arms circled his neck, drawing him down until they breathed in each other's breaths.

Then she gave him a slight push and, with a teasing smile, dangled the car keys.

"Shall we get the motor running?"

"I'm way ahead of you, detective."

And with their arms around each other, they stepped outside, where their shadows blended together in the night.

Turn the page
for an exciting sneak peek of

CHASED BY MOONLIGHT

the next irresistible novel in
Nancy Gideon's
Shape-shifter series

Coming soon from Pocket Books

SANDRA CUMMINGS, TWENTY-TWO, single, a business student at Tulane. Apparently she went to a club off the Square with a group of friends. She left about one thirty and walked to her car alone."

"She should have known better." Charlotte looked at the plastic-draped form, frustration roiling. Why didn't she know better? One too many drinks? The invulnerability of youth? How could her friends let her just walk out into the night by herself? What were they thinking?

Unfortunately, she had a pretty good idea what they'd be thinking when they heard the news. They'd be thinking it was all their fault. And then they'd have to learn to live with it. Lesson learned too damn late, and now just another grim statistic. "Stupid kids," she muttered almost angrily.

She glanced around, her cool, dark eyes efficiently detailing the scene, imagining it the way it would look late at night—not the way it did now, skirted by police tape and obscenely visible to those beginning to crowd behind it. After midnight it would be isolated, empty in favor of the jazz and dance-club party scene closer to the Square. A lonely, shadowed place to die. No place for a twenty-two year old student to be lying under plastic.

"What was so special about her that the chief called me back in?" She glanced at her partner, alerted by his edgy evasiveness. Not much made Alain Babineau fidget. He was the epitome of cool and calm under even the most grisly circumstances. Together they'd seen all the ugly, shocking reminders of what man was willing to do to his fellow man in the name of anger, jealousy, madness, or just plain business.

"She's Simon Cummings' youngest daughter."

"Cummings?" She'd met the aggressively proactive mayoral hopeful at several professional functions. She'd liked his firm, hard line against crime. "A coincidence?"

Something uneasy moved in Babineau's face as he bent and pulled back the plastic. "I don't think so."

She stared down at the partially nude and viciously mutilated body of Sandra Cummings, seeing the signature MO. She didn't need to wait for the pronouncement of cause from the medical examiner, Devlin Dovion. She recognized the work.

Fangs and claws.

"Do you want to drive or shall I?" Babineau asked softly.

LEGERE ENTERPRISES INTERNATIONAL had its business office in a renovated warehouse along the wharf, close to the pulse of its many interests. And many of those interests had been under attack by Simon Cummings. His campaign had stepped up considerably since Jimmy Legere's death and the assumption of power by his long-time bodyguard, Max Savoie.

Savoie was an unknown quantity. Despite his highly visible stance at Legere's back, he'd stayed in the shadows as a silent, simmering threat to anyone who would dare cross his mentor. He literally hadn't existed on paper until Legere's high-priced lawyer arranged for the necessary documents to allow him to take control.

How he would run LE International, and his ability to retain his hold on the far flung and allegedly illegal ventures, was the topic of much debate. Dangerous debate. And though the head that wore the new crown was uneasy, one wouldn't know it when looking at the sleek businessman seated behind a huge teak desk.

"Detectives, what can I do for you this morning?"

In unspoken agreement, Cee Cee remained quiet while her partner, Alain Babineau, squared up to ask questions. From the backup position she could study the elegant Savoie, looking beyond his beautifully tailored gray Armani suit and immaculate grooming to the sharp-edged killer he'd been until a few months ago. The aura of potential violence still shimmered about him despite the careful composition of his ruggedly compelling features. Knowing how much more was hidden behind the steady arrogance of his stare had Cee Cee dreading the confrontation to come.

That, and the fact that she was sleeping with him.

"We're investigating a murder, Mr. Savoie. A young woman was attacked at her car, chased down the Moonwalk, overpowered, raped, and killed."

Max never blinked. "How unfortunate. And this relates to me how? Do I know her? Does she work for me?"

"Her father was Simon Cummings. Get the picture now?"

"Still out of focus. Fine tune, please."

"Her throat was torn out. It appears as if some of her internal organs were . . . eaten."

"Ah. Are you asking if I suddenly got a craving for young coed and decided to go out for a snack?"

"Did you?"

A cool smile. "No. I'm afraid my girlfriend doesn't approve of me assaulting and devouring other women. She's funny that way. I try my best not to irritate her unnecessarily, even though she doesn't seem to have a problem irritating me. Nor do you, apparently, Detective Babineau."

"So you won't mind telling me for the record where you were between one and two this morning."

"I was at my home. In bed. Handling an urgent personal matter. I was not alone." His stony stare never deviated from Babineau's. "Did you need proof, detective? I'm afraid I don't have any Polaroids or video for documentation. Is that something you think I should consider doing, for future reference?"

Alain Babineau was a staright shooter, a good cop and a tough one without being a hard-ass. With his unspoiled good looks—blue eyes, dimples, and compact athletic build—he could have sold anything from toothpaste to boxers. He was protective of his partner in a way that made Savoie grateful and uneasy at the same time. They would never like each other, because of the woman and the badge that stood between them.

"And your time can be vouched for all night?"

"Yes. Every delectable minute of it."

Cee Cee frowned. Max's gaze flickered to her for an instant, registering puzzlement before returning to his interrogator.

"Any other questions, detective, or would you like to gut me right here to see if any pieces of Ms. Cummings come spilling out onto my carpet?"

"I don't think I could get a warrant for that." But his scowl said he wouldn't be above me asking for a sample of his stomach contents. "Can you deny that Simon Cummings has been causing you and your organization a considerable amount of trouble lately?"

"No. He's a tolerable nuisance. But then again, so are you, detective, and I haven't killed and eaten you."

They locked testosterone-fueled stares for a long moment, until a clearly irritated Cee Cee stepped between them. Her demand held a crisp neutrality.

"Did anyone in your employ, with or without your knowledge, undertake the intimidation of Ms. Cummings in order to dissuade her father from continuing his vendetta against your businesses?"

Cold green eyes slashed over to meet hers. "Are you asking if I authorized the rape and murder of an innocent young girl because her father was annoying me? Is that what you're asking, Detective Caissie?"

When she refused to clarify the question, his mood grew glacial.

"The answer is no. This interview is over. If you have any other questions you can contact my attorney. I'm sure you know your way out."

"I'll say this for you, Savoie," Babineau stated in a parting shot. "You certainly are a quick study. You've gotten comfortable real fast behind that desk. Just remember where fast and clever got Jimmy Legere."

Without moving a muscle, fury vibrated the new top thug on the block. "I'll remember. Detective Caissie, a word."

Charlotte wasn't fooled by his smooth manner. He was in a dangerous coil of temper, ready to strike. Still, she nodded to her reluctant partner and remained behind. She began with cautious impartiality, hoping to quickly defuse the situation. "I'm sorry for that, Max. You know it's just part of the drill. I can't help that you top our list of the usual, or rather the unusual, suspects."

But that wasn't what concerned him.

"What was that look for, Charlotte?"

Her competent cop expression puckered with confusion. "What look?"

"When Babineau asked about us being together all night, you made a peculiar face. I don't understand. Explain it to me."

She confronted him directly. "I woke up about quarter to two. You weren't with me."

"What do you mean?"

"You were gone. I didn't think anything of it at the time. I went back to sleep."

"But you're thinking something of it now."

"Of course not."

She was lying; he could practically hear the wheels in her cop brain whirring. His features registered the shock of it briefly before the impenetrable glaze returned. "You think I climbed out of the bed I was sharing with you, came into town to have forced sex with someone else after you'd been supplying it so generously for the previous thirty-six hours, killed her, made a meal of her, came back, washed up, and was all warm and ready to make love to you again?"

How awful he made her sound. It *was* awful. She felt awful, but trying to defend herself would have only made things worse.

She couldn't help remembering the past bodies she'd seen. She couldn't change the fact that she knew what had torn them into pieces. *Who* had torn them into pieces.

He came toward her with a purposeful stride. She held her ground, her heart pounding. She'd never been truly afraid of him, of what he was and what he could do, yet subconscious caution shivered through her soul. He came as close as he could without actually touching her, until she could feel his heat, his strength, his intensity. There was no man alive that she would let do that without thrusting up barriers to protect her space.

But then, Max Savoie was no man.

He asked softly against her ear, "How could you let me put my hands on you if you believed that for even an instant?"

His fingertips rested on the backs of her arms. And she flinched.

With a low oath, he turned away.

"Leave, Charlotte. Just go."

The toneless quality of his voice scared her. "Max?" she asked softly, plaintively.

"What a monster you must think I am. How can you stand me?"

"*Max.*" She reached for him but he shied away, returning to the other side of his desk. When he looked at her again, his face was without expression.

"Don't keep your partner waiting, detective. I'm sure you have more important places you need to be."

He knew she wouldn't just slink away. Not with all that fierce, prideful arrogance that both fascinated and infuriated him.

Charlotte returned his gaze for a long, controlled moment, her stare flat and ungiving. Didn't she realize she could destroy him with just a subtle shift of her expression, a betraying flicker he always prepared for that would plunge from desire to disgust? But she kept her features neutral—those bold, exotically beautiful features that could crush a man's courage with purposeful viciousness or conceal a vulnerable world of pain behind hard onyx eyes. She abruptly broke her rigid stance and strode to the door the way she did everything, with a take-no-prisoners certainty.

After the door closed behind her, he let his breath out in a shaky spasm. He quickly took another one, deep and strong to get on top of all the turmoil writhing around inside him. He'd deal with that later. For now, he had to take care of business.

He pressed the intercom on his desk. "Francis, come in here, please."

Francis Petitjohn was Jimmy Legere's cousin and had supposed himself the heir apparent to the fortune he'd helped make. Finding out that Jimmy had passed his vast holdings to the dangerous enigma he'd taken in as an orphaned child created a difficult tension between the two of them. Difficult and nearly deadly.

"Whatchu need, Max?"

"The truth would be nice."

Max sank back into the big leather chair that had been Petitjohn's up until a month ago. The chair he'd sat in to calmly watch Max twist on the floor in the grip of the poison T-John had used to try to kill him. When Max decided to take the disputed job and the chair instead of T-John's life, Petitjohn had no objections. But he didn't have to like the situation.

"Truth about what?"

"Simon Cummings. Someone killed his daughter last night in a way that was rather telling. Like a gruesome finger pointing in my direction. Whatchu know about it?"

Petitjohn shrugged, looking properly clueless. But then he wasn't exactly the soul of sincerity. Max knew exactly what he was: lying, sneaking, devious, and for the moment, a necessary evil acting as liaison between him and the cautious factions of their criminal world.

The fact that he resembled Jimmy might have had something to do with Max's reluctance to simply dispose of him. He had Legere's wiry build and sharp, cunning features. His voice held that same casual drawl of indifferent contempt for anything that wasn't making him money. He could be charming when he chose to be, or he could be merciless. Both sides made Max most wary.

"I don't know anything about it, Max. First I've heard."

Max tented his hands, resting his chin on his

fingertips. His gaze was still, unnervingly unnatural. "Really? And that's the truth?"

"Yeah."

"Have you been leaning on Cummings?"

"Of course. He's a pain in the ass, like a boil that bothers you every time you try to sit down."

If he'd answered any differently, Max would have known he was lying. As it was, he couldn't be certain.

"Ask around. Find out who did this thing and why. Let them know I don't like it. It's not how I want to do business. Have Marissa send two sizable checks in the daughter's name—one to whatever department she was in at the university, and one to St. Bart's for their women's shelter. Have her reach out very lightly to the family with our condolences."

"That's not how Jimmy would have handled it. Jimmy would have used their grief to apply a little more pressure. He would have considered it a good business opportunity."

Max regarded him narrowly. "I'm not Jimmy. And I will not condone anyone ever harming a woman or child in my name or in my employ. Not ever. Don't make me have to repeat that to you again. I shouldn't have had to say it in the first place and you know why."

T-John said nothing.

Max sighed heavily and sagged back into the leather cushions. "I don't need this right now, Francis. I'm trying to establish a sense of trust here on the docks, and it's like trying to reach under a virgin's skirt while convincing her your intentions are honorable."

Petitjohn smiled slightly, and Max realized he was talking too much and to the wrong person. If he needed a confidant, the man on the other side of the desk was not the one to choose. Unfortunately, the person to whom he wanted to unburden himself was equally unacceptable. And that chewed on him like wharf rats.

"I've got some people to see. I should be back in a couple of hours. Don't talk to the police; don't make any statements to anyone. Deny everything. Make us sound like the aggrieved party. You're good at that."

As Max moved toward the door, Petitjohn drawled, "Whatever you want, Max. Happy to take care of it for you." Echoing words Max had said in all sincerity to Jimmy Legere, twisting them with a touch of a sneer.

Max turned slowly to regard him. His voice was low, almost pleasant.

"Just because I let you go on breathing, don't think that implies any sentimentality or stupidity. I know exactly what you are—and the second you cease to serve a purpose on my behalf, I will rip out your heart and swallow it whole while it's still beating."

"I never doubted that for a minute, Max."

Max paused, gauging Petitjohn's response. The

other man's pulse was racing. He was sweating, breathing in shallow fear-laced snatches. Terror was something Jimmy had taught Max to ply ruthlessly, and as long as T-John was afraid, he'd have a degree of control. For emphasis, he let his stare turn hot and gold while a bloody red swamped the whites of his eyes. With a blink, that look was back to normal.

"Good. Then we understand each other."

Something else occurred to him.

"And if anything happens to Charlotte Caissie, say, if a car runs over her, a safe falls from a second-story window on her, if she contracts some fatal disease, or gets shot in the course of a robbery, I will hold you—and *only* you—personally responsible. And Francis," he added almost conversationally, "you'll beg me to eat your heart raw just so you can die. Got it?"

"Got it, Max."

He left the office, shutting the door softly behind him, and then lingered to hear Francis Petitjohn mutter on the other side.

"And *you'll* get it, too, you smug son of a bitch. So don't get too comfortable in that chair."

Discover love's
magic with

a paranormal romance
from Pocket Books!

Nice Girls Don't Live Forever

22181